The Road to Ruin

THE ROAD TO RUIN

A DAUGHTERS OF DISGRACE
HISTORICAL ROMANCE

BRONWYN STUART

TULE
PUBLISHING

DEDICATION

For my husband and my girls.

Without your never-ending support, I wouldn't be living out
my dreams.
I love you guys!

And to my sister in crime, Kelly Ethan: you helped
brainstorm my sagging middle into a rockin' set of abs and
I'll never forget it.
You're on the love list too!

CHAPTER ONE

WHAT THE DEVIL was she up to now?

They had to be in the worst part of London's seedy wharves and warehouses. The stink of rotten fish mingled with the even ranker filth flowing down the edges of the street. James Trelissick flexed his fingers and then clenched them again, the urge to block his nostrils almost too much. "Are you sure this is the address, miss?"

Her uncovered head leaned through the open window of the closed carriage beneath him and James had to fight an even stronger impulse to whip the horses until they were far away. Vibrant red hair and a fair complexion turned the spoiled young woman into a beacon. At least she'd had sense enough to don a dark cloak over her evening gown, although even a fool half blind and deep in his cups would note her station.

"Your job is not to question, John," she reminded him.

James bit his tongue and held the pair still while his quarry opened her own door and stepped lightly to the blackened ground. It wouldn't do to remind her once again that his name was James or that she should wait until he opened the door for her. Propriety was not something Miss

Germaine would be able to learn at the age of one-and-twenty. You either had it, or you didn't. She did not. He saved his breath and concentrated on the matter at hand.

His military-honed instincts rose to full alert as a shuffle from the right was accompanied by boot heels clicking against cobbles from the left. He should never have brought her to the address she gave him, not in a thousand years, but he couldn't refuse without revealing his true identity.

"I will be some time inside, so you may drive around the corner and wait for me there."

"Not bloody likely," James told her, biting his tongue too late.

"I beg your pardon?" she hissed, her wild green eyes checking the shadows all around.

"I'm not going anywhere without you." He added as an afterthought, "Miss."

"You will do as you're told."

Inclining his head in her direction, James gave the horses a gentle flick with the ancient leather and the carriage moved off quietly, though the clamour of alarm bells in his mind was surely loud enough for even his stubborn mistress to hear. He should have taken her over his knee and spanked some sense into her. If she'd been his sister, he would have her locked in a room with padded walls and declared a bedlamite to keep her from self-inflicted harm.

Once around the corner, not even moving his head in the slightest to look back, James stopped the carriage, tied the reins tight and jumped to the ground. He hit hard but did not pause. As he rounded the back, he rapped two short sharp knocks against the luggage compartment.

"Shite." His man popped out of the compartment and swung his dirt-stained face left and then right. "What the hell is she doing now?"

James shook his head and lifted his woollen cap to rake a hand through his hair. "I have no idea but you can bet it isn't good. Watch the horses; don't move from this spot but be ready to flee as soon as I say the word."

He didn't wait for Hobson's nod or reply. His man would know what to do.

As he ran back to the warehouse his mistress-for-the-moment was intent on entering, he transferred a pistol from his pocket to his hand then pulled his ragged coat sleeve over the weapon. At some stage he would need to use it, of that he was sure. Trouble didn't so much follow Daniella Germaine as she was the trouble herself.

Peering around corners and down dark alleyways, no sound met his ears and no other person came forwards. He found the door to the leaning warehouse and slowed to an unsteady walk when he saw two burly men standing guard.

"Evenin', gentlemen," James said in a servant's accent.

"What do you want? You got no business 'ere." The one on the left puffed his chest out and took a step in James's direction.

"The mistress, she told me to come back and assist her."

The two eyed him dubiously and James hoped like hell he'd said the right thing. "Come on," he whined impatiently, "she'll 'ave me 'ide if I'm not in there yest'dee."

Finally they nodded and opened the door. James held on

to his sigh of relief until he'd walked over the threshold but choked on it when the scene inside rushed to greet him.

Nearby stood a crowd of men joking, laughing, chatting. In front of them, beneath the sloping, decrepit roof, a stage of sorts with a roped-off pen had been erected and topped with an auctioneer's podium. From what he could gather, the crowd were gentlemen, and in their midst lingered Miss Germaine, the bane of his existence and the answer to his many dilemmas. She stood in a dirty warehouse in a gown worth hundreds, surrounded by only men and filth, looking as calm as if she were in her brother's drawing room.

Instead of approaching and asking her the dozen or so questions that first sprang to mind, he held his ground, and his cover. If she for one moment thought him more than a coachman, he would never find his mother or sister.

After only a few more minutes, a nondescript man stepped up to the podium and cleared his throat loudly. The crowd moved closer, the hush instantaneous.

"We're all here for the same reason, gentlemen."

There were titters from those closest to Miss Germaine but the announcer ignored it and went on. "Please remember the rules; and once a girl has been won, she'll be taken off to the back for collection. Cold hard coin is the only currency and no amount is too high for me." He eyed each member of the crowd, waiting for nods of agreement. His gaze paused on Miss Germaine, his beady eyes opening a fraction wider, his wide nostrils flaring, but then he spoke again. "Right then, let's bring 'em in."

James couldn't quite believe his eyes. In filed twelve girls by his count. All were various ages, sizes, skin colours. No two girls had similar features but all wore the same look of fear and loathing.

"The first virgin up for bidding is a delightful little package…"

James stopped listening. What the hell could Daniella Germaine want from an illegal auction such as this? She might have been the daughter of a pirate but she was also the sister of a man knighted by the king. She should have had no knowledge whatsoever of such a thing as a virgin auction. But then Miss Germaine was no ordinary ton daughter.

Ordinary or not, if word got out, if one loose tongue let it slip that she was there, in that den of filthy degenerates, what remained of her shaky reputation would be in tatters and she would be exiled from London society by granddames and daughters alike—something he could not afford to see happen just yet. She had to stay in place for just a few weeks more…

Very covertly and quietly, James began to move towards her. If he could get her out of there before too many noticed her presence, the rumours could be laughed off, a lie woven, an alibi found.

"The bidding starts at twenty pounds. Do I have twenty pounds for this spitfire? Surely she'll be a pleasure to tame."

James didn't stop to wonder at the asking price. Who'd have thought stolen virgins could be had for such a paltry fee? If indeed they were virgins.

"Twenty-five pounds," he heard called from the other side of the room.

"Twenty-six," came a reply.

"You can have her," cackled the first. "I hope she gives you lice, Wetherington."

James shook his head again. He knew Walter Wetherington, and had thought him a fine upstanding fellow in the House of Lords. Clearly what James thought he knew and the truth were two entirely different matters. He ducked his head, put the pistol back in his pocket and pulled his cap farther over his eyes. If Wetherington were in the room there could be any number of others able to recognize him. While he might not risk undoing the hard work he'd had to do to recover his good name from the muck—clearly the gentlemen of the ton were happy to be seen here—but he didn't want to unmask himself to Miss Germaine just yet.

"I should like to bid on her, Wetherington."

Damn that fool girl!

"Miss Germaine," the announcer called with a short bow, and gestured for her to continue.

"Forgive me, gentlemen, Wetherington," she said, as she gave them each an easy smile.

James tried to reach out, to grab a hold of her skirt, her cloak, any scrap of fabric to pull her back and right out the door, but then she started towards the stage.

"May I?" she asked the announcer before climbing the rough timber to stand before the cowering girl.

The silence deafened as each and every man, James included, held his breath waiting for Miss Germaine to speak again.

She didn't make them wait long. "I realize this is quite

unorthodox and I do hope you'll forgive my intrusion but I should like to buy them all."

James choked until the man next to him slapped him hard on the back. His splutters were otherwise lost in an uproar—the gentlemen bidders were all either outraged or overcome by bewilderment.

The announcer was quickest to retain his wits and his eyes sparkled with greed as he checked first Miss Germaine up and down and then the girls waiting their turn. "Three hundred pounds," he said in a way that told everyone he thought the lady would not be able to meet his terms. James, however, knew enough about Daniella Germaine to know she never bluffed.

"Done," she agreed with another nod.

The announcer turned back to the crowd. "It seems, gentlemen, that the lady has just purchased herself the twelve fine virgins I had to offer today. That brings our business to a conclusion until next month."

"On the contrary," Miss Germaine countered, her light tone turning seductive. "There is still one virgin to be bid on."

All she had to do was smile that beguiling smile of hers and the spell was spun. James groaned, removed his cap and raked a hand through his hair. He contemplated taking his gun out and shooting her. Nothing else would make her cease these dangerous games.

"Who?" the announcer asked, looking behind her at the dozen pairs of eyes staring back.

She threw the edges of her cloak back, revealing an evening gown cut more scandalously than the lady was herself, straightened her shoulders and lifted her chin. "Me."

NEVER LET IT be said that Daniella Germaine was afraid of a challenge. Never let it be said she would back down or have her mind turned once it was set on a steady course. Although her heart thumped against her ribs and her mouth was dry, to those watching she would display only the utmost confidence and calm.

"Is this some kind of joke?" the man on the stage next to her stuttered.

"No joke, I assure you. Shall we start the bidding at one hundred pounds?"

"You can't be serious," someone called from the crowd.

"Are you questioning the sincerity of my purpose here, Lord Cumberland, or my virginity?"

Another voice called, "Your father would hunt down any man who dared touch a hair on your pretty head."

She sincerely hoped so but couldn't resist a jibe. "According to the Royal British Navy, my father is dead." It was a good thing she was adept at telling fibs. Her father was still alive—she knew more than to believe the word of a starchy captain looking to be made a general in the war against those benefitting from smuggling and raiding. If he was dead, she would have felt it, or word would have reached her brother and he would have told her.

"No pirate as wily as Richard Germaine would let himself be had or bested by the navy."

Daniella drew herself up to her full height of five foot two inches. "My father was not a pirate, he was a privateer. The rumours about him are wildly unfounded and laughably out of control."

Biting down on her bottom lip to still the sudden tremble there, she inhaled, exhaled and then addressed the gentleman again. "Now, one hundred pounds is the bid and you needn't worry about my father. He's in a shallow grave at the bottom of the ocean and isn't able to harm a flea, let alone a virile gentleman such as yourself."

"In that case, I bid one hundred pounds," the Duke of Leicestershire called, his hands rubbing together in a way that chilled her enthusiasm for her cause.

The auctioneer took over, the chance at easy money too good to give up, and bids came from the left and from the right and even the middle until the amount was a staggering three hundred and twenty pounds.

"The bid is with Mr Pendleton to my right, do I have three hundred and thirty?" the announcer called.

"Three hundred and fifty," a voice said from the shadows at the rear.

"Step into the light, my good man, for your bid to be heard."

Out of the darkness came John, her coachman. Daniella barely contained a shriek of outrage. How dare he intervene? He was going to ruin everything and she had neither the courage nor the funds to make a second attempt at this particular form of disgrace. "You do not have three hundred and fifty pounds," she pointed out. "Pendleton, I do believe you have the bid."

"Do you call me a liar?" John asked.

"I do," she said with a firm nod. "Now hush before you lose your position as well as your pride."

"Three hundred and sixty pounds," Pendleton called.

"Six hundred pounds!"

All eyes swung to John, only now that she looked at him, *really looked*, she couldn't be sure he was actually the man who'd driven her to the auction at all. Her skin crawled as she swung her gaze back to Pendleton with a silent plea. It wasn't supposed to be like this. Her friend Percy was supposed to win her. On a normal day she would never barter her innocence unless she knew it was a gamble she would win. She wasn't stupid. Her calculations to date had been spot-on and flawless. Having plundered Anthony's strongbox, she had precisely three hundred pounds in her reticule to pay for her virgins, and Percy had drawn generously on his next quarter's allowance in the knowledge that her brother would be shamed into paying him back once he learned of his sister's newest, most irredeemable folly. A Germaine paid his—or her—debts.

"Who are you?" the announcer asked the bid holder.

Removing his cap, his hard-eyed stare never wavering from Daniella's, he said, "James Trelissick, Marquess of Lasterton."

"He is not," Daniella shouted over the renewed hubbub as her careful calm shattered to a thousand pieces. "He is my coachman and his name is John. Do not believe his lies if you wish to receive your money." But she was horrified to see him open his filthy coat, reach into his pocket and withdraw a purse.

"Six hundred pounds for Miss Germaine," he said waving it over his head as he approached. "And another four hundred when you feed these girls and deliver them to my estate in Dover. Untouched."

"This is outrageous," Daniella cried. Pendleton was supposed to bid on her. Her brother would have to repay exorbitant sums and wash his hands of her; her father would hear about her antics and rise from the grave to take her in hand. That was the plan. Who the devil was the Marquess of Lasterton to bump her off course?

In a matter of seconds, the said marquess had gripped her arm in his brutish hand and was towing her towards the door. "You can't do this," she rasped, and tried to twist free.

"Who is going to prevent me?" He came to a dead stop, his eyes wide and fierce, his grip tightening a fraction more. "Will you stop me, Wetherington? What would your wife say? What about you, Pendleton? Your poor mother would turn a fit to hear that you bid so callously on the innocence of a lady. I'm betting not one of you will want to mention this incident over breakfast tomorrow."

Daniella let her chin sink to her chest. He had effectively silenced any rumour that would scotch her standing in London—or save her from him. Suddenly her well-thought-out plan seemed naive and silly and her cheeks burned with humiliation.

"I didn't think so," the marquess growled and pulled her so roughly through the door into the damp night that she almost fell.

Quickly, before the two guards could come to their senses, he towed her down the street, around the corner and into her own carriage. Before the door had closed, he yelled, "Plan B," into the breeze and the horses shot off at a furious pace.

Daniella shuffled along the bench seat as far as the space would allow. "Where are you taking me?" she asked, her voice no more than a frightened squeak. Under the circumstances, she wasn't surprised fear had taken over her usually more robust sensibilities.

He looked in her direction for only a second, his gaze shuttered, his mouth a thin line and said only one word. "Home."

CHAPTER TWO

"**M**Y BROTHER'S HOME?" Daniella asked hopefully.

"My home," he replied without so much as a blink, frown, grin or lecherous wink. He displayed nothing but a furious calm in a situation that had quickly spiralled out of control.

"You cannot be serious."

"I can."

Daniella's fear was quickly replaced by anger. "Stop this carriage right now! I demand to be let out at once."

She watched the man across from her reach out a large, dirty hand to sweep the curtain aside. "Do you have any notion of where we are?"

His condescension only served to fuel her fury. "Everyone will know you have taken me."

He lifted a brow and tilted his head in her direction. "Now you fear for your reputation? I assumed destroying it was your single intent when you placed your virtue on the block and opened the bidding."

His eyes lingered on her chest and she blushed anew. Yes, she would have been ruined socially, but her body would have remained untouched. Now her flawless plan was in tatters, and she was no longer in control of herself, let alone her supposed coachman.

Damn him to hell. She pulled the edges of her cloak together with a jerk. "You weren't supposed to be there."

"Neither were you!" he thundered, his fists slamming down on his wide thighs in his first outward show of emotion.

"Not only did you effectively quash the rumours I needed circulating, you have rendered the mitigations I had *in place* impossible." She wanted the gossip to reach her father's ears but only the tales she spun herself, not the ones others did that had a habit of being more about sick fairy tales than actual fact.

"What makes you think they won't speak of tonight's events?"

"I don't know exactly who you are but the fear on their faces was evident. Are you scary?"

"Are you scared?"

Daniella considered this, then shook her head slowly. "I don't think so. If you wanted to hurt me, you would have by now."

The marquess surprised her: he threw his head back and roared with laughter. When finally his uncouth guffaws died down, he pinned her with his gaze, his suddenly husky tone washing over her in waves. "I just purchased your virtue. Why would I assault you in this carriage when I could take you home, tear the clothes from your body, tie you naked to my bed and have you at my mercy? The things I could make you do…"

She gulped. He'd moved forwards with every word, as though he promised all those things could happen, would happen and more. "Take me home," she whispered.

"I am. My home." He sat back with an unnatural grin.

"You can't do that!"

"Again: be sure that I can."

She slowly shifted her gaze from his and looked to the carriage door. If she could get it open, she could leap out into the street and beg someone to help her. But the carriage still moved at a fast pace and she had not the slightest clue as to where they were. Perhaps she could talk her way out of it? "There's been a misunderstanding, my lord."

"Oh?" His disbelief was plainly evident but at least he relaxed against the squabs once again. She would think clearer and faster with a little more distance between them.

"You see, the auction was a setup."

"It was? How so?"

"It's rather a long story but Pendleton was to be the highest bidder. He was supposed to win my...virtue."

"You have a tendre for Pendleton?"

"Good heavens, no. The man is more a brother to me than my own flesh and blood."

"I don't mind telling you, Daniella, that that is the most disgusting thing I've heard all day."

"You may address me as Miss Germaine, if you please, and there is nothing untoward in it. He was to be repaid the money that he bid. There was never going to be a...collection."

"I see."

"Do you?" she asked hopefully, her fingers grasping one another in her lap, twisting painfully.

"Actually, no. Why would you do something like this? What if Pendleton hadn't been the highest bidder?"

"He would have been. We had a clear plan, an agreement."

He threw his arms wide. "What happened to that agreement, Daniella?"

She frowned at the improper use of her first name again. "*Miss Germaine.* You happened. Everything was running very smoothly until you wrecked it."

"I wrecked nothing. I saved you."

"From my friend, my lord? I was in no danger."

She was gratified to see he reluctantly conceded that point, though he clearly had others. "And what of the other girls? What use have you for twelve highly questionable virgins probably being held against their will?"

"I would have set them free." She hadn't expected to buy those girls. Perhaps she should have done more research about the auction before jumping right in but it had seemed the perfect plan. She had just wanted to move the evening forward before losing her nerve completely and then having to wait even longer for another illegal activity to come to attention. Her thinking hadn't exactly kept pace with her actions, a flaw she couldn't seem to shake loose or learn from.

"Set them free to be picked up again and resold? Murdered on the streets? They have no funds. At least eight of them would have been raped and murdered by the time the sun rises."

"Percy would have known what to do with them." An outright lie. Maybe she should have listened when he'd attempted to talk her out of what he regarded quite vehemently as "madness."

"How? Because he is a gentleman? He is nothing more than a milksop and probably a virgin himself. His mother will have him cut off for his part in all of this."

Daniella wanted to shake her head until she blocked out his perfectly sensible words but instead released a frustrated sigh. "Please take me home. You have saved innocent girls; you have saved me—though it was presumptuous of you to think I needed it. You have stopped the gossip and prevented possible murders therefore earning your spot next to God. Can you please take me home?"

"I *am* taking you home."

"Not to your home, damn it, to mine!"

"Tut, tut, a lady should never raise her voice or use vulgar language. Did they teach you nothing aboard that pirate ship?"

She froze. It was one thing that the ton knew she'd been raised aboard a ship but no one had had the courage to ask her outright for details. "I beg your pardon?"

"Do pirates not use manners? Or perhaps just not those your father employs? Does one even employ a pirate? I'm not sure how that works exactly."

"My father is dead."

"We both know better than that."

Suddenly it all made sense. The weight of the world lifted and Daniella laughed. "I understand it all now."

"Could you explain it to me then?"

She stared at the marquess, if that's what he indeed was, with dirt on his hands and face and in his hair, and smiled. "My father sent you to scare me, didn't he?"

"Not at all."

Without thinking, Daniella reached out a hand to rest it on his knee. "You can tell Papa that I'm not going to stop."

"Stop what?"

"You tell him the only way I will cease is if I am back with him. Nothing short of my full reinstatement on board will make me happy."

"You make it sound as though you belong to a regiment."

"His ship is certainly run like one."

"That's interesting to know; thank you for the information."

"So you'll tell him?"

"I suspect you will be able to tell him yourself."

Daniella's hopes lifted and swelled until she could barely contain herself. "Are we going to see him?"

"I do hope so."

"What do you mean? Aren't you taking me to him?" All this back and forth and to and fro made her dizzy. She narrowed her eyes. "You are taking me to see my father, aren't you?"

The marquess shook his head, his dark curls falling over his eyes as he lowered his gaze and straightened the sleeve of his shabby coat. "Not exactly."

"Now I don't understand. Could you explain it to me? Without riddles?"

"I can." He took her hand in his and gave it a squeeze. "When your father finds out I have you, he will come to get you."

"I told you, I don't need to be rescued." She tried to pull her hand away but his warm grasp only tightened more.

"Perhaps you didn't before, but you do now. When your father finds out I hold you to ransom, he will have to come to collect."

"All this for my virtue? I'm not a virgin anyway and he knows it." Her cheeks burned but there was no point him thinking he held a better hand than he did.

"More lies, Daniella? They won't help but you needn't worry. I'm not going to touch you. I need you whole, hale and hearty for my plan to work."

"Your plan?" she squeaked.

"You see, unlike your flimsy scheme, mine is detailed and considered. Even this…nonsense of yours tonight can be turned to my advantage."

She grew cold all of a sudden. "What do you want?"

"Your father stole something of mine and I mean to use you to get it back."

"How do you know he isn't dead as the navy reported?"

"Last I heard he was still floating about making a nuisance of himself and terrorizing the fleet."

"They killed him. It was reported that cannon fire tore the ship apart and all hands went down with the flaming wreckage. You must have read the headlines."

"What else could the British navy report when your father constantly makes them look more foolish than they already do? The public need to think him dead, the navy needs to look to have a win."

"So you have spoken to him? He is alive?"

"I haven't spoken to him but I have heard from someone close to the situation and his heart still beats, his ship still sails."

Relief flooded her. She'd known him smarter than the fleet. "Why do you not simply go and take back what he stole?"

"He would see me coming. With you, I can lure him to me. We will meet on my terms so he can stick no knives in my back."

Daniella bristled but did not bite. Her father would never stab a man in the back. Unless of course he deserved it. She had a feeling the marquess probably did. She may even have to stab him herself if it came to it.

The last she had heard, her father was in retirement. It would have taken something drastic to send him out to engage with the law again, unless that was yet more lies.

"Nothing to say?" the marquess taunted.

"You somehow threatened those men back there into silence. How will he hear about my disappearance and know it was you?"

"Word will be sent. I would save my own name, even if you care nothing for yours. I will control who knows what and when. Even if you are not seen in London again, Sir Anthony will hardly allow the ton to believe you my captive.

He will concoct a plausible story to explain your absence even if he hurries after us to avenge your honour; the details don't matter so much as the outcome."

"You have a high opinion of your influence," she said reluctantly. He'd certainly thought it all through, and allowed for far more contingencies than she had. "What if my father doesn't care? What if he thinks we have merely fled the country? That I have gone willingly?"

"Your father and I have history. He will come because it is I who has you."

"You are arrogant."

He spread his hands out in front of him and shrugged. "You are now my hostage. Your father will show his face and he will bend to my demands. Not arrogance. Merely fact."

"My father hasn't been south of Edinburgh in a decade—he knows better than to come to London. It would mean certain death and he's not going to lay down his life, even to save mine."

"So you're not entirely selfish then? You do think about others some of the time?"

"Don't make the mistake of thinking you know me just because you spent a few months parading as my servant."

He inclined his head in her direction but the look in his shadowed gaze still mocked.

"Are you going to tell me what he has that is so valuable he might risk his own neck to give it back? He's a wanted man in England and over half the continent."

"No. No I'm not."

Daniella huffed and sank back. She waited for ten long

breaths, waited for the marquess to relax, for his breathing to become rhythmic. And then she launched herself towards the carriage door. She kicked out with one foot while her hands closed about the door handle.

But before she could push the timber and glass outwards, before she could jump into the street and hand her fate to whatever lay out there, two hands gripped her hips and effortlessly pulled her backwards. They landed in a heap on the carriage floor, her back pressed against his chest. With a shriek, Daniella began to struggle, to lash out but, wedged as they were between the benches, her struggles did nothing but increase her own panic.

At her ear, the Marquess of Lasterton's hot breath whispered, "I told you, you're mine now."

CHAPTER THREE

T O SAY JAMES was furious would be an understatement. Every part of his body seethed, his blood boiled and if he clenched his teeth any harder, he would finish up with a mouthful of dust.

"Would you—?"

"No," he snapped. His arse hurt as if the devil had slapped it. When they'd gone down, one of Daniella's elbows had landed squarely in his gut, momentarily winding him and taking more than a little of his dignity at the same time. He took in a shaky breath and wondered where in London they were, and how long he would have to hold her on the floor so she didn't try that again.

"Don't you know you could have been killed?" he bit out after a long, tense silence.

"I doubt that," she huffed, the rigid line of her back making her arse bones dig into his thighs. He wondered where her petticoats were—for, as surely as he was a man, the chit wasn't wearing any.

"You're not going anywhere without me."

"And you can't watch me every second of the day. I will not let you kidnap me."

"You don't have any choice in the matter, otherwise the term 'kidnap' wouldn't apply."

She huffed again. "Would you let me up?"

"I find I like it here." His arms slid around her body until he almost embraced her. Perhaps such inappropriate actions would wake up her sense of self-preservation.

Obviously a month of witnessing the wild antics of Daniella Germaine had taken their toll on his sanity. He hadn't been near a woman, a stiff drink or a game of cards in half a year. Right at that moment, when he should have been banging his head against the carriage floor to shake loose some common sense, only two of his longings rose to the surface.

When the carriage came to a halt and the door was thrown wide open, Daniella braced her legs and tried to launch herself through the portal again. This time James let her go. His man would catch her.

"Is everything—? *Oomph.*" Hobson did catch her and then he smoothly hoisted her body over his broad shoulder.

She smothered a screech but pushed in vain at his servant's back. It was too dark for any of his neighbours to see their movements and if Daniella wanted to return to the seven seas she would keep her head down and her mouth shut.

He gestured Hobson up the garden path to the front door. They arrived in the hall of his townhouse just in time to see his butler skid to a stop on the polished tile, his wig askew and his shirt tails only half tucked in.

"Uh…my lord?"

James deliberately ignored his servant's dishevelled appearance since he knew his own was far worse. "Ah, there you are, McDougal. I know it's late but do you think Mrs McDougal might prepare a few sandwiches for Miss Germaine?"

His very staid, very proper butler looked from James to Hobson to the woman hanging over Hobson's shoulder and then back to James again. "And tea, my lord?"

"Tea, Daniella?"

Her muffled response sounded more like "go to hell" than "yes please" so James shook his head and turned down the corridor towards his study, beckoning for Hobson to follow. Opposite the door to his inner sanctum was a small room beneath the stairs with a very sturdy door on it and no window. For an hour or so, Miss Germaine would have to cool her heels while he figured out precisely what his next move would be. Her rash behaviour meant his timeline would have to be as carefully amended as his original campaign had been laid out.

"In there," he said to Hobson, holding the door open.

"Are you sure you couldn't put her in one of the upstairs bedrooms? It would be more comfortable."

He shook his head. He didn't need his partner in crime to go soft on him now. "She was about to throw herself from a fast-moving carriage. I'm sure a second-story window and a fifteen-foot drop to the ground wouldn't deter her from freedom. Put her in."

Hobson lowered Daniella to her feet and waited, hesitation written all over his face and body.

Daniella swiped the hair from her face and stared hard into James's gaze. "You will pay for this."

"I certainly hope so," he replied before gesturing for her to climb over the threshold. "And don't think about starting a fire or any other nonsense because it won't help your cause. In a moment, Mrs McDougal will be along with refreshments and in an hour I'll let you out. Do you understand?"

She huffed but then strangely did his bidding. He'd expected a lot more fight from the daughter of the notorious pirate captain. All she did was square her shoulders and plop down on a stool, her back poker straight against the timber-panelled wall.

His conscience complained when he closed the door and threw the bolt but he pushed the unfamiliar niggling aside. Without a backwards glance to either McDougal or Hobson, standing in the hall with their mouths open, he charged into the study and headed straight for the liquor cabinet.

"That was a little harsh, was it not?" Hobson commented as he sank into a chair in front of an ancient carved mahogany desk.

"Not harsh enough for that wench. Do you have any idea at all what she just did?"

Hobson shook his head.

James sloshed whiskey into two glasses. "First she illegally purchased the filthiest virgins I have ever laid eyes upon." He contemplated the glasses, one for him and one for Hobson, and then with both hands and two smooth movements, drained them both. "She then put her own virtue up for the bidding."

"She did not."

"She did so. Leicestershire almost had her for the paltry sum of three hundred pounds."

"What did you do?"

"I purchased her myself. What else could I have done?"

"You could have let the old earl have her. Odds are her father would have been a mite more upset about him locking her up than you."

James raised his brow because he rather doubted that. "She could—no, would—have been harmed and I could not let that happen."

Hobson took a moment to think before replying and it grated on James's nerves in the most dangerous way. Whenever his man thought, dire consequences and a bucketful of reason ensued.

"You must know this plan of yours isn't going to work."

"It most certainly will—though I admit she is correct: her father likely won't come to us here. By the time anyone knows she is missing, we'll be well on the road north and I expect the good captain will meet us somewhere along the way."

"What will you do when all of these forces come together? How will you escape his vengeance?"

"He won't get close enough for the chance."

Hobson shook his head but asked, "What *exactly* are you going to do?"

"I'm going to swap his daughter for my mother and my sister."

"That easily? What of their reputations?"

"My mother and my sister will survive. We are the only ones who know they are even missing."

"I was also referring to Miss Germaine's."

He knew that. James rolled his eyes. "Hers will also be intact, if not perfectly—whether or not she wishes to return. She seems to have some notion of staying with Germaine. Either way I'll put it out that she was assisting me in some way or another, chaperoned of course, romanticize the whole fiasco."

"She's not going to appreciate that one little bit."

James leaned forwards and picked up a worn piece of paper from the top of his neatly ordered desk. He unfolded the note and stared at his mother's handwriting. Her words were curt, concise and to the point. Exactly three things his mother was not.

"What if they are no longer…alive?" Hobson asked.

He refused to think on it. If it had been any other pirate to snatch them from a passenger ship headed for the Americas, he would be searching for bodies, not living family members. Anyway, the letter attested to the fact they were hale and happy. Right before the *do not look for us* part. "They are alive."

"But taking Miss Germaine—you are playing with fire."

"Her father and his crew are holding my mother and Amelia against their will and it is up to me to get them back. Fire or no."

Thinking of his timid sister made his chest ache. He had been almost ten when she'd come wailing into the world. He and his brother John had been fighting the constraints of the new nursery for over a year, their obligations all changed now their family was titled and respectable. His bedroom had been situated right next to his enchanting little sister's. What no one knew was that he had lain awake at night, waited for her to stir. Then he would sneak into her room and play with her or keep her company until she was tired enough to fall back to sleep.

He'd loved her from the moment he'd laid eyes on her tiny red face screwed up and ready to let loose yet another cry. He'd wrapped his hand around her little fist and hummed to her and she'd quieted. Instantly. It wasn't long before she smiled for him. Laughed for him. Had his very being held tight and precarious in that fist of hers.

"And what of your name?" Hobson said, his loud voice banishing the happy memories. "What if these deeds get out and paint you in a worse light? You are finally starting to banish your past and move into your future."

James snorted. "That sounded alarmingly as though you care, Lieutenant."

Hobson drew himself up, his chest puffed out, and replied, "Only for the women. One such as you, Butcher of the Battle, can look after himself."

"I wish you wouldn't call me that. I would be happy to never hear it again as long as I live." He'd thought of little else but both his names since he received the note from his mother saying that she and Amelia were safe and happy and that he shouldn't search for them. The letter she had been forced to write by her abductor. If his mother had indeed authored the note, it would have gone on for at least four pages and would have said something about where they were and why they had left. There would have been wailing apologies and nonsense about the whys.

It had taken only two days to track them to a merchant ship where they'd paid for passage to the promised land. But news came back that that ship had sunk to the bottom of the ocean, her entire crew and all passengers taken aboard another.

Bloody pirates. They were a menace to everyone who thought to sail across the sea. From there he'd wasted more than a few thousand pounds and two months hiring mercenaries who'd found less than he had himself. One band of roughened men had even returned some of his blunt to him with the advice to stop chasing dead men and get on with his life.

Dead men indeed.

"I must get them back." Why in the world his closest relatives would want to head to the Americas without even offering a goodbye was the biggest puzzle in all that had happened so far. His mother could be flighty but his sister usually kept a level head. She was looking forward to more balls and picnics in the park and had spoken of nothing else in the months he had been home. They had all finally put scandal behind them and resigned themselves to normality and a second season on the town for Amelia when he'd arrived home from his club to find them gone without a trace.

James rubbed a hand against his breastbone. The pain there was uncomfortable. He wished the post-battle numbness would return: at least then he wouldn't have to feel regret or listen to his conscience or worry incessantly. What if *he* was the reason they'd left London? As much as he'd worked hard to return to his witty, charming self, war had changed him. Nightmares that made him cry out in the night left him grumpy and tired. He drank more, smiled less. He knew it. Amelia knew it. His mother did too. Perhaps they couldn't stand the man he'd become?

"Do you really think he holds them because you got away?" It was the first time Hobson had asked the question and he was glad for the distraction.

He'd thought about it too. But as much information as he'd gleaned about this pirate said his prisoners were always ransomed back to their families. He'd wished he'd known that when the ship he travelled on was taken off the coast of Calais. He would have sat on the deck in the weak sunshine like a child and waited for rescue. "Stabbing the captain in the leg was not my finest moment. I should have driven the blade into his black heart." His hands had been so cold and numb. Months spent as an army assassin in Egypt had impaired his resistance to the cold. And he'd seriously believed his life in danger. Butcher of the Battle indeed. He couldn't even dispatch one annoying pirate in the middle of a sea fight.

"It certainly would have made for a quieter retirement," Hobson said glumly.

"I'm a gentleman now. I'm supposed to be staid and boring and bored. I should not be planning an abduction to attract the attention of a bloodthirsty pirate." He refolded the note and placed it in the top drawer of his desk. Taking out his heavy signet from the box where he left it when masquerading as a coachman, he slipped it back on his finger with a sigh. Was it heavier today than it had been the week before?

Hobson clucked his tongue in a way that said he had more to say on the matter but would hold off for another time. James hoped he would hold off forever. He could not predict how long it would take for Captain Richard Germaine to get the notes James planned to send him or what actions her brother would take when he discovered her gone. These variables had been better allowed for in his original plan, but that couldn't be helped.

He would make their journey quite easy to follow but not easily predicted and therefore ambushed. He hoped that whatever Sir Anthony chose to do about his sister's disappearance, their father would fear a man named Butcher enough to rescue her. Just as he was rescuing his gentle Amelia.

Of course there was nothing gentle about Daniella. Where his sister was the most English of girls, with her light brown hair, brown eyes, pale skin, perfect posture and presence, Daniella Germaine was entirely a Scot, with all the fire and immoderation of that lawless race. Her flame-red hair had not been properly tamed once since he'd had the unfortunate pleasure of knowing her. A light tan darkened her skin despite London's dreary skies, freckles spotted her nose and cheeks and the chit didn't walk, she had a stride that ate up ground quicker than a lad's. And the piratical accent—it beggared belief that she'd ever been to a ton party making sounds such as those. Her green eyes were always full of mischief and never had she smiled serenely. She grinned. Constantly. It irked him.

See if she grins now, he thought irritably as he tipped another glass of whiskey down his throat.

"Where to first?" Hobson asked, his hand outstretched for the other glass before James drank it too. Again.

This is where all of his headaches and hard thinking would come to fruition. A full military assault was easier than putting up with that girl. "I believe Gretna Green should be our north. If we stay close to the west coast, he may come inland just far enough to collect his wayward child. We'll make our bargain, a hostage for the hostages, and then we can all go our separate ways. I just wish I knew exactly what it was he wanted."

"And if he doesn't meet us? If he only wants to kill you?"

"If you think I won't use Miss Germaine to save my own arse, you don't know me at all."

"But Gretna? What if he doesn't want her back or doesn't hear that you have her in time? Tell me you're not going to marry the girl."

"Hardly." He shook his head. "But her father doesn't have to know that."

FROM THE COVER of dense shrub, leaning against an ice-cold fence, a man watched the house where only moments before, the strangest scene had played out. Was it not enough the

Butcher had already made two women disappear? He needed a third? Perhaps Lasterton preyed on young women and that was the real reason he was known in military circles as the Butcher?

Where he stood afforded him a partial view of the front door so he settled in to wait. He recognized the young lady who'd been taken inside and agonized over his next course of action. The way he saw it, he had three choices. The first and only choice he should have considered would be to go to the Germaine house and let Sir Anthony know his sister had met with fouler play than she could concoct on her own. Another option was to walk right up to the front door and demand to know what was going on. Always a hothead in times of pressure, the stranger remembered his father's shouted words and drew a deep breath, settling farther into the damp branches.

Right now, there was too much at stake to risk spooking the marquess. He would wait, bide his time, keep watching his movements and, when the moment came to take back what was his, then he would pounce. The marquess had no idea of the trouble hurtling his way.

CHAPTER FOUR

D ANIELLA PEERED INTO all four corners of the small room and nodded her admiration of the housekeeper—there was no dust even here. She didn't like dust. It made her nose itch and her eyes water followed by sneezing fits that would not cease. Even though she had been taken against her will by a stranger, sneezing for the next few hours—or however long they planned to hold her—would not do. She needed a clear head to plan her next move.

The space was completely void of anything except for the wooden stool upon which she now sat, backside cushioned by the thin fabric of her cloak, and a single candle. Escape wasn't an option. Yet.

Should she let this James Trelissick keep her and hope there was indeed something about him that might force her father come after her? Could she take that risk? So far she'd tried everything she could think of to gain her sire's attention and none of it had worked. Perhaps this would.

She wasn't sure she could put herself so entirely in the hands of another though. Especially not one such as him.

Though the carriage had been dark, and his home was not much better lit, Daniella hadn't missed the intensity in his large brown eyes or the tension gripping the hard lines of his body. What puzzled her was why she hadn't discovered his identity when he'd masqueraded as her servant. She should have noticed the way he held himself was different, sure, almost arrogant—or had it been? Had he walked differently as her coachman? Were his acting skills that good or had she been so self-absorbed he had duped her with no effort at all? Now she had the time to dwell on it, she realized he'd stared at her with that unnerving gaze before. And she'd dismissed it. How perfectly obtuse—how perfectly aristocratic—of her.

She cursed under her breath. She could not and would not ever accept a position in English society. If her father had wanted that for her he should have lived a respectable life and never introduced her to the rolling deck of a ship or constant sunshine and crystal-blue waters. He especially should not have let her experience the thrill of a chase or let her taste battle. Now the dreary skies of London left her feeling sad, sullen and incredibly irritable. Well, more than usual. And of late, with the kind of husband her brother talked about finding for his wild sister, she had been more than a little desperate to make it back to the decks of *The Aurora*. A privateer's life should not be denied her simply because she had been born female.

Daniella huffed, leaned her head back against the wall and stretched her feet out beneath her confounded skirts. What she wouldn't give for trousers, to kick her shoes off and wriggle her toes. Well! As to that, there was no one to stop her. She leaned forwards and removed her delicate green shoes and then, feeling decidedly daring, her stockings as well.

The air was cool on her toes and she grinned.

The bonus to this detour in her plans was that her brother couldn't arrange "chance" meetings for her with his cronies. Her grin got wider when she thought about how red Anthony's face would turn when she didn't arrive for her own ball two nights hence.

It would serve him right. His priggish attitude towards his only sister grated on her nerves. He knew as well as any other that there would be no palatable offers for her hand. He should have stood up to their father then and there and refused to host her season rather than giving in to the farce that there was a husband somewhere in London who would make her more respectable. Just because her brother had been knighted for saving the prince didn't mean their family history would be erased or forgotten. More likely the monarch needed to keep peace on the streets and so knighted a reasonably educated, lowborn nobody for seemingly being in the right place at the right time.

Her smile slipped and she sighed, stared at her feet, at the small half-moon scar on the edge of the left one, where she had carelessly stepped on her own dagger while sparring.

Life had been simple once. Happy and content. How she longed to be again but it couldn't happen until she was safely back on the decks of her father's ship. Her brother kept talking about compromise. Search for a husband with a shipping line; marry a naval officer or a man with property close to the coast. Then she might be able to sail some of her days away.

Daniella snorted. Even she was not that naive. Perhaps a Scottish husband would allow a little of her wildness out to play for a time, before any children were born, but an English lord would expect her to embroider and take tea and generally be quite limpid and useless.

Her heart gave a wild thump when suddenly the silence was interrupted by the door lock sliding open with a click. The timber flew wide but she didn't get up, didn't bother to move at all as the deceitful marquess himself stood on the threshold and took stock.

"Making yourself at home?" he said with a raised brow.

Daniella shrugged and wriggled her toes again.

"There are some questions I wish to ask, if you would come this way?"

Daniella looked around and wondered if she should refuse. At least in this tiny room she was safe from his intentions and his anger.

"I'm not going to hurt you."

Damn him. Was he a mind reader too? "But you're not going to let me go either, are you?"

His gaze narrowed and he made as if to say something but instead shook his head.

"Then I shall leave my shoes." She stood and followed him into what appeared to be a cross between a study and a library. The diminutive one who had manhandled her was already seated in front of the desk but rose and bowed his head before waiting for her to sit in the chair next to him.

"I must say, this is all very strange," she remarked as she

settled her skirts to hide her toes. Not very effectively.

"Indeed," agreed her neighbour, as he stared at her ankles.

"Hobson," the marquess warned, his tone low, almost growly.

Ah, so that was his name. Daniella looked to where the marquess perched on the edge of the desk, swirling liquid in a tumbler between his fingers. Her mouth watered.

"May I have a drink?" she asked. "Please?"

"So you do have manners?"

She bristled. "Of course I do."

Hobson choked on a laugh and Daniella had to resist the urge to glare at him. Instead, she saved her glowers for the marquess. "You had questions. Let's get on with it."

"Do you have somewhere more pressing to be?"

"As a matter of fact, I do. The sooner my father hears you have me, the sooner I might get home."

"Home?"

"*The Aurora*," she pointed out with an impatient roll of her eyes. "How about you cease pretending you don't already know everything about me."

This time the marquess sighed, poured her a drink in a matching tumbler, and then sat behind his desk. "Not everything. If I had known what you were up to tonight, I would have abducted you this morning."

"Why didn't you?"

"You sound almost glad to be my hostage."

"Don't mistake me, my lord, I'm not one to easily hand over control, especially not when it comes to my future, but you seem to have a plan that is far better than my own. For the moment, I bow to your superior scheming."

"Why do you want to rejoin your father so badly?" he asked. "I would think some amount of continuity and safety would make a young lady happy."

"Then you would be wrong again. Safe is boring, stability stifling. You wouldn't understand since this is the only life you know."

He snorted and she knew she'd missed something by the expression on his face.

"Where do you think your father is right now?"

"I'm not just going to hand over information like that to someone like you."

"I didn't think so," he said with a wide grin. As much as Daniella tried to ignore it, his grin did things to her insides that she didn't want done. He really was very nice to look at now he was clean. Since arriving in London, she'd not been in the same room as a gentleman in his shirtsleeves other than her brother. Especially not one with his shirtsleeves rolled to his elbows and no necktie. Dark hair sprinkled his wide forearms and chest, similar growth darkening his jaw also. Perhaps he wasn't a gentleman after all?

"Who are you?" she asked, before thinking the better of opening her mouth.

"James Trelissick, the Most Honourable Marquess of Lasterton. I assume you know how to get a message to the captain?"

She shook her head and looked at him narrowly, ignoring the insulting bow he offered with the repeat of his name.

"No. Who were you when you weren't the Marquess of Lasterton?" There was more to his story and she wanted to know what it was. How could she hand over her fate without all the facts?

Hobson chose that moment to intervene. "His lordship was a major in his majesty's army."

"Hobson."

The man stared at Lasterton for a moment and then gave a small nod. She would have to remember that Hobson knew just as much as his master.

"I didn't know marquesses went to war." When *The Aurora* took a ship, the titled were always the fattest and laziest men and she often wondered if they did anything at all for themselves. This marquess was not fat and she doubted very much he suffered from idleness.

"I didn't have the title when my commission was purchased. How do you communicate with the captain when you are away from the ship?"

"I don't. I was forbidden any further contact."

"I don't believe you."

Fury warmed her cheeks. "Don't you think if I had a way to speak to my father, I would have considered that before putting my innocence up for sale?"

"Perhaps he ignored you and you retaliated with your ill-thought-out plan?"

Damn him. That's exactly what she had done. Desperate measures for desperate times. Still, she couldn't very well tell him that. "I am not five years old, sir."

His long sigh floated across the desk. "Yet you behave as

though you are."

Pressing a finger to his temple to ease the growing pain there, James stared at her across the table, trying his hardest to ignore the flash of her ankle as she tucked her feet beneath her. "How do you even know your father hears of your antics?"

So far Miss Germaine had been quite free with her answers, more than he would have been if captured, but this time her gaze shuttered and only her anger showed. "He has me watched."

"How do you know that?" James barely suppressed his eagerness. Maybe her brother had already been informed he had her?

"Because I'm not a simpleton. Send Hobson here to have a look around. I'd wager there is at least one man watching the house."

"Aye, don't even have to look. Felt his eyes on me when we came up the walk. Good at his job too. Didn't realize on the road that we were being followed."

He flicked his gaze from the smugness in Daniella's to the certainty in Hobson's. "And you didn't think to mention something like that?"

"You want the captain to know the miss is with us, don't you?"

"You two seem far too casual with what happened here tonight. Hobson, pirates are dangerous criminals. I should like to know when one loiters around my home. And you,

Miss Germaine, had better hope you're right. Without a sure way to inform your father I have you, we could be stuck together riding up and down the coast for the better half of the month."

"Or we could go straight to him."

He leaned forwards once again. "You said you had no way to contact him."

"I don't—he and my brother made sure of that—but I do know where he docks *The Aurora*, and I happen to know what times of the year he makes for home and how long he usually settles in."

"And where is that?" The chit was a liability. He wondered if that's why her father got rid of her. She talked far too much.

"First, what is the plan? You said you had one."

He nodded. "One I may need to rethink now depending on how far we are to travel."

"Well, I'm not going to tell you where he is. I might yet decide to escape."

James laughed. As much as he didn't want to, he admired her tenacity. "Escape? Not likely."

"You haven't completely convinced me you know what you're doing."

"*Convinced* you?" No, *this* was the reason the captain had dropped her off and sailed away. She was far too cocky.

"You've barely told me anything. In fact, you still haven't told me what my father has that you want back so desperately."

"And nor shall I." He stood and walked around the desk,

or rather, stalked. When he was close enough, he reached out and dragged her chair so she faced him, his large hands on the arms to trap her there. "Just so we're clear on the details, Miss Germaine, I am in charge here. You are my prisoner. There will be no escape. There will be no quarter so long as your father has what is mine. If I have to use you to get his attention, believe me, I will do whatever I must to achieve my ends. Do you understand?"

She gulped once, the smooth line of her throat giving her away. But then she firmed, her back straightened and she rose nose to nose with him, her bare toes sinking into the rug under his feet. "You may think you're in charge, my lord, but you have no idea who you're dealing with. You work on the assumption that my father will care that you have me, though he has in fact abandoned me, and may simply consider you a happy solution to my unmarried state. You can clearly not rely on me as bait, but I have his location and you have the means to travel there. Could an agreement between us not be mutually beneficial?"

James stepped back and crossed his arms over his chest. "Do you remember a fight two years ago, on the Channel, just off the coast of Calais? Your father flew French colours and took an army vessel disguised as a cargo ship?"

She paled.

"I rather thought you would. Your ship sustained damages *as did your captain*."

"You were there?"

"I was."

"You stabbed my father in the leg? That was you?"

"It was."

"If he finds you, he's going to kill you."

He rather doubted that. "I assume that's why he stole from me." Why he toyed with him now.

Curiosity flashed in her eyes while she thought about that. "He's drawing you out? But why?"

The last part of her question he imagined she asked herself but he answered anyway. "I hurt his pride. I escaped his capture and therefore cost him several ransoms. Several very lucrative ransoms. I would be upset with me too."

"But he didn't need the gold and we don't hold to pride the way you English do. He would have admired you for escaping if it hadn't been for…"

"For what?"

She had her head down but he could practically hear her thoughts. "If it hadn't been for what?"

"I can't be right. There must be something else you're not telling me."

He shook his head. He nearly shook her. "There isn't."

"Then you have to tell me what he took of yours. Otherwise it just doesn't make sense."

"What doesn't?" he roared and leaned towards her. His mother and sister depended on him to save them and she was the key. He didn't have time for guessing games.

"Revenge," she whispered, her green eyes wide.

"For escaping? You said he didn't have pride."

"I did not." She slipped past him to lean against the mantel. "I said hurt pride wouldn't make him do something like this."

"But revenge would? I don't understand, Daniella. Why would he risk it? And why now?"

"After you stabbed him, he developed an infection. We thought he would die."

"Well, he shouldn't have attempted to take a ship of returning servicemen. We were on our way home after months and years of fighting only to be drawn into another fray. Your father does not own the ocean. He has no right to take anything he wants."

"No more right than the English to think they own it, or the French to try to claim it. My father lost his leg after that day. He can no longer run the decks of the ship as he used to—he no longer sails as he used to."

He hadn't been aware of that. Guilt pricked through the hard shell of his numbness—one of the few emotions that could. "That is why you're so sure he will be docked?"

She nodded.

"Where?"

"I won't tell you."

"How do I arrange a meeting?"

"Nowhere in England, certainly."

"We stick to the plan and draw him out, get him to meet us. Hobson, search the gardens and see if you can discover the eyes watching Miss Germaine. A live messenger would serve our purpose better than an undelivered note."

"We don't *need* any of that. I tell you I can take you to my father. And if he hates you as much as you imagine, his home ground is the safest place to meet him. He keeps the peace there, and he ensures the rest do too."

"If you knew where he was all this time, why did you not go to him?"

Daniella sighed and the guilt was there to needle him again. "'Tis a twelve-day land journey if the weather is kind. My brother doesn't allow me enough pin money to hire a crew or passage on a ship and overland would be even harder to arrange without his notice. I might make thirty miles but then what? Alone and penniless. My plan was much the same as yours: draw my father out, make him send for me. It hasn't worked, can't you see?"

When her chin drooped all the way to her chest in defeat, James knew what she was thinking. That her father didn't care enough for her to risk his own life.

Nor would he if their situations were reversed.

Daniella frequently behaved recklessly and without thought. Her father probably held out hope that she would one day wake up a woman and act like one. To James that day seemed a long way off.

"I assume we'll find him in Scotland?" It's where most of his intelligence gathering had led him so far.

She nodded.

"Where?" He gritted his teeth.

And she hers. "I won't tell you but I can take you."

"You expect me to blindly follow you into what could be an ambush? A trap? Worse?"

"Don't be ridiculous. I didn't know who you were or what you planned to do—when would I have had the time to create yet another scheme?"

She was right but a smart man never went to battle without weapons or know-how. "Twelve days is too long to travel: we'll go by sea."

"He'll see you coming."

"How? You said he would be docked. Since he is a pirate who wishes to remain undiscovered, he would be moored somewhere shut off, out of the way."

"There are many Scotsmen who still hate the English. Hours after the first one lays eyes on you, the message will be passed along the coast until everyone knows who you are. The news always gets through. How do you think we were so successful?"

"I don't spend my days pondering the inner workings of pirates and thieves."

"We wouldn't have to thieve if we were allowed to be about our business without constant harassment by your king and his exorbitant taxes."

He had to admire her spunk. She was a prisoner yet she acted like a houseguest helping him with complex puzzles and arguing about politics. That was preferable to sullenness but her calm might let them down once they were on their way.

"So we travel by road but send messages by sea?"

"That's right. And after we cross the border, we'll need guards. You would never pass for anything but English and the danger will be high."

"How far into Scotland must we travel? Into the Highlands?"

Daniella smiled and sat back in her chair, her fingers steepled before her. "You can stop asking me our final destination because I'll never reveal it."

"How am I to know which direction to give the driver?"

"You won't. After we cross the border, I'll navigate. You're going to have to trust that I want the same outcome as you do."

"Trust you, a pirate? Once again you mistake your place in this." In truth, James trusted no one save Hobson. It had kept him alive throughout countless campaigns so far.

Daniella stood and James fought to keep his eye from wandering to bare little toes once again peeking from beneath her revealing gown.

"You can't control everything," she pointed out. "Even generals have need of intelligence from the lower ranks." She swished past him into the corridor where Mrs McDougal held a platter of sandwiches and a pot of tea. "Let me know when you decide my place in all of this."

"And then what?"

But she didn't answer. Just climbed back into the room below the stairs, took the tray from his housekeeper's hands and closed the door.

CHAPTER FIVE

IT TOOK ONLY another hour until James was forced to admit he might need Daniella's help if he planned to reach his mother and sister. Each sweep of the minute hand around the clock face was another hour they were in danger, another hour his sister's reputation sustained lasting damage and another hour he blindly stumbled about and prayed they were still alive. He'd wasted enough time on dead-end leads. If he couldn't draw the captain out, he would have to risk marching up and knocking on his door—for which he would need Daniella. He didn't take to inaction kindly and it had been nearly five months since their disappearance. He was a man who charged into battle and came out victorious time and again. So why now, when the players numbered only a handful, did he feel so useless, as though hope had deserted him? Was it because the stakes were the highest he'd ever known or was it because he had no idea where to start the campaign? Perhaps it was because he had to place himself and his family in the hands of a selfish, spoiled girl.

Boot steps on the tile outside his study signalled the return of Hobson. "No sign of anyone outside now. Whoever it was left as quietly as he came."

"Damn. You were both so sure there was a watchman."

"Probably just some drunkard having a piss or something. I think the miss suffers an overactive imagination but I was sure I felt someone watching," Hobson said gruffly.

"If there isn't a spy then no one knows she is missing yet."

"It's only a matter of time before the alarm is raised. The maids have to go to her rooms to feed the fire eventually. And there was someone out there at some stage."

They'd collected and collated knowledge about the inner workings of Sir Anthony's home for a month and now the information would help them. "Germaine might not seem to care for his sister a great deal, but he would already be on the doorstep if it was his spy. He doesn't enjoy appearing the fool." James shook his head. "We'll work this to our favour. I don't want to wait until someone tells Sir Anthony we have his sister. I don't even care if the useless blackguard never knows where she is. As long as we reach the captain and have her to trade, the outcome will be favourable." James sat behind his desk and took out four pieces of parchment. On each of them he wrote the same words of ransom for Captain Germaine to read. He was to prepare his "items of value" to swap them for his daughter.

"These will need to be delivered to the docks. Pay for their passage north and give instructions that they are only to be handed on to Scottish fishermen, the rougher the better."

"Then what?" Hobson asked.

James stood, flicked open his watch and met the gaze of his oldest and most trusted friend. "It is two o'clock now; if we can be on the road within the next few hours we'll have a good head start. If Anthony does discover her missing before then, he can give chase. He'll say she has retired, ill, I imagine. That way she can choose to return to the Marriage Mart if indeed this story of preferring the sea is the hogwash it smells like."

"So we are for Gretna?" Hobson asked.

"Forget Gretna for the moment. We'll head in that direction but once we cross the border we'll let Daniella navigate."

"And if she is leading us into a trap?"

"If we see it in time, we make for Gretna and wait it out in a public place full of both English and Scottish witnesses. If her father took Amelia and Mother to draw me out, if this is some kind of revenge attempt, he will either wait for us or meet us halfway."

"Why don't you just compromise and marry her? Then her father will have to give the women back. He won't hurt his little girl's husband or his kin."

"Firstly, she is a pirate and a hoyden, not the wife of a marquess. Secondly, you assume Captain Germaine has a moral compass where I think he would be just as happy to see his daughter widowed to inherit my money. I would play into his hands and get myself killed and all he would have to do is drive the knife in."

Hobson's eyes opened wide for a moment and then he guffawed loudly. Once his laughter died down, he grew serious. "How do you think he worked out that it was you who stabbed him that day? He weren't exactly asking questions."

"That stupidity was my own fault. I identified myself in the hopes he would find his conscience and let us live without a fight."

"By all reports, he does enjoy a fight. What makes you think you'll be the victor in this one?"

"How many battles have I lost?"

"None."

"If the man had brains at all, he would never have invited me into a fray."

"You can't win them all, James."

He smiled then, a cold tightening of his lips. "Oh yes I can."

DANIELLA WAS FAR less than prepared when the door to her prison opened and once again Lasterton filled the doorway. Clean-shaven and dressed more like a king than a servant, he peered down his nose at her. "You have ten minutes to refresh yourself and then we leave."

No please or thank you? "You can't expect me to cross the country in this gown." She had liked it because it was daring and made her feel beautiful and desirable but here, with him, she was just cold and half-dressed.

"There is another gown waiting for you."

"Whose?" she asked, as she narrowed her eyes at him.

"My sister is a different shape from you but it will have to do."

"I do hope she doesn't object to you lending her clothing

to a stranger."

He shrugged but his shoulders were tense and a fleeting wariness flickered in his eyes for a moment before he answered. "She and my mother are travelling the continent. I dare say she'll purchase a hundred more and discard all the others as unfashionable upon her return."

Daniella bit her tongue against a sharp reply about English women having far more allowance than good sense but she couldn't afford to fight with him. It was already going to be difficult sitting across from him in a carriage for near on two weeks. If they set off on bad terms it would be that much harder. "Very well, if you're sure she won't mind."

By the end of fifteen minutes, Daniella swore and cursed fashionable ladies as though they were responsible for all the trouble she now found herself in. Twisting this way and that, stretching her arms over her head, behind her back, across her shoulders, she still couldn't reach the row of tiny buttons that marched mockingly up the back of the pale blue gown. Holding her breath didn't help either since her stays had already done their job of pulling her tight.

The gown was quite low in the neckline and was cinched just below her bust to drop to the floor around her ankles. She couldn't even do up most of the buttons and then pull the dress up because it was too small for her. The sister must be a very tall, very slender Amazon.

A knock startled her so she cursed the door as well as the man who almost certainly stood on the other side.

"I need a few more minutes," she called through clenched teeth.

THE ROAD TO RUIN

THE ROAD TO RUIN

"We need to go now."

"Well, I'm not ready."

The handle on the door turned but it held since she'd locked it from the inside.

"Miss Germaine, open the door."

"Not yet," she huffed and renewed her struggles in earnest. She could wield a sword in waves higher than a ship, yet a little row of pearls was going to prove her undoing.

"Open the door this instant."

She ignored him, her fingertips finally touching the edge of one button. More seconds passed but she was able to push one more through the impossibly small corresponding hole. A sigh of relief escaped her as she let her arms relax so the blood could flow again. The dress sagged everywhere it wouldn't if the damned thing had laces or was her own size.

"I'm coming in there, Daniella. If you have a leg out of the window, I *will* drag you back in."

Not for one moment had she considered escaping the house, just the nuisance gown. "I just need a little more time."

The lock clicked and he barged in, his eyes going first to the still-closed window and then to her, where she stood before the basin. He raised his brows but didn't ask, didn't say a word.

"I can't get the bloody buttons done up on this bloody dress that doesn't bloody fit!" she exploded, turning in a frustrated circle, her arms once again wrapping around her body.

"Language, Daniella," he admonished with half a grin.

"Why didn't you ring for the housekeeper?"

"I don't need help; I'll be done in a moment."

"We don't have time for this," he muttered. "Turn around."

"I don't think so."

"Turn. Around."

His tone was so commanding, so demanding, she could do nothing else but comply. He really did sound like a general.

At the first brush of his warm fingers against her shift, she twitched. Their situation was most improper. She smiled.

"You are not supposed to enjoy this," he murmured, bending to his task so that his hot breath whispered over her back.

"Enjoy what? I don't think I'm going to be able to breathe deeply again for days. Surely your sister has a wider dress than this one?"

"No. This is the most, ah, commodious I could find."

Daniella felt short as a squab, as her bare toes were swamped by the frilled hem. "Do you stretch her on a rack?"

She wasn't prepared for his chuckle. If she had been prepared, she would have thought of something else before his warm breath skated over her skin and a blush heated her cheeks. Before all she could think about was melting into him and thinking how to make him chuckle again.

Damn. *Those* were the kind of thoughts that saw her stranded in London in the first place.

Making eyes at a deckhand had evidently been the proof her father needed to finally see her as a woman rather than a child and to therefore ship her off to the capital to find a husband before she found more trouble. What would the captain make of her blushing at her abductor?

"I do not. Amelia is, to her horror, naturally very tall and very slim."

"English men are attracted to buxom women," she said matter-of-factly before thinking the better of it.

"Many of us are, yes," he replied as the last button slipped home.

She turned slowly, her breath held more from anticipation rather than the too-tight dress. "Oh?" That one word came out more a squeak than the sophisticated question she meant it. He was so close, the flecks of honey glinted in the brown around his pupils.

He shook his head. She followed the action with eyes that surely betrayed her.

"I'm sorry. That's the response I always give Amelia when she complains about being gangly. She is rarely grateful for my honesty."

So he talked to her the same way as to his sister? Even though disappointment drooped her shoulders, there was a part of her that was not unhappy he treated her thus.

"You said we were out of time?"

"We do have to be on our way. The horses will grow restless and soon the streets will fill with servants and such." He turned and walked out of the room without waiting to see if she was finally ready or if she would even follow.

She wanted to drive a knife into his shoulder then and there. Daniella drew a breath in, exhaled, counted to five and stared at the window. She knew she wouldn't make it far but it looked enticing nonetheless.

By the time she reached the bottom of the curving staircase, Lasterton stood with her slippers dangling from his fingertips, irritation pinching his features. She fought the urge to poke her tongue out at him.

The front door opened and Hobson's head appeared. "The bags are strapped. We're ready to go when you lot are."

Her captor nodded once and started for the door. "Put it around to the staff that if anyone asks for me once we're gone, I'm on my way to Scotland via the North Road."

She slipped her feet into her shoes then followed him across the hall.

"Wait behind the door while I check for passers-by," he said, and she nodded.

At his signal, she ducked under his arm and pattered down the front stairs to the waiting carriage. Hoof beats sounded down around the corner—she froze, but Lasterton, right behind her, grasped her about the waist and tossed her into the shelter of the conveyance, then jumped in before she had even decided which way was up.

"You need to be gentler with the miss," a female voice admonished from across the small space as the carriage lurched into motion.

"She could have climbed in herself," Trelissick pointed out with a shrug.

Once Daniella could see again she threw a glare at the marquess, but he was busy looking out the window at the passing buildings beginning to be lit by the rising sun. She guessed it to be somewhere around six in the morning. Sitting across from her was Mrs McDougal. Some more conciliation could only help her cause.

"Thank you for thinking to bring me a chaperone. It isn't necessary, but it is a kindness."

This time he did turn his gaze to her but it was too dark for her to read his eyes. "Mrs McDougal is here solely to ensure I don't have to marry you if we should be seen by members of the upper echelons."

She drew in an outraged breath. "In case you hadn't noticed, I am not the marrying type."

Mrs McDougal huffed but obviously knew better than to speak for her master.

"You're never going to marry?" he asked.

She shook her head. "Probably not."

"What are you going to do for the rest of your life?"

"Now that my father has retired, I plan to take charge of *The Aurora* and sail the seas. I won't need a husband to see that happen."

"Your father may have objections to that."

This time it was her turn to shrug. "He'll come around to my way of thinking."

"You do know you don't rule the world, don't you?"

"What is that supposed to mean?"

"In the month I've been watching you, you haven't taken a care for anyone else's welfare or social standing at all. Your behaviour reflects poorly on your brother, indeed on everyone you associate with. There are others to consider when you sell your virginity in a warehouse on the docks."

She gulped. She stuttered. Her cheeks warmed. "You don't understand."

"Oh, there you are wrong. I understand you think you know better than everyone else. I understand you value your reputation with no more than a passing thought. I understand you have been indulged for far too long. It's little wonder your father dropped you off and then staged his own death to be rid of you."

JAMES SHOULD HAVE stopped talking. He should have closed his eyes and pretended to sleep until their first stop. But something in him had snapped and he couldn't patch it up. How the hell was he to have predicted what would happen when faced with the smooth expanse of her back emerging from her shift? She was his hostage—at best his collaborator—not his mistress.

In the four weeks he'd watched her, he hadn't once looked at her as anything but a means to rescue his mother and sister. Why now, after kidnapping the girl, did his desires have to awaken? He shuddered. The easiest way to lose all he held dear was to think of Daniella Germaine as anything but a hostage. The next was to make her furious. He watched as she drew herself upright on the seat, her back straight and her pert little chin in the air.

"My father," she spat, "did not wish to be rid of me. He wishes for me a better life."

James rolled his eyes—anything to lift them from where her chest rose but the dress did not. "So life on a pirate ship isn't as glamorous as one is led to believe?"

"Privateer ship," she corrected, her passion and fire only adding to her allure.

"Oh yes, I apologize for not making the distinction." A snort from his left and he turned his raised brow on Mrs McDougal, who fought laughter with an impish grin.

"There is a difference, you know."

"I know the difference but I wonder if you do? In the history of boats on the sea quite a few have claimed to be privateers but most were nothing but pirates with special letters from this king or that. Did your father have any such letters?"

Daniella nodded in triumph. "He did."

"From whom?"

"The King of Spain."

James shook his head and made a *tsk tsk* sound. "He hands those things out like sweets so he can expand his coffers with ill-got gains. I'll tell you if the English were to capture your ship, or even the Americans, that piece of paper would be burned along with the rest of her."

Her look changed from triumph to fury again and she crossed her arms in defiance.

James closed his eyes and rested his head against the squabs. For the first time in his life he wished his sister, Amelia, was rounder. At least then her dress would have fit Daniella instead of squashing those breasts inwards and upwards. He made a mental note to retrieve a pelisse or coat from the luggage at the first stop. He made another to ensure his sister wore a fichu in all of her gowns in the future.

Daniella didn't argue with him anymore as the coach rattled its way through the streets of London heading north. The only sound came from Mrs McDougal's knitting needles ticking as she worked on what loosely resembled a scarf.

The last twelve hours had been such a drain on his nerves and his temper. He hoped the weather stayed clear and they made good time so he could be rid of the troublesome chit all the sooner. How could any young lady think it a good idea to sell her innocence, even if the sale were staged? There were shameless members of the demimonde who wouldn't behave as rashly as Miss Germaine. When he got back to London, he would seek out Pendleton and box the pup's ears for his encouragement of her scheme.

If he made it back to London.

As much as James didn't want to dwell on the morbid side of what he set out to do, he had to face the fact that if this went wrong, he would be going back to his home in a timber box with a ball in his heart or a blade in his back. If Miss Germaine didn't betray and murder him, he was sure her father would have a good crack at it. Amelia and his mother were dear to him but if he had a daughter and someone made off with her, held her for ransom, he would be out for blood too. Thoughts of young women being treated badly led his mind to wander to the other virgins from the auction block and he swore, his eyes opening wide. He hadn't sent warning to Wigby at his estate to expect them. Damn the fool girl.

Lord, he hoped the captain really did want her back once

this was all over and done with.

Sir Anthony Germaine rubbed a hand over his brow and sighed. He'd had the night from hell and hadn't yet retired, the glass in his hand long since empty and the sun high in the morning sky. Not for the first time he thought about packing up his London townhouse and moving far away. Somewhere he could be accepted for the man he was rather than the tales of his father's past. There had to be some part of the world the Germaine name wasn't known.

Of course, the events of the previous night made it impossible for him to run anywhere.

Anthony flexed his toes and had to bite his tongue against sudden and blinding pain in his ankle. Broken. That was the doctor's educated guess. Stupid. That was his cousin Darcy's opinion. Irreparably soiled. The young lady's father's words. The young lady he had fallen on when he'd attempted to climb over a balustrade in a garden to avoid another woman's furious glares. He'd hit the ground hard, smashed his ankle on a boulder unseen in the dark and collided with the once honourable Miss Something-or-rather. Elmira? Alvira? He'd never seen the chit in his life, but all in the space of ten seconds, they had become affianced.

Never mind that it was a mistake, a misunderstanding of monumental proportions. She had been alone in the garden and when she shrieked, a passer-by (a vicar strolling with his wife no less) had discovered the pair in each other's arms. Elmira. Yes, that was her name. She had instinctively reached out to steady him as he barrelled into her. They hadn't been hugging or kissing or any other such scandalous action. He hadn't even caught her name until her father was summoned and her mother cried while the miss herself just stared at everyone in confusion. Was she a simpleton or had she been merely swept up in the madness the same as he had?

So there he sat, a debilitating headache from the spirits and a sick stomach from a lack of food, or perhaps it was an overabundance of fear and stupidity that made him feel ill. He wanted to be a respected and respectable member of society. He had saved the prince's life for God's sake. But nothing he did made up for his father's past antics or his half-sister's current disasters. Perhaps Miss Elmira's father would have him killed rather than wed his daughter to the son of a pirate? One could hold on to the hope.

"Brahm!" he called over his shoulder. His butler usually hovered somewhere close but theirs wasn't a large house so in any case he had no doubt he would be heard.

"Yes, Sir Anthony?" he replied seconds later as he entered the room.

"Has my sister risen from her bed yet? I have need of her." He almost laughed aloud at his own words. Was he seriously considering asking her advice in all of this?

"The lady has not yet come down to break her fast."

"Wake her at once and send her to me."

"If you're sure, milord?"

Anthony stared at him. Even his own staff didn't give him the respect they should, forever questioning his every command. He knew they meant well but it wasn't as if he had to like it.

"At once, milord."

Minutes passed in which Anthony poured himself another drink from the decanter on the little table at his side. He may as well get comfortable since he would not be able to walk for at least a month, after which he would swap this shackle for another more permanent one.

A commotion in the open doorway gained his undivided attention as Brahm entered, followed by a footman and two maids, one in tears, the other wringing a cloth between her hands.

"What has Daniella done this time?" Anthony asked, mentally bracing for another shock. Why so many in one morning?

Brahm drew a deep, steadying breath and then stepped forwards. "It seems that Miss Germaine did not make it home last night, milord."

"At all?" came Anthony's mild response.

The crying maid came forwards as well. "She told me not to wait up for her, that she'd be late, but she never said nothing about not coming back at all."

Damn her. "Send for Pendleton: that boy always seems to know Daniella's movements and exploits."

As he said the words, a furious knocking sounded at the front door. Anthony made to stand but the pain shot up his leg and with a mighty curse he fell back into the chair. "That will be the runners," he muttered under his breath as he gestured for the butler to see what it was about. His sister had probably been arrested. Again.

His butler wasn't the most circumspect around but he knew his place and he knew society so when voices became raised in the portico, Anthony damned his broken ankle to hell. Daniella needed to be horsewhipped and soon.

Brahm skidded to a halt outside the door. "A captain is here to see you." He got no more words out as the captain in question charged into the room, his hat still on his head, his filthy boots leaving mud tracks on the Aubusson. In the middle of all of the disaster, the man held a sheet of folded paper in his hands.

"And you are?" Anthony prompted after he dismissed his staff with a gesture.

"Darius. I was a friend of your father's a long time ago."

"A pirate friend?"

The stranger laughed and took a seat without invitation directly opposite Anthony. "At one stage of my life, yes."

"What brings you by?" Anthony clenched his teeth; all this civility made him feel as though his skull would crack.

"My bosun was this morning given an interesting note to be carried to Scotland and put in the hands of Captain Richard Germaine."

"And you're here telling me this why? My father and I don't communicate regularly so you can deliver the note yourself."

"The note concerns Daniella. Is she here?"

Anthony shook his head, torn between keeping his sister's unknown whereabouts a secret and sending a search party out for her, which would create yet another scandal. "She is indisposed."

Darius narrowed his eyes and reclined against the back of the settee. "You're sure about that?"

"Just what exactly is in that note? I take it you read it?" Pirates rarely observed even the most sacred niceties of postal etiquette.

"I did. Do you know the Marquess of Lasterton? A James Trelissick?"

"Not personally. I've heard of him but we haven't yet crossed paths."

"So you know of no reason he would kidnap your sister in order to initiate a trade of some sort?"

Anthony leaned forwards in his chair, his hands clenched on his knees. "The devil you say?"

"It says right here, right above the seal of said gentleman, that he has taken Daniella and will meet the captain at Gretna in two weeks and he had better have the marquess's belongings or she will find herself in a lot more trouble than where he found her."

Anthony's head thumped as he closed his eyes. "What has she done now?"

"There was a whisper of a tale, a red-headed gentlewoman selling her virginity at an auction last night. Heard the news over my morning ale down at the docks. Of course I wouldn't put a lot of stock in the man's words, only he had more coin to throw about than he did sense to keep his mouth shut."

She *didn't*? She probably did. Anthony groaned.

"I can tell you that Daniella did not leave by boat. The marquess's house is being closed up and the servants are remarkably tight-lipped. They'll only say that the master heads for the country. His carriage isn't in his stables but yours is."

"My carriage? In his stable?" The effects of so much liquor and very little movement began to take a toll and the room spun violently. She would be the death of him. He knew she wanted to leave London, but with Lasterton? Anthony wasn't even aware the two had been previously introduced. What would the Butcher want with his sister anyway? Her virginity, paid for? He almost snorted.

"So you'll go after her? You know, after you retrieve your carriage that is," Darius said.

Anthony shook his head. He couldn't even chase a mouse around the room let alone a carriage across the countryside. "I can't leave town. I'll be called out. I won't ever be able to return."

"What are you talking about, man? She's your sister."

"Half-sister..." he replied with vague sentiment. "I've a suspected broken ankle and now a fiancée. Daniella got herself into this mess. She will have to get herself out. She's a cunning bit of baggage; I'm sure she'll be back by the end of the day with a great adventurous scandal to talk about and another black mark against her name. And mine."

"So you would leave her to her fate?" Darius asked him.

Anthony nodded; his chest squeezed. "I have no choice, not this time. Lasterton is an army man, perhaps he will instil a measure of discipline into the girl."

Darius laughed but it lacked humour and warmth. "That might not be all he instils in her."

"If you care for my sister and call yourself a friend of my father's, why do you not go after her yourself?"

"I've a ship and men to think about and a job to do in England. I didn't come here planning to chase your sister God-knows-where."

"No one ever plans when it comes to Daniella."

Anthony almost winced when a thoughtful look crossed the other man's face.

"If I do go after your sister and bring her back here—"

"Not here," Anthony said firmly. "If you find her, take her to Father. She won't be welcome back in London if even one whisper of this gets out amongst the ton."

Darius nodded slowly. "If I set off after her, you will owe me a favour."

Anthony narrowed his eyes, cursing when Darius's form blurred before him. "What kind of favour? I don't have funds to speak of and I'll soon be either dead or married at the end of a pistol point. What could I possibly do for you?"

He shrugged. "I don't know yet but if I come to you, no matter the favour, you will say yes?"

"If it is within my power, then yes, damn you, the answer is yes."

"Excellent." The filthy pirate stood and rubbed his hands together.

It dawned on his very slow senses that Anthony had just been duped somehow. "You would have gone after her anyway, wouldn't you?"

"Probably." The grin that accompanied the words made Anthony want to grab the man by the neck, but he wasn't a violent sort. Not usually.

He had a feeling that was all going to change in the coming months…

CHAPTER SIX

B Y MIDAFTERNOON, DANIELLA had had enough of the carriage. She'd had enough of Mrs McDougal's incessant clicking as she knitted what appeared to be very large, coarse socks, and she'd had enough of the borrowed dress threatening to take more of her breath away. After their first stop, Lasterton had jumped down from the carriage with the order for her to stay put, still treating her like a child or a hound. When next he appeared, he thrust a thick hooded cloak into her hands with a curt command to don it.

"But I'm not cold," she'd complained.

He gave her a look that said he didn't care one bit for her comfort. "Put it on or stay in the carriage. It's your choice."

God how she hated that carriage. The sway of a ship as the vessel rode the waves was what she was used to, not bumps and groans and creaks over cobbles and dirt. Or the way the carriage lurched when they were off or when one of the horses lost its rhythm and tried to find it again. Swinging the cloak around her shoulders, she tied it tight, lifted the hood and followed Mrs McDougal from the nightmarish conveyance.

"We will eat a light meal and then be on our way again,"

the marquess said in that tone that was not to be argued with. He pinned Daniella with a hard glare. "You will do as you're told. You will not try to sway anyone over to your side, no thoughts of escaping me to get to your father quicker are to fill your head—and do not tell anyone your real name. Is that understood?"

"Aye aye, captain," she said with a little salute. What an arrogant man to think he could order everyone around with nary a please or thank you in it. She wondered if he was always this cranky or if it was the situation itself rendering him unbearable. When he'd spoken to her as though she was nothing more than an incorrigible bairn she'd wanted to kick his shins or worse. He was refusing to understand that she only wanted to be on the decks of her ship. Why any woman would want to live her life according to the ton's set of rules she had no idea. It was like a smoky prison of their own making and she didn't want a bit of it.

But she would let men like Lasterton think they ruled all those around them if it gained her place back on the decks of *The Aurora*.

As much as she despised his heavy-handedness, she did like that the marquess had them on a tight schedule. If they could decrease by even one moment her time in that carriage she would be thanking God.

As they filed in to a clean and bright taproom, Lasterton ordered refreshments to be served in a private dining room— only to be told the only one the inn boasted was already occupied. While he and the landlord bartered on suitable eating areas, Daniella looked around at the occupants of the room for any sign of one of her father's men, though she hadn't seen a familiar face in weeks. And why was her brother taking so long to come after her? Surely he would have discovered her missing by now and be in pursuit?

Not that that was at all what she wanted.

If *Saint* Germaine found her first, he would drag her back to the city and a marriage agreement before she could blink. After all, she tarnished his near-perfect reputation with her schemes. Even the marquess's superior attitude and arrogance would be preferable to that fate.

She gripped the edges of her hood and pulled the fabric farther over her face.

"This way, m'dear." Lasterton held out his arm for her to take. She really should have been listening to the excuse he'd given the innkeeper. Were they married? Was she his sister or cousin? They should have discussed ruses before now so she knew how to act.

Rather than ruining whatever story he'd spun, she silently took his arm and let him lead her to a small but cosy sitting room. There were only soft sofas and a few chairs around a small table as furniture but the fire was built and it beckoned. She hadn't felt the cold before but she did now. She suspected the sudden chill shivering its way down her spine had more to do with foreboding than it did the air temperature.

After the innkeeper promised sustenance and closed the door, Daniella turned on the marquess, despite the presence of his staff. "Are we working together or not? Will you please tell me what stories you are spreading around before we leave the carriage?"

"Keep your voice down. I don't want to be followed too closely. We'll leave a different tale each time we stop."

He really was better at this than she had been. She refused to look at either Hobson or Mrs McDougal, already knowing the smirks they were undoubtedly wearing.

"We cannot risk someone coming to your aid. Whether you are a willing hostage or not, I'll not let anyone interfere in this."

Daniella nodded and turned to the fire for comfort. She wouldn't remind him she only remained his hostage while it suited her. If at any time she thought he meant her harm, she would escape. But where would she go? She had no money. No belongings. Nothing but her name and her father's reputation. It's why she'd attempted to sell her virginity. It's why she sought deeper disgrace. If she had the funds of a marquess, she would have simply booked passage on a ship and run back to him again and again.

Until they reached Scotland, where the humblest of farm boys knew and respected Captain Richard Germaine, she was at Lasterton's mercy.

There was no more time to think about anyone's mercy as the innkeeper's wife came into the room bearing a tray of pies and ale. Not one of their party moved until the small-statured lady closed the door behind her.

Trelissick cleared his throat. "Everyone eat. This will be our last stop before nightfall."

Hobson and Mrs McDougal each picked up a plate without hesitation and sank into chairs to eat.

As tenterhooks dug deeper, Daniella took a plate, but the constant tension of the day left her feeling vaguely uneasy and she picked only at the top crust. She worried that if she did eat, she would see the food again in not much time at all such were her nerves.

"You have to keep your strength up, Daniella."

The way he said her name so softly did things to her already upset stomach. "You aren't eating," she pointed out, more to distract herself than him.

He shook his head.

"Nervous?" she asked.

"Not so much nervous as terrified."

She was surprised. "Terrified? Of what?"

"Whom, is more like it. This could go badly at any time for either one of us. For all of us really. Your brother could even now be in pursuit with his pistols already loaded."

"You don't know much about my brother then," she said wryly.

"If you were my sister, I would avenge your honour."

The way he said the words, she knew he meant it. She warmed slightly towards him. "The only reason my brother would want me back is to marry me to one of his old friends and so be rid of me." And she did mean old.

"Where was Anthony when you were aboard the pirate ship?" Lasterton asked her.

Grinding her teeth with frustration, Daniella longed to remind him once again that *The Aurora* was a privateer ship. It had been many a year since they had flown the Jolly Roger: they had a bountiful enough time sailing for the King of Spain. The greedy monarch had no way to discern how much they kept for themselves and how much they returned to his shores.

"My half-brother was away at Eton by the time I was born. He is much older than me."

"So you have different mothers?"

"We *had* different mothers."

"What happened to your mother?"

"She died." Her stomach did a flip-flop and she put her plate back on the table.

Trelissick waited but Daniella didn't elaborate. Her mother was no privateer. She was a common Scottish woman of indiscriminate morals and Daniella hadn't seen her since she was four years old.

Daniella inwardly groaned and nearly rolled her eyes. Behind closed doors, being a pirate's daughter was exciting and thrilling for the empty-headed debutantes. She should have told them all about her lowborn mother trading her only daughter for jewels and coins and scuppered her chances of a London marriage once and for all. Why did she always choose for herself the most difficult paths?

"Daniella?" Lasterton called her name.

"I'm sorry." She shook her head. "I was woolgathering. What did you say?"

"I said I'm sorry to upset you. I shouldn't ask you such questions when it is none of my business."

"Tell me about your family," she prompted, wishing for silence but hoping at least to be allowed to listen rather than speak.

He swallowed: she saw his throat working as his skin paled. Abruptly, he reached into his pocket and withdrew his watch. "Time to go." Then he rose and walked from the room.

Daniella was left to follow with Hobson, who had eaten only a little, and Mrs McDougal, who had all but polished her plate with a dry crust of bread. Were they not nervous about discovery, terrified of pursuit?

When she flicked a glance at them, they both seemed quite content, as though this wasn't the first time they'd kidnapped a lady. She gulped. She hoped it was the first time they had kidnapped a lady.

The next hours in the confines of the carriage were very nearly Daniella's undoing. Every bump in the road, every loud noise between Hobson and the driver made her breath hitch in her throat. She didn't want her brother catching them up and dragging her back to London. He would never leave her to live a life of her choosing, and now that she'd broken free of the capital the idea of returning made her heart ache.

She sighed and settled back into the soft velvet. Her brother wanted nothing more than an advantageous marriage for her. When she had asked him about independence, he'd scoffed and told her a good husband was all she should hope for, that women are dependent by their very nature and wouldn't get far in the world on their own. If the truth were to be told, she would have entertained the idea of a man she liked enough to put up with day after day. She might have even married a rich (and complacent) man so she would have money enough to disappear and set sail for her father's inlet once a year. But no one wanted her. Not one offer had been made. Not even from the more lecherous members of the ton—at least not until it had only been her virginity they were required to take. She was undesirable.

Unwanted.

It was about time her father saw that in her wild up-bringing, her freckles and red hair, and took her back. At least on the decks of a ship, she would be happy and free.

She supposed she could ask Lasterton why even he apparently didn't believe her about that. But it wasn't a question one blurted out over carriage seats.

APPARENTLY WHAT ONE did blurt out over carriage seats was bad pie.

James hadn't wanted to stop until traveling became dangerous due to the dark but when Mrs McDougal began to cast up her accounts right there in the carriage, he was forced to re-evaluate for the day.

"Hobson?" he called through the open carriage window.

There was no reply.

He rapped sharply on the ceiling with his knuckles and the vehicle slowed and moved off to the edge of the road. He'd barely taken the breath needed to order Mrs McDougal out before the door was open and the poor woman on her knees in the damp grass.

He threw a glance towards Daniella, who sat poker straight against the squabs, face implacable, hands in her lap like a demure lady. He nearly snorted.

They hadn't shared two words in five hours. He hadn't wanted to bring up her family and see the anguish in her eyes again. He was equally worried about her pressing about his own relations so he'd leaned his head back and pretended to sleep.

He'd suddenly turned the coward over a few innocent inquiries but in this confined space, he had nowhere to run, nowhere to hide from her bright, prying eyes. He wouldn't have the matter brought up only to have to shut her down. Telling her about his mother and sister or his brother and father would get him nowhere. In fact, she would be less inclined to play the part of his hostage, he was sure.

"You should see to Mrs McDougal," Daniella pointed out with an irritated flick of her hand.

As soon as James jumped down from the carriage he looked around for Hobson, but the man was nowhere to be seen.

"Willie?" he called up to the driver.

The carriage tilted and then Willie's bald head popped over the edge. "Milord?"

"What happened to Hobson?"

"Oh, he got sick a mile or so back and jumped off for a spell."

"Why was I not informed?"

"Begging your pardon, milord, but you was sleeping. He didn't want to disturb you."

Damn that blasted innkeeper for feeding them all bad food. He wouldn't countenance the sickness to have come from his own kitchens since Mrs McDougal herself prepared most of the meals when he was in. And there was the fact that he felt absolutely fine. Well, his irritation beggared belief but apart from that, he was fine.

"Daniella? Do you feel as though you might be ill?"

"Not at all. I would need more provocation than a bouncy carriage to see my breakfast again, thank you."

He wanted to point out that she hadn't partaken in breakfast. In fact, he hadn't yet seen her eat much at all. He lowered his tone to a better measure of gentle and addressed his retainer. "Mrs McDougal, are you going to be all right?"

She didn't answer for a long moment and he found himself looking away lest he begin to feel queasy after all. Blood and innards he could deal with; vomit was another matter.

"Hurts like the devil it does," was followed by a low moan and yet more bad pie.

They could not go on like that but neither could they linger by the roadside. James searched the road behind them but there was no sign of Hobson. They couldn't turn the carriage around on the narrow road and he was fairly sure they were closer to a village ahead than they were to those they had passed. They would have to press on.

Raking a hand through his already mussed hair, James went to the rear of the carriage and emptied a small bucket that hung on a hook there. He was no stranger to travel sickness since his sister suffered on long journeys.

His hands stilled. God, he hoped she was all right.

"James?" Daniella's voice reached him and he shook away his distracting thoughts.

"I didn't give you leave to address me so personally, madam." He sounded like a schoolgirl. Did she witness his moment of vulnerability?

"You insist on calling me by my Christian name; am I not allowed to do the same, *James*?"

Her smirk as she enunciated his name almost made him smile in return. She tried to irk him on purpose and he actually appreciated the sentiment in that moment. "Trelissick is my name. Only my mother calls me James."

"So stuffy. Not Lasterton? Since that is your title?"

"I ask them not to." He still didn't feel like Lasterton. Like a toffy gentleman. The genteel, poor child, soldier and second son in him were still far more present than the titled man.

"I think I'll call you Jimmy. I knew a Jimmy once."

"You will do no such thing."

"Very well: James it is. What says your perfect plan about all of this?" She gestured to the still-retching Mrs McDougal.

He held up the bucket.

"I'll ride up the top then," Daniella said, her suddenly not-so-bright green eyes switching from the bucket and back to Mrs McDougal.

"You will do no such thing," he said again as he turned back to the carriage and used the lip of the bucket to scrape the mess from the floor. Would he keep having to say those six words to her all week? "You will ride in the carriage with me and Mrs McDougal will ride up top."

"What if she falls?"

James's gaze never left Daniella's as he called over her

shoulder, "Mrs McDougal, would you ride up top with Willie? We'll stop at the first inn we happen across."

"I would appreciate that, my lord."

James raised a brow and waited for any more protest or bright ideas from Daniella.

"Let us be off then," she called.

"I give the orders around here, Miss Germaine."

"Aye aye," she said with another salute. How he hated that salute. He began to get the impression she really wanted to stick up only one of the two fingers she held to her forehead.

CHAPTER SEVEN

A S NIGHT DREW in, poor Mrs McDougal at last fell
asleep in a cot at the end of the bed where Daniella now
lay at a small posting inn known as the Black Sheep. Hobson
had arrived an hour after them, looking the worse for wear
but not quite as sick as Mrs McDougal. It was decided that
the pie was definitely to blame since Daniella and James were
feeling fine.

The emotion Daniella did not feel was relief. She just
wanted something to happen. Anything really. She wanted
one of her father's spies to make himself known. She wanted
to get to Scotland already and be done with the nervous
butterflies taking up residence in her stomach. She hated
uncertainty almost as much as she hated London.

As if summoned by her frustration, the lock turned and
the door opened a fraction.

"May I enter?"

Daniella smiled at the hesitation in Lastert—no,
Trelissick's voice. She'd thought his titled power and self-
importance ran too deep for such courtesy, as she had already
witnessed in so many blustering dukes and earls of the ton,
but James was different. Only just, but there was enough

disparity to draw a comparison. She pulled the bedcovers up to her shoulders. "You may."

He looked so uneasy as he entered the room, leaving the door open wide—less like a military peer facing battle than an ordinary man facing a woman sat up in her bed.

"I'm sorry, I shouldn't have come," he said immediately upon seeing her.

"Pish," she said with a huff. It wasn't as though she was naked.

Her cheeks warmed.

"I wondered if Mrs McDougal will be well enough to travel on the morrow."

There wasn't an actual question there but Daniella didn't enjoy the awkward silence that followed. "I don't think she will be going anywhere anytime soon."

Trelissick leaned over the cot to see the woman's face and then straightened with a shake of his head. "Who would have guessed one little pie could upset the plan so spectacularly?"

In his voice was defeat. She knew the feeling well. "How long do you think we will have to wait here?"

"We can't wait. We have to press on otherwise your brother might catch up to us and force an early confrontation."

"Will you give me over to him if that happens?" she asked, immediately dreading the answer.

Trelissick met her eyes with his for the first time since entering the room and shook his head. "I don't think so."

"You must think him dreadfully weak."

"Is he?"

She considered her answer as she lay back against the pillows. Her brother was an intelligent man of sharp words and cold shoulders. A perfect politician but a poor fighter. He would never have made a decent pirate had it come to it. He couldn't throw a knife or aim a cannon…but he could make Daniella doubt herself and all she did with mere syllables.

"My brother has his fine points but in a fight I would wager money on your side." Out of loyalty alone she should have told him that her brother was fierce and noble and would fight to his very last breath for her, but it was not believable. He had been knighted for saving the prince's carriage but it was common knowledge that even that had been nothing more than smoke and mirrors and well-placed bribes.

"You are the strangest woman I have ever met."

"Thank you?" she replied.

"Perhaps you are lying so that if I face your brother over pistols I'll let my guard down?"

"Believe me or no, I was serious when I said I would cooperate. If you knew how desperately I want to be away from London, you would understand."

"Why don't you make me understand? Was there a beau? Perhaps a gentleman for whom you had a tendre, but who felt differently in return?"

"Not quite." Daniella laughed. "What about you? Is there a lady wondering where you are tonight? Perhaps a mistress waiting for her bauble?"

"You should not know about mistresses and you certainly should not talk about them with a gentleman."

"Can I talk about them with a lady?"

Trelissick choked, on laughter or outrage she had no idea since he chose that moment to turn towards the window and the dark night beyond. "Did your brother never engage a companion or tutor for you?"

"I know how to read and write and I don't need a governess."

"I meant to teach you a lady's manners. To teach you not to talk about mistresses or sell your virginity or ride astride in a dress through the park."

She'd forgotten his presence in the background as she'd attempted to disgrace herself again and again. "You were there for the race with Callington, weren't you?"

"He should have known better. And I should have taken you over my knee that very day."

Daniella blushed but replied with indignation, "The prig should never have challenged me in the first place."

"How did that come about?" He leaned against the wall, his hands behind his back as he waited for her story.

"The earl was bragging about his horse being the fastest in all of Britain."

"And you just had to prove him wrong?"

"Well, I did, didn't I?"

"Where did you learn to ride like that?"

"I didn't spend my whole life on board a ship. When the weather turned and we were forced to make for land, I enjoyed the normal pursuits of a child."

"A boy child," Trelissick flatly pointed out.

"My father never did know what to do with a girl."

"One should probably not teach her how to use a sword."

"I had to be able to protect myself, otherwise he would not have had me on the ship in the first place."

"You shouldn't have been there in the first place. It was irresponsible of him to drag you into danger."

Daniella bristled anew. "You have no clue what you are talking about. What was he supposed to do? Abandon me to a nanny? Live a pauper just because my mother had the mischance to bear him a girl and then—?" She bit back the words "abandon her" just in time. He did not seem to notice.

"That's not what I meant."

"What did you mean?"

"Only that a pirate's life is not for a girl."

Those were her father's words exactly the night he'd told her of her fate. They had fought all day after he banished Jimmy the deckhand from the ship for kissing her. That they'd happened to dress before their discovery was the only reason the handsome and charming Jimmy was still alive and not deep-sea fish food. But her father wasn't a simpleton. He'd discovered part of their relationship and put an end to it before she found herself with child. Or, and in his opinion even worse, married to a pirate.

But she was only having fun. She'd never considered marrying at all. She wasn't the daughter of a nobleman or an heiress or a helpless lady in need of a husband. It wasn't until her father's threats became reality that she began to think about what marriage would be like.

She'd only come up with one answer so far. Stifling.

What husband was ever going to let her sail her own ship for months at a time or scramble about the rigging in trousers and a shirt?

Not a one.

"I'm sorry." Trelissick spoke into the silence. "I didn't mean to upset you again."

"It's not you. It's the whole situation. I prefer to make my own choices." The admission probably wasn't one she should have made out loud but her insides felt as though they could explode with tension and nervous anticipation. She had grown up with a company of friends to confide in. A ship was a small home compared to the mansions on Mayfair but it was never lonely. She had never known loneliness before moving to London. She may not have had female friends, but she was a chatterer, and right now, with James staring at her with pity in his eyes, she wanted to pour her heart out and make him understand why she had gone to such lengths as to sell her supposed virginity.

What she wanted was to speak with her father. She wanted to feel his tight embrace and the scratch of his beard on her cheek as he told her everything was going to be all right.

"Oh good God, please tell me you aren't going to cry."

The horrified tone of Trelissick's voice pulled her back to the present, to the room at an inn where she was held hostage and would spend the night with a woman who smelled like stale vomit and sweat.

"I do not cry," she replied. Even though her eyes burned and her throat felt as though it was stuck fast with a rock in it, she would not cry. Ever.

Trelissick exhaled with what sounded like the relief she had earlier longed for. "Get some rest. We leave first thing in the morning."

"What about Mrs McDougal and Hobson? You can't expect them to travel."

"They are going to stay here."

It dawned on her exactly what he didn't say and Daniella wasn't sure if she wanted to crow with joy or shrink back in fear. Alone. She would be alone with Trelissick in that carriage for hours on end each day. What was left of her reputation would finally wither and die, never to be revived again. She smiled.

"You needn't look so happy about it." He sighed. "We might be able to find another chaperone in the next village."

"Are you worried for my reputation?" She laughed.

Trelissick turned the door handle and looked back one last time. The picture she must have made with her frizzed hair wild about her shoulders and the blankets tucked under her chin.

"I'm worried for mine." And then he left, closing the door as quietly as he'd come.

All of Daniella's happiness disappeared in that moment and she shivered. She hadn't thought of his standing in the ton. Would his name sustain damage when linked with hers or would it bring the matchmakers out with rewards for removing her influence from their daughter's lives?

Only time would tell.

JAMES HAD NO idea what the hell he was doing anymore. Just one hiccup in his plan and it all fell to pieces. It had never happened to him before. He always had contingencies for his contingencies when going into battle. Daniella Germaine was going to be the end of him.

Pondering her situation required ale and a lot of it so he found himself perched on the edge of a rough stool at the inn's bar indulging like he shouldn't. He would only drink to forget her siren's call. To forget she was a victim in this saga and not its instigator.

At the sight of her red-rimmed eyes, he was ready to absolve her of her indiscretions and push her back to her brother's embrace…except that that wasn't what she wanted. After seeing her in a state of complete dishevelment and ready for bed—with obviously not much in the way of clothing on—it wasn't what he wanted either.

When he'd first insinuated himself into her life he'd honestly thought her capers were those of a spoiled brat. The occasional anguish shadowing her eyes said it might be so much more.

James could understand the lures of freedom, especially as one who also felt the constraints of high society, but it was the world they'd both been landed in, whether Daniella accepted it or not. It was a club whose members had great privilege and greater responsibility, even if many revelled in the first at the expense of the second. She owed it to family and society to marry well and breed. And apart from any of that he wondered if she had stopped for even one moment to consider what she would do if her father turned her away.

Again. There had to be very good reasons for the captain ignoring her, unless he simply hoped, given time and distance, she would accept her fate.

James snorted and tossed back the last of the ale in his mug and then gestured to the serving girl for just one more.

His own father had talked about phases and moods and the makings of a man when James had announced he was joining the war effort. Never one to assert his authority, and only newly ascended to the title his cousin had held until his untimely death, his father had purchased him a commission and wished him well. They all had new lives to lead and their mark to make on the world and in society. So James had said goodbye to his father, his brother John, his sister Amelia and his mother and left for parts unknown.

He was excited to fight for his country and put Bonaparte back in his cage but had he known what he would miss, the price of his leaving, or what he'd eventually come home to and come home as, he would have done without the excitement. He would have burned that commission and settled into being the spare. And, in hindsight, carousing with women, horse races and taunting the watch with his ton peers had to be better than being trained as a killing machine in His Majesty's Army. At least if he'd played the part of a womanizing brat, he might have saved two people he loved rather than killing hundreds of strangers.

He reached for the new tankard and gulped the entire contents without taking a breath. To be drunk was better than entertaining those thoughts.

"You look like a man who has the weight of the world on

his shoulders," a deep voice with more than a hint of the Highlands to it commented from his right.

James squinted at the stranger, worried for a moment that they had indeed been followed, but then dismissed the notion. They'd had a good head start and no one knew which way they travelled. He'd told his staff they were heading up the North Road but he'd lied. It was too obvious and he wanted to travel closer to the coast.

"Nothing another ale won't fix," James replied, with another gesture to the serving girl. This would definitely be his last. Traveling the next morning after a hard night would add to his discomfort.

"May I join you?" the newcomer asked even as he pulled up the stool next to James.

"Why not?" Drinking really was a lonely business and Hobson was sleeping upstairs in the room next to Daniella's, still slightly green from the bad pie.

He groaned when he thought of Daniella. He hoped she didn't get it into her head to pick the lock. He straightened and put his mug down. Could the chit pick locks? He wouldn't put it past her. Just where in the hell had she found out about virgin auctions anyway?

"So are you heading to London or away?" the stranger asked. He had his own tankard now and gulped almost as much as James did.

"Away." His answer was curt. He knew more than a thing or two about discretion.

"Do you have an estate up the coast?"

"You ask too many questions," James commented while

looking down his nose at the lad. Any more than one was too many.

The boy couldn't yet be two-and-twenty but he spoke with the voice of a man. His blond hair and striking blue eyes were at odds with that heathen accent. Most Scots looked more like Daniella, with flaming hair and green eyes the colour of spring pastures.

James groaned again and took another swig of ale.

"That look can only be associated with a woman," the Scot commented with a sympathetic chuckle.

"Bloody chit is going to be the death of me."

He laughed again. "But worth the trouble I'm sure."

"Not this one."

"Your wife?"

James shook his head. He realized he liked this nosy stranger. The man had an air of friendship about him. James was a very good judge of character. The war had done that to him.

Playing the Butcher had done that to him.

"It can't be that bad, friend."

It was. If only the man knew where he'd been, what he'd seen and done. Even now after leaving the Butcher well behind in France, he sat there, a kidnapper of defenceless women.

He snorted again. Daniella was a lot of things but defenceless was not one of them.

"Your sister then? I have seven of the creatures and they are certainly pushing my poor da into an early grave."

"Seven?" James had thought being one of three children

growing up tedious but seven? "How many of you are there in all?"

"Eleven children my ma and da can lay claim to. Seven lasses, four lads."

"No wonder you are heading to London. How do you stand to be in a house with that many siblings?"

The stranger chuckled as he took another drink. "We don't have houses in the Highlands. We have castles. Big ones. A boy can get lost if he wants not to be found. And then there's the riding and swimming and exploring. It's a brave life."

"I'm Trelissick." He offered his hand in greeting. They hadn't left a crumb at this inn yet and if the talkative lad was traveling back towards London, he might come in useful. James had to put his plan back together and quickly.

"Patrick McDonald."

"So is it business or pleasure that takes you to the capital, Patrick?"

"I've been and I'm returning home now, in fact, Trelissick. It was business. I was to find a bride in London and bring her back to the Highlands."

"A bride? Good God, why would you want to do that, man?"

"Good lasses are scarce in our parts."

"Unless you count your sisters."

"It is frowned upon to marry your own sister."

A bark of laughter slipped through his lips and went a long way to raising his spirits. "So you went to London to find a wife. Drastic. Are you in need of an heir?"

"One day, yes, but not yet. I promised my mother I would attempt to settle down. She suggested I take a trip to London. Who was I to decline her generous offer of a lazy tarriance?"

"So what's next?" James liked that he could take his mind off his own worries and empathize with someone else's misfortune for a change. It had been six months since his mother and sister had disappeared. Six long months of worry and getting nowhere. He wished she'd been there to nag him to settle down.

"Now I go home," Patrick said with a nod.

"You didn't find a wife then?" James wished he wasn't on his way to being foxed. A strange emotion passed over the other man's eyes but then was gone. James was too slow this evening to attempt to read what was there.

"I did."

"What happened? You can't just begin the story at the end and not tell the rest."

"I'm afraid I was a horse's arse and didn't recognize love when it was crying all over my shirtfront. By the time I did, the lass didn't want me anymore."

"Cocked it up well and good by the sounds."

Patrick nodded.

"Why didn't you stay and fight for her?" God, he sounded like a romanticist. He was drunk.

"I tried. But it was too late. Now it is all a huge mess. Distance might help me see what my next move should be."

He was right. James knew why his plan had fallen apart. He was too involved. Too close to it all, and since he had the most to lose, he was blinded. What was he missing?

"I don't suppose you are in need of company for the road?" James asked as he eyed the young man's dirty clothing and muddy boots. From the cut of his cloth, the boy was in need of funds and James was in need of an outrider.

"I wouldn't say no but I don't sit well in a fancy carriage. I assume that one in the stables is yours?"

"It is. My man has taken ill and I require someone reliable to lag behind. Someone who will ride like the devil to warn me if there is pursuit."

"Are you running from someone? The girl? Don't tell me you were to be leg-shackled too?"

"It is a very long and a very complicated story," James said with a sigh. Already the ale had prompted him to do something he normally would not. The lad was a stranger. What if he lied about the girl in London and followed them for the captain or Sir Anthony?

James took another look at Patrick but the ale was beginning to make the lad look as though he was about thirty-five, with four eyes and two heads. He'd had more than was wise. "Sleep first and we can decide in the morning. If we're all going the same way anyway, we may as well make a traveling party." He sounded like a fop or a dandy. Damn it all to hell. Two days with Miss Germaine and he was not himself at all. What would more than twelve do to him, he wondered…

CHAPTER EIGHT

WHEN DANIELLA AWOKE the next morning, Mrs McDougal snored softly in her pallet but none of her previous colour had returned. In fact, the woman still looked more than a little green and her skin was coated with a slick sheen of sweat.

Good, thought Daniella, breathing only through her mouth to escape the God-awful smell. It was uncharitable but between pounding the feather stuffing from her pillow, and tossing and turning for half the night, she had come to the conclusion that being alone with Trelissick might be the very thing to push her to her limits of patience but it would do wonders to the gossip. If even one person saw them alone, either alighting the carriage or taking lunch together, word would travel and the closer they got to the border, the better chances her father would have of hearing it.

If she'd only known she could have provoked the marquess to kidnap her a lot sooner.

She rolled from the bed and began to put on the ridiculous dress from the day before. She knew it was fruitless to think she could manage on her own but she tried anyway.

Before long, the lock turned and the door opened a fraction. "Are you awake?"

"You can come in." He really wasn't a very good kidnapper. He hadn't even checked to see if the window opened (it did) or how far the drop was to the ground (she could have made it without breaking bones). She could have escaped, stolen one of his horses, and been halfway back to London or off to Scotland before anyone knew she had left.

Daniella wanted to smugly point out his shortcomings but wisely refrained by biting down on her bottom lip. She still hadn't decided in her own mind how much control he actually had and how much he thought he did.

"You will need to help me with my dress." She gave him her back and stood completely still as he did the buttons. This time she ignored the warmth of his fingers and his breath on her neck. "Did you bring any other gowns for me?"

"No."

"I can't wear this one for the whole journey. And what of the cold as we approach Scotland? I thought you said you were a great schemer."

"I have been to war, madam, not Scotland. Men do not complain about the cold when their very lives are in danger."

She smiled at his tone, at his outrage that she could doubt his skills. "Well?" she prompted.

He finished with her buttons and went to lean over Mrs McDougal where she still lay. "The innkeeper says there is a village ahead with a celebrated dressmaker. We will stop there for whatever you need."

"We don't have the time to wait around."

"Then you had better hope the proprietor has something already made."

She hoped the dressmaker had *trousers* already made.

"Come, we will break fast and then be on our way."

He was very abrupt this morning, not at all the man who had chuckled the night before and left her room in fear of his reputation. He was more the army major facing a day of bloodshed with a dark shadow on his jaw and red rims around his eyes. He actually looked half ferocious in the dawn light. No, not ferocious. Boiling with frustration.

Daniella shivered and cold fingers of foreboding squeezed at her nape.

They weren't anywhere near far enough from London to breathe easy over pursuit. The pie sickness and today's gown shopping were going to put them behind but she couldn't face Scotland without warm clothing. She couldn't keep facing Trelissick with her borrowed dress sagging either.

They left Mrs McDougal and Hobson upstairs and head-ed down to a small dining room, Daniella hidden in the cloak from the day before. Her stomach growled despite the fact she had received an overflowing tray of supper delivered the previous night.

When they entered the room, flooded with morning light and smelling divinely like tea and toast, Daniella stopped so abruptly Trelissick bumped into her.

"This room seems to be occupied."

Trelissick pushed her farther into the room with a hand at the small of her back and then closed the door. "This is Patrick. He is going to take Hobson's place for a few days."

"Hello, Patrick, I am—*Oomph*." She whirled and glared at Trelissick, who had shoved her. Hard.

"Well, my *lord*?" She would do his bidding but she didn't have to like it or comply with grace.

"Patrick, this is Daniella." He left off her surname and the newcomer didn't ask for it, although his brows were high as he looked between Trelissick and her.

"The events of the last few days have been taxing on her," the marquess offered by way of explanation.

Patrick inclined his head and went back to eating his breakfast without question. Daniella huffed and glared again at Trelissick before sitting at the table where her breakfast had already been placed. Ham, eggs and toast. Simple, but it smelled heavenly. She was even prepared to risk food poisoning, so great was her returning hunger.

No one tarried. Tea was gulped rather than sipped, every last scrap eaten as though it was their last meal and not another word was spoken.

Before they left the room, Trelissick pulled her hood so far forwards she almost couldn't see where she was going and had to follow his shining boots out into the yard, where the carriage already waited.

Hobson waited with it.

"You are staying here," Trelissick told him in a tone that brooked no argument.

Except Hobson must have been used to arguing with Mr I'm In Charge Of The Universe. "You need me to come along. I'll sit alongside Willie and rest for a spell."

"And what of Mrs McDougal? How will she return

home?"

"I'm not going back to the city with her. She's a big gel and can make it without a nanny. I gave her money enough to hire a sparkling new carriage and riders to accompany her if that is her wish."

"You have it all sorted, haven't you?"

Hobson grinned but his pale face gave truth to the lie that he felt better.

"Very well, but if you're going to be sick, you'll have to carry the bucket."

"Already up there."

"I will ride with Miss—" he stopped himself "—with Daniella, Patrick will ride behind and you will go with Willie."

Hobson shuffled forwards a few steps until he was close enough to talk into Trelissick's ear. Daniella leaned in to hear what was said.

"Are you sure this boy can be trusted?"

"No more than the girl can be."

Daniella gasped in outrage but the answer seemed suitable to Hobson. He climbed the carriage and dropped down next to the driver's seat, his mussed hair blowing in the wind, his booted feet crossed at the ankles.

Trelissick opened the carriage door and bowed to her in his first real public show of chivalry. "After you, m'dear."

Her chin rose as she stepped up without taking the hand he offered and settled herself against the squabs in the farthest corner from the door. When she could no longer stand the silence, she snapped, "What of this Patrick? How do you know he isn't an agent for my father sent to check up on me?"

"Is he?"

James lifted his head and stared at Daniella for a moment too long. He had resolved not to let her draw his temper out today but resisting that was an almost impossible feat.

She shook her head after a few moments. "I don't know. He isn't one of my brother's cronies nor one of my father's regular sailors."

"I think he's just an ordinary lad in need of a few guineas and company for the road." If he disappeared without word, then James would know he'd wrongly placed his trust in the boy.

"I hope not."

"If he is a spy for your father, why not steal you away in the dead of night?"

Daniella smiled that knowing smile that made him itch to shake her. "My father would know I don't require his assistance to escape you if he'd been watching so far."

"Wrong. I sat outside your door last night so no such attempt by you or he would have worked."

She rolled her eyes and he had to curl his fingers into his palms. She really needed a good shake. It might rattle her common sense loose from wherever it had fallen.

"You don't think much like a military man. Were you very good at it?" She gaped with more theatrics than a Vauxhall actress. "Don't tell me you were an officer? One of those who stayed in a tent while the others risked their necks for king and country?"

"You show your youth when you mock something you know nothing about."

"And you show your ineptitude when you leave me in a room with an unlocked window and an unconscious chaperone. My father is probably rolling on the floor with laughter waiting for me to tire of you and make my own way." The next emotion to cross her big green eyes was a thoughtfulness that worried him.

"You are not going anywhere on your own. I wouldn't even give you one day until you were molested or worse."

Her cheeks tinged with pink and James settled back, confident he'd won the argument.

For now.

THE STRANGER WHO was no longer quite a stranger rode at the rear of the carriage for a few miles and overheard the heated conversation drifting from inside. He wondered for a brief moment if he should have warned the marquess that the countryside knew everything he and the girl spoke of.

Willing allies. Who would have thought?

He let some distance grow between him and the now quiet carriage so he could think clearly. Seeing the crested conveyance leaving the city as he'd made his way back to Trelissick's townhouse had been a stroke of luck indeed. Only now he had no clothing and not enough food in his saddlebags to last very long. The effect was that he appeared penniless and in need of a traveling party.

He couldn't have planned it more perfectly.

Now all he had to do was divine the right time to recruit Miss Germaine and find out what the hell was going on.

Once they'd left London, he became less convinced about the facts of the whole situation, but for the moment he would have to wait it out. It wouldn't do for Trelissick to start asking questions about why he was asking questions.

If the all-powerful marquess knew who he really was, it would be Patrick's life at risk. But that was a chance he would take willingly now honour was at stake. He had disgraced himself and his name but he would find redemption. And if it turned out he was too late for redemption? Then he would have revenge. He wasn't leaving Trelissick's side without one or the other.

CHAPTER NINE

THE TRIP TO Worcester felt agonizingly slow to James. He was desperately tired and wanted to doze but he just could not relax enough to let his guard down when it came to Daniella. He still had no clue as to why she was so…so…willing. He simply could not accept that any woman would prefer shipboard life to a settled home with a comfortable husband and children to love. All women were born with that ambition stitched into their bones and no unconventional upbringing or hoydenish streak could pick it out.

Daniella's attitude in the last day or so showed she was confident she held the power in their exchange. She had shown the ton she was a spoiled brat in need of a firm hand, and possibly a spanking, but as she sat opposite him, her back straight, her little chin high in the air, he wondered just what her strength and stubbornness would cost him. And his family.

He shook his head and let it fall back once again against the squabs. He hoped he was doing the right thing in all of this. Never would he just give up. As long as there was the hope that his mother and sister were alive then he would fight.

As the carriage began to slow beneath him, James lifted the curtain back on the window to reveal cottages and pastures sown with the season's crops soaking up a light rain. They were approaching the edge of the town and he figured now was the best time to lay down the law with Daniella.

When he glanced back to where she sat at the end of the bench on the corner furthest from the door, she glared right back at him. He wondered if she was still upset that he hadn't shared all of his intentions with her. His current plan really was very simple. If any rumours were to reach ears in London, they would be so scattered and puzzling that no one would know which were true and which were lies. Then when he returned to London, indeed *if* he returned, the wildest of the gossip could be laughed off and the tamer could be woven into a credible story. No irrevocable damage would have been done to his sister's name or, for that matter, to Daniella's. She might profess not to care but as a man of honour he would not contribute to the wrecking of a lady's prospects.

Gossip was hideous. A person's reputation could be irretrievably lost if a rumour was strong enough—truth rarely came into it. Indeed the harder a person fought to deny the gossip, the guiltier she appeared. For twelve months James had laboured to restore his family name, to restore dignity and honour so his sister could make a good match and they could each go about their lives. He wanted to see his beloved family again, but he knew restoring them without too much malicious chatter was his obligation as much as it was his desire.

"Do you know," her voice sounded as if from a distance, pulling him back to the carriage, to their predicament, "if you told me what it is my father has of yours, it would make it easier for me to assist you."

He shook his head again. "I don't need your assistance for that. Only your directions after we cross the border." When she opened her mouth to argue, he held his hand up between them. "Although your cooperation does help."

She snapped her mouth shut.

"When we arrive at the modiste, we must be quick. I want to be back on the road within the hour."

"And what if there are no dresses ready-made?"

He looked her up and down from her dainty, albeit ruined, slippers to his sister's ill-fitting dress right up to her wild untamed hair. "You had better hope there are. And get yourself a hairbrush and pins as well."

Self-conscious at his words, she reached up to smooth her hair but then seemed to think the better of it, her hand dropping back to her lap. "Anything else, Your Majesty?"

He was saved when the carriage came to a stop and Hobson opened the door. He was still pale but appeared to be holding up.

"We're here, milord."

"Good. One hour is all we have. Hobson, I'll need you to gather us some food so we don't have to stop again until sunset. Patrick can stand guard by the carriage and Willie can stay where he is just in case we have to depart quickly." He waited for Hobson to nod his understanding and then turned back to Daniella. "Are you ready?"

"What is my part to be today?"

"I think you will be my paramour in need of a more suitable wardrobe."

Her lips lifted at the edges. "It is as well I plan never to return to your precious London, then."

"Just play along."

She nodded once but the smile never left her lips.

"And please don't improvise. The less you say, the better it will be and the less identifiable we will be to anyone asking after us. Let me do the talking."

"As you wish."

Her easy acquiescence was a concern but they didn't have time to stand about and argue.

When James jumped to the ground to hand her out, Patrick had caught them up and reined in his mount, waiting for his orders.

"I'll need you stay here and stand guard with Willie. If we're not out in one hour, come rushing in with an urgent message."

Patrick raised his brows but nodded and made himself more comfortable in the saddle.

Daniella emerged, put her hand in his, and let him help her to the cobbled ground. She was as regal as a princess in a ball gown. She looked more a pauper in a potato sack; he could have chosen her a better, newer, grander dress from his sister's collection but he had been of a mind to punish her in harmless ways at least.

Misgivings sat low in his belly as he pushed through the

single door of the modiste's establishment. This is what he hated about not having a clear plan. In battle it was easy to predict the men's reactions, his own and the enemy's, but in this battle, where women were not only involved but key players, he wasn't equipped with the necessary knowledge to pre-empt them.

"Bonjour, monsieur, madame, I am Madame Perèt. How can we help you today?"

Madame Perèt was a small, lithe woman with greying hair and wrinkles framing intelligent eyes. Her French accent rang rather truer than those of many London lady's maids.

"My…" he hesitated for effect "…wife, needs a suitable wardrobe for travel and I was told you were the lady we needed to see?"

The lady in question looked his "wife" up and down before addressing him once again.

"Are you traveling to London or away from?"

"To London," James lied, "but then we may travel back, so we will need some warm items."

"Will she be attending balls and such?"

James didn't miss the imperceptible rising of the modiste's brows nor the tightening of her shoulders. Just as he suspected, this madame was another on the edge of her seat to await gossip. A tale she could share with her friends and be the first to spin what she wanted about the gentleman and the woman he claimed as his wife even though Daniella wore no ring.

"No. She will not."

"As you wish."

He switched his gaze from Madame Perèt back to Daniella, who wore a small smirk. "I will leave you to choose your gowns, m'dear."

"Oh no," Daniella purred in a way that made his hair stand on end. "You must stay and help. After all, it is your money we spend, darling."

"I trust you," he grated out.

Daniella gave the modiste a mock look of frustration and then sauntered over to him. Did she really just *saunter*? After *purring*?

"Very well, then, I shall have everything made up in pink." She ran a finger slowly down his cheek to his chin. "The marquess absolutely loathes pink, do you not, darling? And I believe breeches may also be in order, no?"

His teeth ground in his mouth and it took all of his strength not to shake her. They were supposed to leave rumour and innuendo, not their names and addresses. "No pink and certainly no breeches."

Better than an actress on the stage, she squealed and jumped on the spot, clapping her hands together. "So you'll stay and help with the gown choices?"

"I suppose I must."

"Excellent. Let us get started."

The modiste watched the exchange with perplexity. James wanted to rake his hand through his hair until the urge to throttle his hostage left him but that would show Madame Perèt that Daniella's taunts had substance to them. So far the modiste didn't look as though she would ask questions but the hour had barely begun. He had a feeling he was in for far more than colour choices but he sat and fixed a smile to his face. It would be a very long hour indeed.

HIS PARAMOUR, WAS she? Fine. Let him see some *amour* firsthand then.

He could have told the modiste she was his ward or niece or something along those lines. Their ages weren't so close. She guessed the marquess to be around three-and-thirty—he couldn't have risen so high in the army if he was much younger.

Which reminded her that he hadn't actually spoken about the army and she hadn't had a chance to interrogate Hobson either. There was still a great deal she didn't know, which made it difficult to know whether Trelissick was friend or indeed foe. What if her father gave his precious items back and Trelissick refused to let her go? He had no reason to keep her—unless this wasn't only about a trade and there really was more to the tale? It was so frustrating not knowing.

"Do you wish for privacy, madame?"

Just as Daniella was about to nod and thank the woman, Trelissick interrupted. "I really don't want to let my *wife* from my sight, if you don't mind?"

Daniella knew it for the challenge it was. He meant to discomfit her into being good. "Of course, whatever my *husband* wants. After all, he has seen my skin before."

When his Adam's apple bobbed in his throat, Daniella smiled her victory. But only for a moment. A man's form was something she was used to from her time on the ship. The hands often discarded their shirts on a hot day. But she certainly hadn't. Anytime she even rolled her sleeves too high or loosened the ties on her shirt too far, her father had been there to remind her of her sex. As if she could ever forget. She wondered if James had ever removed his shirt to toil. Would the dark hair on his forearms cover his chest and the ridges of his abdomen as well…?

She stood silently, not once breaking eye contact with Trelissick, until the modiste returned with several ready-made dresses for her to try. She gave her back to the modiste and Madame Perèt deftly undid each tiny button down her back. When she felt the borrowed gown sag, she gave a little wriggle until it dropped to the floor around her ankles with a whoosh.

That left Daniella in nothing more than an almost transparent shift and barely there stays. The gown she had worn to the virgin auction was made of silk so fine it was translucent, and it wasn't designed for substantial underthings. As she lifted her chin and pretended she was comfortable in her near nakedness, his jaw tightened but he didn't look away. He kept his eyes glued to her face and forced a wider smile.

For the next forty minutes Daniella tried to ignore Trelissick as much as she could. She didn't make eye contact again, but did as the modiste instructed. She tried to choose out gowns that she could fasten herself but ladies' fashion just didn't allow for doing much on one's own.

"Do you have anything that is not so extravagant?" she asked Madame Perèt.

"Such as?"

"Such as a sturdy gown for walking or working?"

The modiste looked back at Trelissick. "Why would the...lady...wish for a gown like this?"

"My wife enjoys gardening and worries when the maids cannot remove the stains."

"You should not worry about such things, madame. Your husband will simply buy you a new gown, no?"

Trelissick nodded. Daniella glared. "Since my maid had to stay behind, who will help me with these dresses?"

He rose and came towards her, a predatory look replacing his earlier annoyance. "I'm sure I will be able to manage."

"You can't. It's not appropriate."

"As you said, I have seen your skin. And since we sleep in the same bed—" he raised his hand, his thumb smoothly stroking her cheek in a caress more intimate than she had managed earlier "—I will be there to help you in *and out* of your clothes."

It was Daniella's turn to gulp. "You won't always be there." It more hope than a question.

"Yes I will, *ma chère*."

The world stopped moving about her in that moment. She knew he was trying to get a response out of her, daring her to put an end to the charade but also knowing she could not, she was lost. The warmth of his fingers on her neck, of his breath against her chin, caused her heart to race, caused her to sway into him until her chest was almost leaning against his, her eyes on his mouth as she waited for his next move.

But then Trelissick snatched his hand away and stepped back. She nearly stumbled without his support. What the hell?

"We'll take two day gowns, the riding habit and the nightgown. My wife will also need underthings, shoes if you have them and a woollen cloak. Hers is not suitable for cold nights." He snapped out the orders and it was clear the army major had returned. Thank the Lord. She wasn't sure how much longer it would have been until she forgot where she was and begged him to kiss her.

CHAPTER TEN

WHAT WAS WRONG with him? He wasn't a child. He didn't accept a challenge when the challenger was clearly insane. What else could explain her behaviour? Had she been trying to prove something to him by tricking him into staying while she undressed?

He sure as hell had proven to her that he was in charge and that all his faculties were in order. But only just.

"I bet you're happy." The bane of his existence sulked in her corner of the carriage, arms crossed over her now covered chest, sullenness drawing her mouth into a frown as her body rocked with the motion of the road.

"Happy?" He bloody well was not. The, ah, *state* their little act had left him in had hurt. A lot. His arousal had been almost impossible to hide from Daniella and the modiste.

"Imagine the fury when my father discovers I am your harlot."

"I don't think your father will actually learn of any of this before I hand you back to him. You can deal with all of that down the track. Any pursuers, on the other hand, will hear of chaperoned siblings in one town and an outrageous marquess and his doxy in another." Perhaps if she understood that part of his plan she would stop tormenting him.

"Anthony will have your head." Though she didn't sound entirely convinced of that herself.

"You think he'll blame me? He'll know you are the bad influence, not me."

"Do you even know my brother?"

He had seen Germaine from afar. At a horse race. Despite saving the prince's life, he was not universally accepted yet, especially as all of London knew who his father was. Who *their* father was. "Not personally, no."

"He'll force you to marry me if he catches us up before we get to Scotland."

"I doubt that." Of course it was a possibility. But what he didn't know was whether Germaine would hold his sister's honour high enough to call him out. Would he risk his neck for a sister who sold her virginity? Who swam in the moonlight in nothing more than her skin for half of London to see? A sister who tried to disgrace herself within the circles he wanted to be a part of? Hell, even James needed to shore up his place in those influential groups. For two years he had tried his hardest to erase the blemish his brother had left on their lives when his addiction to opiates became known. The Trelissick name had been nearly drowned in scandal when Bow Street investigated whether his brother had killed their father and then himself, or whether the reverse was true. He could have told them his father was incapable of hurting anyone, let alone his eldest son.

The story they'd concocted had concluded robbery but it

had taken quite a substantial bribe. Not many believed the official causes of death and speculation spread faster than a sandstorm in the desert.

The last letter James received from his father was a plea for him to return and help him to help John. He wanted James to cash in his commission and return to the family seat.

But he hadn't done it. In London, as the spare, he was next to nothing. He hadn't been able to make a difference to anything or anyone. Anytime he wanted to try something new or daring, he would be encouraged down another path. The second sons of England weren't destined for bigger things. They were to stand in their brother's shadow. They were to stand in the bubble of possibility of a tragedy befalling. Only then could they become visible and worthy.

His father never asked for more than his unending commitment to the Trelissick name and then the Lasterton title. If James hadn't been filled with ambition, he would have been there to save both his brother and his father. Instead, he had been at war, killing, maiming, working for his mad king and uncaring country. It was almost as if his father thought him the same as Daniella did. An officer sitting in a tent while the men around him charged to their deaths.

Instead of preventing their disgrace, he had added to it. Rumours of the Butcher had drifted back to his homeland even before John's murderous rampage. Soldiers whispered to their families that he was a saviour, the last resort when the battle had gone against them in Egypt and the field needed to be levelled back out again. Some of the ton worried that the bloodshed had gone to his head, that these interloper Trelissicks would never easily wear the shoes a dead cousin had vacated. Those were the people who were closer in their character assessment of him.

He was the assassin who moved about in the night and eliminated enemies in silence, without conscience or regret.

And while he was killing Bonaparte loyalists, his brother had been killing his father and their good name. Perhaps he should have dragged John with him into the army.

"Are you going to answer me?"

He snapped his gaze back to Daniella. He hadn't even heard her question.

"Why did you let that woman believe we are lovers? Why not a husband and wife?"

James didn't want to consider that too closely, so he went on the attack. "Why did you auction your innocence? You had to know there would be other consequences if your father didn't succumb and give you your way. What would your brother do? Beat you? Lock you up? Send you away? Perhaps seeing you live secluded as a nun would be preferable to your father than having you back on his ship?"

She bit her lip and he knew satisfaction. She hadn't considered that either. Silly girl.

"Why did your father leave you in England if he no longer sails? Why not settle and let you pick your choice of a husband from a nearby town?"

"He no longer sails as a pirate. I do believe he makes occasional runs off the coast for provisions but he no longer sails for Spain or anyone else."

"You didn't answer my question."

"And you still haven't answered mine. I could have been your niece, your ward, your neighbour, a woman you found on the road. It makes no sense."

"It isn't supposed to make sense. As I said, a different story in every village. It will help us if there is pursuit. In one town they will look for a man with his ward, in the next they are looking for a marquess—my thanks to you for revealing that by the way—and his paramour. In the next they will not know to look for a lord and his servants. It helps to cover our tracks with confusion. I don't need anyone to catch up with us until we reach Scotland, and nor do you." It's why they weren't taking any direct route, zigzagging slightly from shire to shire but staying close to the coast. "Now, why did you not honour your father's wishes and simply marry a respectable man, if you won't tell me why he insisted you do so in London?"

"I don't want to talk about this anymore. I believe I shall rest my eyes for a spell."

"Eventually you have to tell me the full story, Daniella."

"No, I don't." She closed her eyes, effectively shutting him out from her thoughts, and leaned her head back against the squabs.

There had to be more to it than what she told him. What woman after reaching the sparkling beauty of the ton would not want to be a part of it? Some part of his mind whispered that the women of the ton were about as useless as second sons but it was different for men. Women of upper society only had to keep their beauty, have at least two sons and run a household in order to live an easy life. Daniella was lucky her brother had been knighted otherwise she might have wound up cleaning chamber pots.

Why didn't she see her father had done her a favour by leaving her in London? That he wanted the best for his only daughter?

Until James got the whole story, the whys and what ifs would be unsatisfying and as endless as eternity.

DANIELLA DID HER best to pretend to be asleep but the farce was short-lived. When they were only hours from their next stop for the night, the carriage jolted and then shuddered as it came to a sudden stop, the horses whinnying their discontent.

Trelissick had his head out of the door as he yelled up to the driver's box. "What is going on? Why have we stopped?"

It was Hobson who answered. "There's a tree in the road, and we won't get past until we shift it."

Trelissick snatched his head back into the carriage and closed the door. He lowered his voice to a whisper. "Do not move or speak. If anything happens to me, run into the woods and stay hidden. Wait there until Patrick catches up."

"Why? What is it?"

"A fallen tree blocks the road when there has been no storm and no wind? This could be a trap."

"By my father?" she asked hopefully.

"Not by your bloody father," he hissed. "How would he get ahead of us to set a trap?"

"Give me a gun then: I can help."

"No. You stay here." He stood and reached under the seat where he sat and pulled out a small pistol. He checked the shot and then stuck it in the back of his trousers, tucking his dark coat back over it before looking at her one last time, his glittering gaze fierce. "Stay."

Daniella thought about it for all of three seconds after he left then jumped to her feet in search of another weapon. If it was a trap and there was a group of men with pillage on their minds she would help. She would not cower in the carriage like a lady. She would not run and hide either. If it was her father's men then Trelissick was likely to get himself killed over her. She could live with a lot of things, bad and terrible, but she would not have his blood on her conscience.

The murmur of voices soon reached her but she couldn't be sure it wasn't Trelissick talking to Hobson. She slowed her efforts in her search for a weapon so the carriage didn't bounce and give her away.

The voices were getting closer now but were almost drowned out by the thumping of her heart and the roar of blood in her ears. Were they actually in serious danger? This was not what she wanted. Others should not be physically harmed over her.

Finally she found a second loaded pistol under a blanket beneath the bench where she had sat. She would have only one shot but would be sure to make it count.

Daniella held her breath and muttered a prayer to whoever listened, that she would be safe, that her father had come to retrieve her at last, and then she swung the carriage door open and jumped to the hard ground.

CHAPTER ELEVEN

"WELL, WELL, WELL. What do have here then?"

James swallowed a groan and slowly edged his way from behind the tree that hid him while he got the number of their foe.

"Hello, gentlemen. To what do I owe this pleasure?" Daniella's voice was smooth, in control, melodic. James swallowed another groan. He'd told her to stay put. The vixen listened to no one.

Between them stood six large men and a good deal of distance if he had to act quickly. James was tall at over six feet but these men would match him in height and weight, he was sure. They were hopelessly outnumbered and now had the added distraction of Daniella to throw into the fight.

"Might you need some assistance, miss?" One of the tall men took a step towards her and bowed low, the others laughing at his back.

She held her ground. "Assistance? With what?"

"We could relieve you of your fine jewels and be on our way. No one comes to harm and everyone is happy. Well, except for you that is, without your fine jewels."

James could see her gaze narrow as she pinned the man

who spoke with her eyes. "You aren't my father's men, are you?"

"And who might your father be, lass?"

"Have you heard of Captain Germaine?"

"The pirate?" This was followed by guffaws of laughter. "I heard he died. Couldn't have happened to a nicer gentleman really."

"He is a privateer, actually, and he isn't dead. Merely..." she waved her hand "...indisposed."

"Well he ain't here is he, so I'll be having your jewels."

Daniella held her hands out and then pulled the edges of her cloak back to reveal her smooth, pale neck. "As you can see, I have no fine jewels."

"She took 'em off and 'id them in the carriage," one man accused with a menacing step towards her.

Did she not realize they inched closer as she made small talk? Soon they would surround her and she would be at their mercy.

"You're welcome to search the carriage."

No they bloody weren't!

"How is it that a fine lady such as yourself, daughter of a successful pirate perhaps, comes to be on this road all on your own? Where is your husband or maid or whatever?"

"I'm no fine lady. I already told you, I'm Captain Germaine's daughter. No jewels, no money, no nothing. As to the whys, I've been kidnapped." Her mouth lifted in a smile. "I'm a hostage, hence nothing fine."

The men stopped advancing and laughed so hard one had to bend over at the waist to catch his breath. Daniella tapped her foot and crossed her arms over her chest.

"Looks like we got us a cracked one."

"I beg your pardon. I'm perfectly sane, thank you very much."

"Lass, you can't kidnap yourself and there isn't anyone else about."

"Are you sure about that?" At her words, chaos erupted. A shot sounded from the opposite side of the road and one of the men went down with a surprised squawk. A little farther down from there, while the men were busy taking shelter, another shot took down another brigand.

James fired his shot and removed another from the equation. It was only then that he stepped clear of the woods on the road's side and made his presence known. Now their numbers were even. "We have you surrounded. Give up, go home, live to fight another day."

The man who'd addressed Daniella ran to her and threw his arm around her neck, using her as a shield. The way her cloak fanned out meant that James could see nothing behind her, couldn't tell if the man had a gun or a knife to her back. The other two brigands both trained their guns on him but neither fired. Interesting.

James called out, "You will have to let her go. She can only make one of us a hostage and she is already mine."

"Stop right there or I'll kill her," the man shouted back.

He paused and held out his hands, his heart in his throat. He had to fight to appear calm and keep his fingers straight. She should have stayed in the bloody carriage, then he and his men would have had the thieves circled once they came closer. She put herself in danger unnecessarily. "It really would be terribly inconvenient for me and I don't take well to inconvenience."

The other two brigands leaped out of his way as he finally continued his approach but he was careful not to let either of them behind him. They stood in an awkward diamond shape with Daniella in the middle.

"You killed my men."

James nodded. "When it is kill or be killed, I prefer to make the first move. The tree wasn't very original, by the way. Had ambush written all over it."

The ruffian showed surprise as his gaze flitted from James to the tree and back again.

"It would have also behooved you to be closer when we stopped rather than coming from...? Where did you come from?" He was dealing with simpletons. He should have known by the fact that only six men thought to hold up a carriage with an unknown number of occupants. If it had been full, they would have been outnumbered and outgunned with the driver and another man up top.

Hobson was right now waiting for his signal, Willie with him in the dense forest.

"How about we agree that no one won here today and go our separate ways? We have nothing of value save our lives so why not walk away with them?"

"You're lying. Rich nabob like you must have some blunt."

James shook his head. "Not a farthing and not a shiny jewel in sight." He held out his arms again to show that he indeed had nothing on his person. Nothing that showed anyway. Only the signet on his little finger could be seen, and he wasn't giving that away. His watch was secreted in his pocket and his money was in the carriage. Thank God the men hadn't searched it when Daniella had invited them to.

The ruffian swore a blue streak but his grip on Daniella tightened. She showed no panic at all as she was jostled. Her hands went to her skirts, he assumed to avoid stumbling.

"Are you all right, m'dear?" he asked her in a low voice.

"Are we done with this?" came her reply.

James raised his brows at her but then nodded. "I rather think we are."

Out of her dress pocket, Daniella drew a pistol and without a glance behind or any hesitation, tucked the thing close to her side and pulled the trigger.

The brigand released her with a strangled cry and fell to the ground, his hands immediately going to his abdomen, where her bullet had dug deep.

James rushed one of the remaining two men just as Daniella launched herself at the other. He lost sight of her but knew Hobson would be only seconds away as he wrestled with his own bandit. He landed a few good punches but this wasn't his opponent's first outing. They both went down, James on top with a right hook to the other man's jaw.

Ordinarily, his punch should have at least had the man seeing stars but in less than a second, he was on his back while the brute pummelled him. He couldn't disable the man; he needed his hands to protect his face and head. A glancing blow slipped from his cheekbone to his ear but as the man atop him lost his balance, James flipped him over, took hold of his head and slammed it into the ground. He slammed again and again until the brute's eyes rolled back in his head and his body went limp.

James was breathing hard, his face hurt, the skin of his knuckles split open; and when he looked up to see where Daniella was, to make sure she was all right, shock hit him harder than any fist could. Hobson had his arms around her and had lifted her right off the ground as he dragged her away from the man in the dirt—the man she had been kicking with the hard toe of her new boot. As soon as she stopped struggling, Hobson put her down but then the crazy girl ran back and landed another kick to the ribs, her skirts held in her hands as she swung her leg with power.

Astonishment unlike anything he had ever experienced washed over him and he began to laugh. He climbed off the unconscious man and fell to his back still laughing and still fighting to catch his breath.

He would hate to be on the receiving end of one of those kicks but she hadn't been lying when she said she could look after herself. The minx looked to be enjoying the fight.

THE SOUND THAT brought Daniella back to the present was as unwelcome as it was unsettling.

"What are you laughing at? I could have been killed," she shouted.

Trelissick sat up and stared at her as though two heads had sprouted from her shoulders. "If you had thought your life in danger, why didn't you stay in the carriage as I instructed?"

"You left me in there alone. Anything could have happened!"

"We were watching." He gestured to Hobson and Willie who were now dragging the bodies from the road. "The only potential danger was these ruffians being actually any good at what they set out to do."

"How do you know that?" How could he possibly know what the outcome would have been? She could have been shot, stabbed, raped, all of the above.

"If these bandits were worth their salt, they would have killed me when I exited the carriage and Hobson as he jumped down and indeed Willie before we even made the fallen tree. It's what I would have done. Lucky for us they weren't even close."

She raised her hands to her hips. "Have you ever been on the side of the road readying an ambush? How much battle did you actually see?"

"That—" he pointed to one of the dead men "—is not my first kill."

"They don't call him the Butcher for no reason, lass." This from Hobson.

"Yes, why do they call you that?"

"Never mind that now. We have to get this mess sorted out so we can push on. We've lost a lot of time here." The glare he threw at Hobson would have killed had it sharp edges.

Daniella almost smiled. She really was going to get some

answers out of Hobson. It was the second time Trelissick's man had spoken out of turn.

James had shot that man without regret or compunction. So had she, but many a man had died by her blade. On the open sea it was kill or be killed. There was no friendly wave when one ship passed another. If two got that close, it was because one wanted to board the other. Plain. Simple. Deadly. Now she had to wonder how many men Trelissick had killed in his time in the army. It was far better for her sanity to assume he had been an officer in a tent at a table of maps while others died at his behest. She'd thought he was being defensive when she hurled that accusation at him.

She turned to ask Hobson more now that Trelissick was on the other side of the road but pain smarted at her side and she staggered. "Ouch."

"What is it, lass?" Hobson rushed to her, his hand at her elbow.

When she peeled her new cloak back, her dress was blackened around the edge of a hole in the fabric. With the excitement of the fight now wearing off, it hurt like the devil and burned like hell.

"Your pistol must have touched you when it discharged."

"It's nothing, just a scratch." She waved Hobson away and tried to pull her cloak back but Trelissick had seen the exchange and looked furious as he stomped towards her.

"Why didn't you mention the fact that you were hurt?"

"It's just a scratch. I'll be fine. Anyway, you're hurt too. You just may be bleeding more than me."

He raised his hand to his nose and when he pulled it

away his fingers were red. "It's nothing. Lucky punch is all."

She raised her brows and snorted in disbelief. He was already bruising.

"Ladies should not snort, Daniella."

"I think I just proved beyond a doubt that I am not a lady; and you are actually hurt."

"Never mind me, what of you? How deep does the burn go?"

Before she knew what he was about, he had the burned edges of the gown in his hands and was trying to see right past her garments.

"I told you, it's nothing." She swatted his hands away.

"Let's make an exchange. I can inspect your wounds and you can inspect mine."

"You just said yours were nothing."

"Doesn't hurt to have someone take a look though, does it? It wouldn't help either of our causes if one of us were to develop an infection. Or worse."

"Not here," she said, looking around as though more inept thieves lurked in the shadows. "When we stop for the night, you may look at my scratch."

His brows rose for a moment but then his mouth drew into a tight line as it had so many times in the last few days. He nodded once and then turned away to survey the scene.

Hoof beats sounded and everyone scattered without a word. Trelissick hauled Daniella into the tree line with a hand over her mouth and his arm around her waist pulling her close. Hobson and Willie disappeared to the other side of the road.

Relief poured through her when she saw Patrick rein in with a curse.

"What are we going to do now?" she asked when the men finally had the tree moved out of their path enough to move on. "Should we alert the authorities in the next town?"

Trelissick shook his head at the same time as Hobson did.

"You're just going to leave them here like this?"

"We don't have time to stop, lass. The magistrate would ask questions—he would have us stay in town for days."

"Hobson's right. Someone else will come along and they can report the bodies. We've moved neither them nor the tree far enough for anyone to just barrel past."

It seemed wrong to Daniella, but then again, a battle at sea saw all those lost go overboard. Holding on to bodies only brought disease. "Very well, let's be gone from here. It gives me a very bad feeling." Not because she had killed a man but because there wasn't one who remained alive to tell the story of why they were there. Her father would never hire such obviously dismal excuses for criminals but she wouldn't put it past her brother to thoroughly muck it up. If he had a finger on any kind of illegal activities, she would eat her favourite bonnet. He was after all a peer, a man knighted by the king himself. She was about to snort but recalled Trelissick's words about ladies.

Damn the men in her life. Damn them all to hell.

CHAPTER TWELVE

WHY COULDN'T IT all be simple? Why couldn't they stick to his plan to get them to Scotland without interference from inconvenient elements? First the bad food, then the highway robbery attempt—and now a storm had blown in and dumped rain and hail the entire afternoon. Even if it did cease, the way would still be too treacherous for the carriage to risk. They could slide off the road, lose a wheel, snap an axle—anything could happen. Even now they should have stopped, but they had yet to find a town and the carriage was too small to shelter them all. To top the dreadful day off, James was beginning to think they were lost.

It seemed they were in the middle of nowhere. The only structure they had passed in the last two hours had been an old barn, apparently abandoned. The map showed a fork in the road leading closer to the coast but they must have passed it already.

His only consolation, if one could label it that, was that if he couldn't travel due to the weather, then neither could Daniella's brother, although by now James had his doubts that Germaine pursued at all.

Were it him, he wouldn't rest for one second until he'd

caught up. Indeed he hadn't rested since he'd discovered his mother and sister gone. Each and every moment of the day had seen him plotting ways to get them back and then drive a knife right into the heart of that damned pirate.

James, or rather the Butcher, would be hailed a hero for eliminating a menace.

"Are you cold?" Daniella asked from the dimness.

He must have shuddered or betrayed some movement so he shook his head. "Just thinking."

"About the storm? Don't tell me you're afraid of a little thunder and lightning?"

He forced a chuckle as he pushed murderous thoughts away. "Not at all."

"Then what were you thinking about?"

"I was thinking how lucky it was today that we weren't all killed."

"How would you get your precious items back then?"

"Well, for one, I'd be dead and no longer in need of them."

"And two?"

"There is no two. Death is pretty final, don't you think? Perhaps except in the case of your father. How many lives has he used up so far?"

"I believe this is his third meeting with Davy Jones in as many years. Who knows how many more men have laid false claim to sinking him."

"Does it ever get tiring?"

"What?"

"The never-ending danger? The never knowing if you'll

live out the day?"

"Why don't you tell me? The Butcher must have had some experience with that himself."

"You've made it abundantly clear that you have no knowledge of war or the Butcher."

"Will you tell me? I'd like to know."

"No. You would not. It is not a subject for a lady." And when he realized she would protest her status in that regard, he added, "Or for any woman."

Another hour passed, the steady beating of rain on the roof of the carriage the only sound to penetrate the tension. When they slowed to a stop Hobson opened the door and stuck his dripping head in. "What should we do? We haven't seen a town since this morning and not a marker to show how much longer it will be until we reach one. Willie thinks we should go back to that barn we passed: the horses are getting tired and cold."

He hated the idea of it. Hated even more that they would have to turn the carriage around in this weather and then backtrack so far, but it would be worse to be on a strange road after dark with their destination unknown. They must have taken a wrong turn somewhere along the way. Already it was obvious the light would fade much quicker with the black clouds roiling above them. They would have no time to figure out where they were and remedy their direction.

James nodded, stood, reached under the seat where he had earlier removed the pistol and pulled out a greatcoat. "Stay here this time. Please," he added. "We'll turn around and then find shelter."

"I have no wish to catch my death out there in that," she said. Her look conveyed he, on the other hand, should definitely venture out into it.

A very real smile found its way to his lips as he stepped into driving rain and fading light. She was filled with mischief and fire and he rather thought he liked that about her. Even though he really didn't want to.

QUITE A GREAT deal of time later they finally reached the decrepit barn they had passed earlier. It seemed like yesterday that they had fought and killed the men on the road. Daniella was beyond weary but she hadn't been able to sleep. Not knowing if they could be stuck on the side of the road, all four of them huddled in the carriage, until morning. It hadn't bothered her when Mrs McDougal had fallen ill and been left behind. It wasn't until after the battle with the thieves that she'd realized just how hopelessly outnumbered she was. Four men and only one woman. Hobson was the only one she wasn't at all afraid to be alone with. He'd been kind to her where Trelissick had been gruff and moody. She didn't know Patrick but there was something about the way he stared at her that made her skin crawl. It wasn't leering as such: almost as if he worked to decipher her secrets from afar. Willie she knew nothing about but if he was in Trelissick's employ then he couldn't be all bad. Could he?

This was what Daniella traditionally referred to as her bout of doubts. It only ever hit her after she'd already gone ahead with a scandal or challenge or something equally wrong-headed. The uneasiness had tried to encroach several times already but she kept pushing it back, thought of something else, did something else. But now as they pulled into the dark barn with God knew what animal calling it home, the bout of doubts flew at her full force.

She wanted to call out that she was quite happy to continue on the road but Trelissick had warned her to stay quiet on the off chance the structure was inhabited. He was so bossy and serious all the time.

Except when he had flirted with her at the dressmaker's.

He wouldn't call it flirting but she would. His eyes had sparkled and his grin had shaved years off his face and his mouth had transfixed her. She couldn't help but rise to his playfulness. He had obviously at one time been a boy and then a young man. What had happened to turn him into a veritable rock? Was it this Butcher business?

When she'd first agreed to be his hostage she had planned to wait until they drew closer to their destination and then she was going to flee—she could not guarantee he would really hand her to her father and was determined to get herself home—but the fight with the thieves would have ended a whole lot differently had she been on her own.

This side of the border, she was certainly better off with him than without him. She would never tell Trelissick that though.

Daniella was startled from her thoughts when the carriage door flew open. She raised her dagger against the blinding light from a lantern, ready to use it if she had to.

"Where did you get that?" Trelissick's voice reached her, full of furious exasperation.

"I took it from one of the dead men."

"Are you planning on stabbing me in the back with it?"

She smiled as she dropped the blade to her lap, ensuring he knew the thought had occurred to her. "Not today."

His gaze held hers steady for more than a few beats of her heart while droplets of water fell from his hair to roll down his face and neck. He then stepped back so she could jump down. He didn't offer his hand as he had when they had been in town. Not the gentleman then?

"Patrick started a fire for us right down the end of the barn if you'd like to get warm."

"I'd actually like to change my clothes if you don't mind." Her "little scratch" was still on fire just above her hip, and her dress was stiff with the blood that had dried there.

"I still want to check your wound."

"You really don't need to and yours looks to be doing much better." The rain had washed away the blood on his face, leaving only light bruises to show that he had been in a fight at all. His nose wasn't any more crooked than it had been before and he was using his hand with the scabbed knuckles just fine.

"I'm not asking permission, Daniella."

She huffed but he was deadly serious. She damned him again. "Very well. Bring me my bag and we'll get this over with so you can get dry and I can get warm."

She didn't wait for arguments or acquiescence, just

climbed back into the carriage.

"What are you doing?" Trelissick called after her.

"I'm not going to stand naked out there for the whole world to see."

"You don't have to be naked at all."

She smiled to herself. He actually sounded as if he was going to grow prudish on her. "I am cold and filthy. I wish to change into something that will stop my teeth chattering all night long."

Harsh mutters reached her ears but she couldn't make out his words; she wondered if he was cursing her right back. The carriage dipped a little and then sprang upright again and he was back, standing in the doorway, a lantern in one hand, two bags in the other.

She raised her brow at the second bag. He better not be thinking of undressing as well. She gulped.

"This one has the medical supplies," he said as though reading her mind. Or perhaps just her expression.

As Trelissick climbed back into the carriage and closed the door behind him, the small area seemed to shrink in size, sparking a small flame of hysteria in her chest. "Why don't you wait outside until I am presentable and then I shall call you back in?"

"Why don't you take off your things and I will close my eyes?"

"Can I trust you to keep them closed?"

He chuckled. She liked the sound of it.

"I give you my word but if I think you are hiding injuries from me, there will be consequences."

She straightened up. After all, what could he do to her that hadn't already been done? He really had no idea what she had been subjected to in her life aboard ship. Not one clue at all. He must think she'd embroidered below decks while the men played pirate. "Am I supposed to be scared?"

"Are you scared of anything?" he asked as he turned away from her and put his head in his hands.

She began to undo the buttons marching down the front of her gown as she considered her answer. "Well, I don't much care for spiders. And there was this one time we were off the coast near India and… Well, you don't actually need to hear about that."

"You've seen much of the world, haven't you, Daniella?"

"I have. Beautiful green coasts and deserted islands and towering cliffs and the bluest waters you couldn't even dream up on a good day."

"Is that what you miss the most?"

She wriggled the dress over her knees and then off her feet and sat back down in her underthings. He'd already seen her shift and stays. "I miss my father the most. I would have given it all up had he just kept me by him."

"Did he not discuss it with you first?"

She laughed long and loud then. "There was no discussion. The captain has the final say aboard *The Aurora*."

"If he's not to be argued with then why are you being so defiant now? Is it for him or the ship? Or is there another reason entirely?"

Daniella pulled on the first dress she found in her bag, discarding the nightgown: it was far too cold for that. She was doing up the buttons when she remembered he was there for a reason other than annoying her. "Both," she replied, beginning the task of undoing them again. "I do not belong in London. Hell, I am beginning to believe that no one belongs in London. There is no happiness, only order. No freedom, no contentment, no acceptance."

"Are those the things you wish for then?"

She wasn't sure what she wanted anymore, and even if she was, wishing wasn't going to get it for her. If a body wanted something in life, she had to work hard to make it happen. "I tried to fit in when I first arrived. There were so many rules and I couldn't keep them straight in my head. I had no help other than from Anthony and he was really no help at all. I was doomed from the first wobbly step I took."

"Doomed in what way?" He was looking at her now. Her gown was undone and while she hadn't managed to pull it all the way down to her waist, he kept contact with her eyes.

She cocked her head to one side and sighed. "I am undesirable."

CHAPTER THIRTEEN

TRELISSICK CHOKED AND spluttered and at first Daniella thought he was laughing but it became clear from the way his eyes bulged that she had shocked him. "What did I say?" she asked.

"You are not undesirable."

"I heard the men talking about me and that is exactly what they said." She remembered that conversation because she had wanted the ground to open up and swallow her whole. It was the first time in her entire life that she had been made to feel miserable and ugly and unwanted.

"Who said that? And when?"

"At some ball I was dragged along to with Anthony. I heard them say that with my freckles and tanned skin and wildness, I was undesirable."

"Ah, I think I see."

She glared sharply at him, ready to slap him if he even for one moment agreed with those dogs. Not that his opinions mattered that much to her, she reminded herself.

"They weren't saying you were undesirable. They must have called you *an* undesirable. As in, not good for a wife."

Her cheeks burned with humiliation and she was suddenly sorry she'd raised the subject. "And why not? How is that any better?"

"You don't understand how it works in London. A man takes a docile wife. He wants her to be obedient and efficient and quiet. She runs the household and bears the heirs. She does not sell her virginity or ride astride in the park. She doesn't challenge gentlemen to duels or swim naked in the moonlight."

She wished he would forget that particular night ever happened. "I know all of that and anyway I don't want to be some staid man's even more staid wife."

"I'm afraid that is how it works, Daniella. You can't break so many years of tradition or thinking."

"So you are going to go home after you retrieve your items and find yourself a lap dog?"

He shook his head, donned a patronizing glare and folded his hands over his knee. "I am going to find a woman who will make me smile at the breakfast table and who can run my house and birth the children who will carry on my name. It is what titled men do. I am the last of my line so it is what I must do."

"And before you were titled? What did you want to do then?"

She saw it in his eyes. Whether he meant to show it or not, regret flitted over his face, and she knew this hadn't always been his future. Once upon a time he probably would have had it all figured out, the second son. How many men walked around thinking their older brothers would die young?

"It doesn't matter what I wanted. This is the way it has to be."

"Says who?"

"Says society. Says my sister, who must make a good marriage. Says my mother, who wishes for nothing more than to bounce a grandchild on her knee. Says the House of Lords, who need the titled to make fair and just decisions about the future of the empire and her people. I have responsibilities. I cannot shirk them just because I saw it turning out differently."

Trelissick sighed then. Mostly with resignation. "Let us get this done so we can warm ourselves by the fire."

Darkness shrouded them and, as it did, the temperature dropped. She would not like to grow too cold lest she never warm up again.

"Let me see then."

She'd left her petticoats on so she wasn't worried about him seeing more than he should. When she'd spoken of nakedness, she had only been trying to irk him into backing down about her scratch. It did not need this level of attention. Even the time she had stepped on her own dagger by accident it hadn't warranted this level of concern.

"That is more than a scratch," he commented upon seeing the scrape on her side.

"It is not." She tried to pull the dress back on, having fulfilled her part of the bargain they had struck, but he had other ideas.

"You need to remove this." He tugged on the linen of her shift, moving her entire torso. "The area must be cleaned properly."

"I will be fine."

"I am not asking you, Daniella. Take it off."

"No."

Trelissick's nostrils flared and Daniella almost backed away from the sound his teeth made as they ground together.

"We can do this the difficult way, or you can make it easy for yourself and remove it," he said.

"I won't do it. It isn't decent."

"Not decent? You wouldn't know decent if it bit you on the buttocks. Take it off now, or I will do it for you."

She hadn't noticed her discarded dagger in his hands. Not for one second did she doubt he would cut her out of her dress. Her new dress, and the only one she had left. She didn't hurry but she did remove the dress. "I'll need a blanket."

Since they sat on the same seat, Trelissick leaned forwards and removed a blanket from beneath the seat where she had sat all day. He had every necessity in those small spaces. He threw the blanket at her and then turned his head once again.

"Why do you have to be so stubborn all the time? Can you not see when the people around you know better?"

Her fists balled in the coarse fabric. "Better for whom? You? Anthony? My father? What is actually good for me isn't what you might think. You've never experienced freedom the way I have, only to have it snatched from your grasp."

"If society did more than speculate how deeply you were involved with pirates, we wouldn't be having this discussion.

If your father had ever been captured red-handed rather than taunting and eluding, you would be in prison, already dead or on your way to the colonies. You curse your brother yet his knighthood protects you now."

With one last tug, she was free of all of her clothing, naked as the day she was born, the blanket itching against her skin. Her cheeks began to heat but she lifted her chin and pushed aside embarrassment. So far, James Trelissick had treated her somewhere between a sibling and a problem. Even in the dress shop, he had pulled away from her as though she carried a disease. He wasn't likely to ravish her in his carriage with his men just outside.

Securing the blanket beneath her armpits with one arm, she maneuvered the rest of the blanket so it would split open at her side but not far enough that he would see everything she had to offer.

"I am ready," she said into the thick silence.

His back lifted with the force of his inhaled breath and as he turned Daniella closed her eyes. Never in her life had she felt this level of scrutiny and embarrassment.

She would not call it shame and attach it to her actions. Not ever.

IN ALL HIS life in London, on the battlefields, in the countries he had been to, he had never met anyone so full of blind stupidity. Did she really not think the skirmish they had had earlier in the day could have turned fatal for any one of them or did she just not care? James certainly had. His heart squeezed uncomfortably in chest as he thought of all the ways she could have been hurt. Not for the first time he wondered if Daniella's inability to take real threats seriously was the true reason she had been dumped in London. Being wrapped in petticoats and politeness was almost the same as a padded room. She wasn't supposed to be able to find any harm.

And harm was exactly what she had done that man today. And herself.

He tried not to touch her skin at all as he peeled the edges of the blanket back. "You have quite a burn here, Daniella. Why did you hold the gun so close?" He would not think about the paleness of her hip or the ridges of her ribs or the warmth she emanated. She could have been a lot more seriously injured and that was what he should concentrate on.

"I did what I had to do; there wasn't time for measurements or concentration," she said.

As she inhaled, the blanket lifted and her thigh came into view. His heart thumped painfully but he set to cleaning the area, instantly relieved the wound wasn't nearly as bad as he'd first surmised. "That's why you were to stay in the carriage."

"Then you would have been killed."

"I'm touched you think so highly of me as to come to my rescue."

"I need you right now just as much as you need me, perhaps more."

She had to stop being so honest with him but he was

grateful she saw it that way. He might live to see days beyond this week after all. "I'm going to apply a salve to the burn but you won't be able to put your dress back on tonight— binding it will only make it hurt more."

Daniella pulled the edges of the blanket back together so he couldn't touch her. "If you think I am going to spend the whole night in nothing but this blanket, Trelissick, you can think again."

"James."

"What?"

"I want you to call me James." It had been childishness that made him revert to propriety and he was done with it. "Trelissick is...stuffy. And you did purchase a nightgown." He pulled at the blanket but she held fast, her fist on the inside of the wool.

"I will be cold."

"You can sleep next to the fire."

"And my back?"

"Why do you make such a deal out of this? I will sleep at your back. Between me and the fire, you will be warm and safe."

"Who will stand watch?"

"Could we please stop arguing?" He was tired and hungry and wet. "Let me apply the salve so we can get warm. You can berate me more then."

"Very well."

James took the edges of the blanket and once again pulled them apart. She flinched when he touched his fingers to the burn but said nothing. He expected a curse at the very least.

Despite the angry redness, her skin was still smoother than smooth and James found himself rubbing the salve into areas not affected. As his circles grew bigger, he grew more mesmerized. Had he ever touched a woman so soft yet so unyielding? Beneath his hands lay the tension of corded muscle covered in satin. No pudginess or overindulgence lined her hip, only strength and stamina.

It wasn't Daniella who put a halt to his exploration—although she should have—it was Patrick knocking hard against the carriage door that drew him back to the present. Once again he met her eyes but this time it was simple to name what he saw there.

Desire.

Yearning.

Need.

Emotions sure to destroy his plans and far too many lives.

He rubbed his hands down the front of his coarse, damp trousers to be rid of the salve and the feeling of her on his fingertips. "I'll leave you to dress in your nightgown."

She only nodded. She did not move, did not argue. Seems he'd finally rendered her speechless.

CHAPTER FOURTEEN

THE FOLLOWING DAY dawned bright and clear, the storm passing in the night, but Daniella was miserable. Her face was all puffy and her throat itched abominably. Trelissick kept scolding her about keeping dry and warm, and no matter how many times she tried to tell him it was the hay and dust that affected her, he kept up his steady diatribe about looking after herself better and how a dead hostage was no good to him at all. The strangest part was how chatty he was this morning. After sneezing all night long, she didn't think anyone was well rested.

The dark smudges beneath his eyes attested to the sleepless night but there was something else about his mood this morning she couldn't quite place.

His concern, if it was genuine, was almost touching. At least she'd finally convinced him she needed fresh air to clear her head and he'd let her ride up top with Willie for most of the morning. The sun on her face and the wind in her hair almost made her forget her troubles and remember the decks of the ship and the freedom she'd once owned.

One good thing about the day was that Willie wanted to chatter and that helped to distract her. He asked her questions about her father and she answered: even if he only asked for Trelissick's benefit, she had nothing to hide save her father's port location. She shared stories about storms and chases and disease and he in turn told her about Trelissick and his brother when they were lads. Willie had served the old marquess before James's father had ascended to the title. She guessed him to be approaching seventy years in age.

"What happened to the marquess's brother?" she asked.

"Poor lad went quite mad with the drugs."

"You mean the heir? Trelissick's older brother?"

Willie clucked his tongue and shook his head. The horses pulled at the reins and adjusted their stride as they picked up speed on a straight stretch of road. "Weren't never made to be a marquess, that one. Didn't have the balls, beggin' your pardon."

"That's quite all right." She waved for him to continue and when he didn't, she spoke. "Is that when Trelissick returned from the war?"

"Had to. His mam and Miss Amelia needed a man when the brother and father were found dead."

Daniella gasped. "What happened?"

"No one is real sure. Heard the gunshots and found both the master and the boy in the study. Dead."

"That's awful. How did Trelissick's mother take it?"

"Finally found her strength, that woman. Aye, she had some help but she still arranged the funerals, covered up the truth and had the army send for the other boy, held it all together."

"No wonder she is traveling the continent. I take it she rather needed a holiday after the shock of that."

Willie looked sideways at her, shook his head and then turned his eyes back to the road.

"What?" she asked. "What aren't you telling me?"

"Mayhap the master should be telling you the rest of the story."

Damn. She had been quite involved with the tale. Did she dare ask Trelissick the rest? As certain as she was that she would once again man the decks of *The Aurora*, she was sure there was much more to the story than what she had heard so far. How did the two men wind up dead? Were they murdered? Did they kill each other somehow? What truth did Willie allude to?

Poor James. The scandal must have added to the heart-break. Perhaps it was the reason for his mother and sister's trip abroad. He must have sent them away for their own good. Much like her father had done to her but theirs was a holiday and hers was a prison.

She wasn't nearly as naive as she'd have others think. She wanted to regain her place aboard the ship but she had no interest in sailing for the king of Spain once she did. She'd shared her grand trade plans with her father, to try their hand at legitimate dealings while they had the blunt to back themselves and buy their first load of precious cargo. He'd laughed at her. Told her no one would barter with a woman, let alone one as young as her. She'd spent every day for a year or more thinking about the ways they might take advantage of wars raging all over the world. She'd made plans on maps, drawn up list upon list upon list. As soon as word of Anthony's knighthood reached them, her father sent her away.

He'd obviously spent those days thinking of ways to rid himself of his overly optimistic daughter. Hand her off to some gentrified lord who could keep her caged and safe. After the loss of his leg, he changed, the captain.

Daniella shook her head and bit the inside of her lip. James did that to him. In some roundabout way, James was the root of her current problem.

They might be cooperating for now, but she would not romanticize James. For the last month, he had masqueraded as her servant with the intent to draw out her father and, when that failed, he'd kidnapped her. He was no hero in this no matter what had happened to his family or what motivated him.

Then why was it so difficult this morning to see him as anything but?

THE ONLY THING better than a bed to sleep in and four walls and a roof to keep out the wind and rain was the inn they discovered later that afternoon nestled in a hamlet on the edges of the cliffs off the coast just south of Frodsham or Fidsham or maybe even Shamfrod.

Before she settled in, Daniella needed to walk. She needed to breathe in the fresh scents of the ocean and pretend for one moment that there was nothing odd in her current situation. That there was no pull between her and Trelissick.

Between her and James.

How could she have any kind of warm feelings for this man who used her so callously?

You're using him too…

She damned her subconscious to the deepest depths of the ocean. He was her means to an end and she was his. That was it. That was all there could ever be between them. They weren't friends. To even think about more meant the end to something else entirely.

Her freedom.

Daniella shook the thoughts free from her mind. Marriage would never be the answer for her. If she thought the constraints of London stifling, she would be absolutely smothered under a husband's rule. Especially his. He had already made it more than clear what he wished for in a wife. A breeding machine and a housekeeper. Oh, and a pretty face. Not a freckled, tanned hoyden with scars and calluses and a keen sense of adventure.

If she were ever to marry, her husband would have to make her feel wanted. Desirable. Needed for more than babies and warm meals. He would have to admire her tenacity and welcome her opinions, her advice. She supposed it would be nice to feel wanted again. She felt that with Jimmy the deckhand. He'd always stared at her with such gentleness and barely concealed hunger. She'd felt safe giving herself over to him. It had felt right.

James had only twice stared at her with anything but anger and it hadn't spelled gentle. The hungry expression in his eyes at the dressmaker's and again in the carriage when he'd soothed her burn had scared him. It was the only reason he would have pulled away like he had. The reason he hadn't touched her since. Not to hand her into the carriage or even to guide her into a room. He'd put up a tall, wide barrier and she'd no idea if she wanted to push it over or not. Suddenly the pretty papered walls closed in on her. She crossed the timber boards and threw open the window, leaning her head right out and gulping the night air. With her arms resting on the weather-worn sill, she closed her eyes and tried to pretend she was home, on her ship, with her father pacing the boards above with two good legs and chatting to his crew, giving orders for the night, laughing at the day's mishaps.

She tasted the salt on her tongue and smelled the freshness in the air but try as she might, she could not forget where she was, what she was. The more time she spent with the marquess, the cloudier her thoughts became. Never had she thought of anything but the ocean, her father, her ship. Why did he have to make her think about responsibilities and reputations and how a lady should and should not act?

A lady would never climb down a wall and walk barefoot through the sand. She was sure of it.

When they'd arrived in the late afternoon, the light was still strong enough to see the side of the building. It faced out over an ocean still turbulent from the recent stormy weather and was constructed of mismatched stone. Hopefully it would provide the footholds she needed to drop down to the roof below.

Even if her door hadn't been locked, she couldn't risk leaving by way of the corridor. She also wouldn't give

Trelissick the satisfaction of thinking he'd caught her escaping.

All was dark now but she would have to be very quiet and very careful. The barns were to the rear of the building and, so far as she could tell, the kitchens, tap and bar stretched across the opposite side from her room. She hoisted up her skirt to undo her petticoats and sighed with relief when they floated about her ankles. She stepped out of the fabric, dropped the hem of her gown and then picked the petticoats up and hid them beneath the bedclothes. If Trelissick happened by earlier than he'd promised, then perhaps he would think her asleep and leave her in peace.

Perhaps he should have consented to the walk when she'd asked him. His answer had been drivel about the dark, the rain, the waves crashing down on the sandy beach. "It is too dangerous." "Someone might recognize one of us." "The day has been trying enough." He'd practically driven her to climbing down the outside of the building.

With one more glance out the window into the dark, she threw her leg over the sill, balanced on her bare toes, then lifted the other one out. Slowly, she felt around with one foot and then the other, lifted one hand and then the other, confounding her outer skirt to the bottom of the ocean with her earlier thoughts, until she felt the solid expanse of cold slate beneath her foot.

From there she lay on her stomach and inched back over the side of the roof, hoping that what she dangled from wasn't the kitchen or a dining-room eave. Though it was dark, a body hanging in front of a window would be easily seen and the alarm raised.

After what felt like hours, she finally stood on solid ground, her body flat against a windowless wall as she caught her breath. Thank God she hadn't landed in a rose garden or woodpile.

The moon sat low and full in the sky as light clouds sped towards the opposite horizon and lit the path between the trees to the ocean. Not hesitating a moment longer, Daniella broke into a run to cross the yard and only slowed when she thought she would be hidden beneath the tree's thin canopy.

As she walked in the direction of the crashing waves, the sound so familiar she wanted to cry, she wondered where her father was, what her brother was doing, whether they searched for her or not. She kept thinking Anthony should have caught up to them by now and, though she had no intention of going anywhere with him, she was desolate to think he wasn't coming. That no one was coming. Even worse was the feeling she deserved it. All of it.

Her life was so wildly out of control and she had no choices left to her to gain it back. A chill settled on her arms and, as she crossed them over her chest, her toe caught the edge of an exposed tree root impossible to see in the dark. She stumbled. Before she could fall in the dirt, one strong arm snaked across her middle at the same time a hand closed over her mouth.

Her first thought was to kick out, to scream and throw her body weight away from her attacker. But then she sagged with relief. Her father had come at last.

TO CROW HIS victory would have been far too loud but it's what Patrick wanted to do. Just as he wondered how he was ever going to get Daniella away from Trelissick, she fell right into his arms.

"Don't struggle, lass. Will ye scream if I take my hand away?"

She shook her head, her mouth curving into a smile against his hand. He dropped it away and pulled her off the path behind the trunk of a large tree.

As soon as he stepped away from her, she came towards him and punched him in the nose.

"What did ye do that for?"

"You could have told me you were one of my father's men," she huffed, holding her hand and beginning to pace.

"I'm not. I don't even know your father." His eyes swam with moisture as he gingerly felt the bridge of his nose to be sure the chit hadn't broken it. Damn, that had hurt.

"You don't have to lie; I won't tell James."

"Come now, lass, I don't believe that for even a hen's heartbeat."

She stopped, threw him a glare and then continued her pacing.

"With luck, you won't see him again anyway." Patrick took her arm and began towing her back towards the barn. But what to do with her while he saddled his horse? And what of supplies? They would need more than the dried bread and small amount of clean water he had left from the day's ride.

"Where is my father? Is he near? Did he come by carriage

or by ship?"

"I told you already, lass, I don't know your father. Yet." Patrick transferred his grip from her arm to her wrist but still he pulled her along.

Daniella reclaimed her wits and resisted, throwing all of her inconsiderable body weight in the opposite direction until he was forced to stop or drag her along the ground. "What is going on?"

He tugged on her arm, maybe a little harder than he should have, but they had to be away from there before she was missed and a search organized. "We have to go. Now."

She tugged again, her feet digging in. "I was not escaping. I'm going for a walk. You can tell Trelissick that I will come back in one hour if he should ask."

"You're not escaping?" This time he stopped. He turned and regarded her with a raised brow.

"No. I just want to dip my feet in the ocean. I'm not used to being stuck in a carriage with His Highness for days on end."

"We don't have time for this. I have to get you away from here."

"Why?"

After hours of Patrick pressing home that he couldn't fully help to protect Daniella if he didn't have all the facts, Hobson had finally revealed why the party travelled together. When he heard what Lasterton was hoping to recover from Captain Germaine, he'd barely been able to hide his fury.

Was there no line the marquess, the Butcher, wouldn't cross? There, in the harsh truth, was the reason Patrick hadn't been able to find any trace of Amelia. Whatever he'd feared her brother had done—sent her to a convent; even smothered her, as murderous as the dead eldest Trelissick—he certainly hadn't imagined he'd let her be taken by pirates. When he realized she was gone, he'd had nothing to go on and no one to ask. He had tried to gather information from the household but Trelissick had few servants in the city and he couldn't risk his questions getting back to the marquess. Then the damned man had gone to ground and Patrick had wasted months traveling back and forth between Trelissick's country estate and his house in the capital. One night his watching had paid off when the marquess had snuck into his own house via the servants' entrance to the kitchens, dressed in dirty trousers, a shirt that had once been white and a coat that could barely be described as such. Not exactly the actions of a ton gentleman.

Patrick stared at Daniella, exasperated. "Why? Why would you want to stay with a man such as he? I can take you to your father but we have to go now."

"But you just said you don't know my father."

"I don't. I just want Amelia back."

"Amelia? The marquess's sister? What has she to do with my father?"

"Do you know nothing?"

"I have never been so confused! I thought Amelia and James's mother were traveling on the continent?"

"Did you never wonder why the marquess truly has you?"

"My father has something of his and James is to swap me

for…" Realization dawned on her face and her eyes widened. "You're wrong. What would he…? How would he…? No. I don't believe it."

"Believe it, lass, heard it from Hobson myself this afternoon. A daughter in exchange for a mother and sister."

She paused, clearly evaluating this new information. "You can't take me to him: it isn't the same."

"Same what? Why can I not be the one to trade you?"

"You have no leverage. My father will order you to return me to London. There is no danger about you."

That should have smarted but it didn't. Now he was the confused one. "What is the danger behind Trelissick?"

Daniella shook her head and squeezed her eyes shut and Patrick had to curl his fingers so as not to scare the truth from her.

"It's a long story," she said with a sigh.

"Here's the story as I know it. Your da has Amelia and I am going to get her back before all of this scheming sends her to the bottom of the ocean. I have to find her. She is— She is not…strong."

"If the captain does have her, he won't hurt her."

"He's a bloody pirate! And if he harms a hair on her head, he will have me to answer to!"

Patrick ground his teeth as Daniella shook her head, her expression one of defeat, of resignation, of exhaustion. "Why do men think they can solve every problem with threats? If my father holds Amelia, he does so for a good reason."

Patrick made to interrupt but Daniella raised a hand between them and shook her head.

"It is not in his nature to hurt a defenceless woman. Despite what you've heard about pirates, my father's crew are not defilers of young ladies nor burners of villages nor killers of children. If, and I do mean if because I am beginning to think you are all quite mad, *if* he has Amelia and has not ransomed her, then his quarrel is with Trelissick and not you. You have not earned yourself his nickname. You did not stab my father in the leg so that he lost it. You did not take his livelihood and adventure away from him. Trelissick did. Trelissick is the only one who can hand me over. My father will not like that he has me but he will not particularly care if you do."

The possibilities swam in his mind until he wanted to pull his hair out. She was right. Damn the chit. But the Butcher could not be trusted and Daniella should have known that more clearly than anyone.

A stunning realization hit him and he staggered, his hand against the trunk of a nearby tree.

"What's the matter? Patrick? I'm sorry this isn't going the way you thought it would."

He shook his head. Trelissick was never going to give him Amelia. Even if the marquess did get his sister back, there was no way he was going to say goodbye to her and hand her over to him. Patrick would still be minus the one woman he knew he had to have. The only woman who could provide him with both redemption and love.

And damn it all, now Daniella knew who he was. He should never have spilled his secrets before getting her away from there.

"Say something, please?" Her soft touch on his arm had him lifting his gaze. Worry filled her eyes and her lips were pressed together in a tight line.

"When did it all get so difficult?" he asked.

"I know when that happened for me, but when did it go so wrong for you?"

He would tell her nothing else. He shook his head and asked, "Where do we go from here?"

"Well, it seems I will be getting no walk tonight. I have to go back before Trelissick discovers me gone."

"What will you tell him about me?"

"I won't tell him anything. You must care for Amelia a great deal and I won't stand in the way of that but you can't do this again. I have no wish to escape the marquess yet, or possibly at all. I have even less desire for him to watch my every single move so closely that I never get any peace."

"Are you sure this is the best way? What if you're wrong about Trelissick? We could be wasting precious time."

"I promise you, on my own life, no harm will come to Amelia if my father holds her."

Patrick wanted to trust her, he did. Her big green eyes shone with sincerity in the moonlight but she was the daughter of a pirate who was tangling with a man known across half the continent as the Butcher. If he had the chance to take Amelia away from it all, he would do it. By any means necessary.

CHAPTER FIFTEEN

B Y THE LIGHT of the full moon, James never took his eyes from Daniella's form. What the hell was the chit up to now? The only reason he hadn't jumped out the window and chased after her was because this particular cove went nowhere and the waters were too dangerous for a ship to get close. The innkeeper had given him a very long and detailed history lesson while James gulped down his ale as though the bottom of the mug held the answers he sought.

Unless she thought to climb the cliffs on either side of the sand, she would be coming back. Only a few minutes passed and the puzzle grew more complicated as Patrick also slipped into the woods between the inn and the ocean. James couldn't see as far as the sand and after twenty minutes of tense waiting, he was about to join the two and find out what the bloody hell they were about when Daniella re-emerged from the cover of the trees.

If this was her brilliant getaway plan then she had learned nothing about scheming at all. Good thing for him.

When she stopped at the base of the building and pulled her skirt up and tied it in a knot, James saw red.

He crept from his room and used the key to unlock her

door. As soon as he stepped into the space, the breeze from the open window was cool on his chest without a waistcoat or coat to cover the fine fabric. How in the hell she had made it from the sill to the ground he had no clue but if she didn't break her neck climbing back up, he was thinking about doing it for her.

As he made his way to the bed to wait for her to come back through the window, unable to simply stand by and watch her fall, which was certainly a possibility he could do nothing about, he noticed something odd. It looked as though someone was already beneath the covers. A closer inspection revealed layers of petticoats in the rough shape of a sleeping woman.

James raked a hand through his hair and pulled on the strands. He was definitely going to kill her.

He made to blow out the candle but hesitated. The little dagger she had stolen from the dead man sat there on the bed stand as though it shouldn't be in her hand right now. He picked it up, snuffed the candle and crept towards the window. He aligned his body so he was flush against the wall, his back to the corner.

Then he waited.

Quicker than he thought possible, one slim, very bare leg poked through the opening, five little toes bending and pointing as she stretched her foot to the floor. James held himself at the ready in the shadows, dagger in one hand, the other clenched into a tight fist.

By the time the other naked leg came through the window, James had had more than enough. There she stood, attempting to catch her breath, her skirt pulled almost all the way up to her derriere, hands gripping the sill. She hadn't seen him yet but she must have known something wasn't quite right. She looked towards the bed and the candle, a frown pinching her lips and eyes together as her breath held. As soon as her hands were free of the window frame, James pounced.

His free arm wrapped around her stomach and she shrieked and began to struggle. He brought the knife to the delicate skin of her throat and she went as still as the dead.

"What are you doing, you filthy cur?" she hissed.

"Tut tut, I wouldn't say too much, my dear—I fear this knife to be very sharp."

"Let me go."

"What were you doing outside just now?"

"I went for a walk."

"Liar!" He tightened his arm around her and held the knife that little bit closer.

A shudder racked her and he had to use all his power not to pull the blade away and offer his apologies. He'd meant to scare her for a moment, not give her an apoplexy.

"All I wanted was to take a walk."

"I don't believe you," he murmured, his mouth close to the lush skin of her neck. He'd bet the sea air would have infused the spot right beneath her lobe.

"If I wasn't taking a walk, what was I doing?"

He had to keep his head. "Why don't you tell me? You and McDonald must be quite the chums now."

She flinched beneath his palm. "He saw me out there

and thought I was escaping."

"So why didn't he raise the alarm then?"

"Because unlike you, he believed I was truly going for a walk and accompanied me. Please let me go. You're actually going to hurt me."

"Why aren't you afraid of anything?" he asked with frustration. Her voice held no fear at all. "Anything could have happened to you out there. Anyone could have come upon you and you would have been unarmed and at the devil's mercy."

"I am at no devil's mercy." The half laugh that followed her words did nothing to calm his fury.

"You are at my mercy."

"You need me, therefore you won't do anything to harm me."

He wasn't sure if it was the boy in him, the man, or the Butcher, who responded to her cocky statement. He dropped his arm to gently stroke the bare skin of her thigh where her dress was still knotted. At first his touch was soft, controlled, as was he. "Invincibility is a trait of the gods, Daniella, not the daughter of a pirate. If I wanted you, I could take you and so could any other man with muscle on his arm."

"Don't you dare." Her whispered words held no conviction whatsoever and he wondered if he was winning this battle or if she only led him to believe he could.

"Oh, I dare." His fingers tightened around her leg, his thumb inching closer to her undoing with every firm caress.

"You said you wouldn't do this."

"When did I say that?"

"You don't even find me attractive."

Inching closer and closer, his thumb finally brushed against the edge of the barely there drawers beneath her hiked-up skirts. Only the thin scrap of fabric saved her at this point. "Attraction has nothing to do with this. Someone needs to teach you a lesson."

In his arms, she groaned, her head falling back onto his shoulder, her breasts arching against the confines of her dress. "A lesson about what?" she asked breathlessly, her body tight and tense as she responded to him rather than cowering from him.

"That a man is a man and he cannot be trusted." He lifted his hand from her leg and brushed it up and over her stomach to gently squeeze her breast. "That you cannot control every situation you get yourself into." He squeezed again and almost smiled when she arched into his hand, her backside rubbing over his growing erection. "That you are not invincible."

He loosened the ties at her neckline and yanked on the fabric, satisfied when it ripped. Reaching in, he cupped her naked skin, rolled her pebbled nipple in his fingertip. Her sharp intake of breath said she still wasn't scared of him or the situation. The realization pulled him from the haze of the edge and he wondered if this was about teaching her a lesson or finally giving in to the lust he felt when she was near.

He turned her in his arms quickly and pushed her onto the bed. "Are you still feeling invincible?" he asked.

"You're not going to hurt me." Her eyes opened and she pulled the edges of her wrecked gown together and started to rise but James jumped onto the bed, straddled her so she couldn't rise, his hand to her shoulder to push her back down. He wanted to see just a touch of fear in her eyes. He wanted to know there was a shred of self-preservation in there somewhere, something to tell him that she did think about the consequences of her actions at some point and that she wasn't a danger to herself and to him.

"What the hell are you doing? I get it. I understand the lesson."

"Not yet."

"James, let me go now."

"I don't want to." He spun the knife in his hand until the blade pointed up and then slid it beneath the front of the gown and chemise.

"Don't—"

In less than three seconds, she was bared to him from the waist up, her clumsy attempts to cover herself no use at all.

He trailed the edge of the knife between her breasts right down to her navel. "Shall we continue?"

She lifted her chin, resilience and fury lighting them bright green from within. "So you see me naked? What next? Are you going to stop at humiliation or are you going to rape me too?"

He had gone much further than he should have and she was far stronger, and more stubborn, than he'd thought. Unless it was all an act? A slip of a girl couldn't keep this up, but a skilled actress could hide her fear, the daughter of a pirate who was used to getting her own way in all things could too. He would have to change tactics.

"I DON'T HAVE to force you."

Despite the effort to hold on to her fury, Daniella's bravado slipped and she gulped. "What do you mean by that?" Despite her voice being level and sure, despite the fact her fingers didn't tremble and her hands were steady as she held them against her skin, she was beside herself. In what way, it still wasn't entirely evident. At one moment she felt the thrill of the chase and would have gladly followed, the next, fury at his actions, the next, the heat pooled low in her belly and made her want to let him have his way with her. Any way he wished.

"I am going to make you want me."

She raised a brow. "What kind of lesson would that be?"

"What makes you so sure of yourself, Daniella?" He threw the knife to the floor and slid his way down her body until his chest rested against hers. His delicious weight pressed her into the mattress, her hands over her breasts and his pelvis digging in. He ground his erection against her softness. The two layers of fabric may as well have been nonexistent for the exquisite friction his movements created.

This is what had seen her thrown off her father's ship. The wanton within her who couldn't help but yearn for completion had corrupted until her life was ruined. Jimmy had been dropped off the side of the boat to swim his way to the nearest island and she had been dumped on her brother's doorstep in London. If she gave in to this thing that grew between her and James, her father would likely have them married at the point of a sword.

"As enjoyable as this might be, we must stop."

"You think words will save you now?" he asked. "If you flee my protection and a band of ruffians comes upon you, how will you get away? Saying please and thank you won't help."

"I'll use my dagger. I can fight."

"You don't have your dagger," he pointed out with a flick of his head in the direction of the discarded weapon. A long lick to the side to the side of her neck, from her collar-bone to her earlobe, sent a thrill right through her.

"Stop that," she warned him.

"You're in no position to give orders, Daniella. If I was a ruffian, your skirts would be up over your head by now. You should be grateful I'm somewhat of a gentleman."

"Not this minute, you're not!"

"And you're still not getting it. Men are stronger than women; it's a simple fact. Try to buck me off. Try to unseat me. Show me you can fight for your life."

"I'll hurt you," she said.

He smiled. "You cannot."

His eyes closed to her investigation, his head lowering so slowly she wondered what he was about. Then it hit her. She only had to call his bluff.

Daniella reached up as though to push him away but at the last sank her fingers into his soft hair and pulled his lips down to hers. Her tongue delved into the warmth of his mouth with a groan. He tasted of liquor and man, of risk and danger, of heat and pleasure. His growing stubble rasped her skin and she felt the pull all the way to her sex.

When his iron grip closed about her wrists, she let her head fall back as he slammed her arms onto the coverlet and pinned her where she lay, his panting breath harsh in the silence, warm against her nose. "You mean to play games with me, Daniella? How do you know this is one you can win?"

"This—" she wriggled her hips "—has naught to do with games. And you would do well to remember you started it. The question is will you finish it?"

"Have you any idea what you ask of me?"

"I'm not asking, James." She smiled. "It is inevitable now."

"You think me that weak?"

"I think you are a man. I offer my surrender as a woman."

"Complete surrender?"

She smirked as she leaned up and nipped his lip, wanting more of his taste on her tongue but knowing this was indeed a game. One only the gentleman in him could call a stop to. "Only in this."

He sat up, straightening his shirt and dusting himself off. "I was hoping for more, but I'll take it."

JAMES ENJOYED SEEING Daniella realize he had duped her. Her green eyes opened wide and her hands fisted.

"Take what?" she asked, both eyes narrowed, the promise of pleasures and playing fading quickly now though her lips and cheeks betrayed what had happened between them.

"You thought you could drive me to the edge and then pull back? Humiliate me? You'll never have my full surrender."

James sighed and let his gaze drop to the twin globes of her breasts, magnificent in the pale moonlight. He damned his self-control to the deepest depths of hell. Why could he not just let go? Take what he wanted? He went to the candle and lit it. "You are a better actress than I thought."

"Thank you."

"For all your bravado, you can't do this alone. If you were to arrive alone on your father's doorstep—or gangplank in this case—he would have you back in your brother's home with a larger dowry and more desperation than ever to marry you off. We have to work together rather than against one another."

She sat on the edge of the bed now, a coarse brown blanket over her shoulders clutched tight in her grasp. Good. He couldn't bear to look at what he'd done to her dress all in the name of teaching her a lesson "You know I'm right," he continued. "No more joining in fights or climbing out of windows."

Her head tilted, her eyes searching his. "For a moment you were scared. That I would get away?" A hint of triumph ghosted across her swollen lips.

"I was scared you would break your neck." And he didn't mind admitting that much.

She laughed then, surprising him as usual. "I first climbed the rigging when I was four years old. Probably six times higher than your highest tree. I was perfectly safe."

"And if you'd fallen? Hobson, Willie, Patrick and I

would be right now burying your body in an unmarked grave."

She scoffed a little, then relented. "All right. There is a very slim chance that might have happened."

He sat on the bed next to her and bumped his shoulder against hers. "And what of the injury to your side from yesterday? Have you reopened the wound?"

"The scratch is fine. Your salve ensured it is healing well." She paused for a moment. "I'm beginning to hate it when you make reasonable sense."

He was beginning to hate that he couldn't correctly gauge her reactions. Why wasn't she screaming at him? She should have been reaching for the chamber pot to brain him.

James knew he should feel remorse, Butcher or not. He should feel sorry that he used her in his scheme. It was less likely than she was aware to end her way—which he'd always known. Germaine was likely enough to return the Trelissick women but he would surely never set his daughter back on the ocean. Amelia was worth more than Daniella's happiness to James. He could and would trade his already shattered conscience for her any day of the year.

He was more than half tempted to drive his own dagger into the back of the captain and take back what was his. But he didn't kill senselessly. Not anymore.

But he could. He was sure of that much.

CHAPTER SIXTEEN

I F THE TRUTH were to actually pass her lips, Daniella would have admitted she was confused. The wrath of the Butcher had been waiting for her in her room but now James, the man, sat on her bed and teased her like a brother. And more than that, he had again stopped her before she did something regrettable with her "virtue."

Oh, it would have been fun though. A red-hot haze of lust still thrummed in her veins, though it was cooling slightly.

At first she'd thought his refusal of her personal. After lying atop her and hearing her wanton, brazen words, he'd changed his mind and rolled away. But when he'd lit the candle and her eyes had dropped, the tell-tale bulge in his breeches told her he wanted her well enough. But he had resisted.

She'd thought him weak when faced with a willing woman but it was she who was weak. He was a gentleman through and through, despite the Butcher business. She wasn't even sure she really had glimpsed the ruthless assassin after all in the depths of his eyes. Perhaps the ferocity and fierceness he'd displayed had been his gentlemanly, brotherly, protective instincts but in overdrive.

She could now understand why he'd gone to such lengths to take her hostage. His items weren't items at all. He fought for his family. She had to admire that about him.

She wished her brother had ever shown that particular emotion for her. She wished her brother had ever looked upon her in a way that wasn't calculating, adding up her worth to the House of Lords, to him, to his cronies and his social standing. She wished the men around her saw her as a woman and not a bargaining chip.

At that moment, she wished James saw her as more than a female to be protected.

"You should get some sleep: tomorrow is going to be another long day." His voice was low and smooth, gentle.

"I will bid you good night then." She rose and went to the washbasin in the corner of the room intending to prepare for bed, to remove yet another ruined gown. But he didn't move. James just sat there and stared at her, his eyes narrowed, his hands fisted on his thighs.

A thrum of anticipation reheated her cooled blood. Her grip loosened on the blanket around her shoulders, letting in the cool night air.

"I think I will sleep here tonight."

Her heart rate faltered, her hands paused in midair. "Oh?"

"Don't get any strange ideas, Daniella. I am not going to share a bed with you. I'll sleep by the door."

The look in his eyes told her he actually meant *against* the door. "I thought we were achieving a level of trust?"

"We are. But I am taking no chances tonight."

So much for her brotherly gentleman. He nodded in her direction and then turned. She thought he would make himself comfortable by the door as he'd said but she'd had to goad him. Instead he placed the dagger on the small night table and, still wearing his boots, breeches and shirt, lay down on the blankets, his hands behind his head.

With a glare and a humph, Daniella retrieved her cotton nightgown and retreated to the relative safety of the dressing screen. She would not argue with him anymore tonight. If he wanted to sleep on the bed, then she would sleep on the floor. When she dropped the blanket the ruined gown almost made her gasp. It had been quite exquisite, despite her intense hatred of layers of skirts.

"What do you expect me to wear tomorrow?" she called.

Silence greeted her question before he let out a long, audible sigh. "I really don't know."

"You could have been gentler."

"Where would the fun be in that?"

She almost chuckled. Almost. The light-hearted banter, the niceness of his voice versus his actions, added to the confusion.

Changing into the nightgown, she dropped the ruined gown to the floor, picked up the blanket and emerged. She felt naked. Or rather, exposed. Despite her earlier words, she knew he was capable of forcing her. She wasn't as strong as he was. She wasn't as calculating or manipulative either.

She wondered who was more desperate. Desperation made a person do silly things. Like sell her fake virginity at an illegal auction.

She avoided looking at him as she snuffed the candle. In the darkness, she wrapped the blanket around her and slid down the door to sit on the floor. "Can I ask you a question?"

"Can I stop you?"

"I doubt it."

"I'll answer your questions but not while you are sitting on the cold, hard floor."

"Care to trade places?"

"I do not."

She huffed again. Why must he always make her feel like a petulant child? "I cannot share a bed with you, James."

"Worried for your reputation?"

More like worried for her sanity. He'd driven her to the knife's edge with his performance earlier. Her body still hummed and throbbed in all the wrong places.

"You will need to sleep, Daniella. I need you alert."

Fine. She rose with all the dignity of a princess and approached the bed. "You take up too much room."

"Stop stalling and get in. I can hear your teeth chattering."

She bit down on her bottom lip but did his bidding. The floor had been very cold and a draft had breezed in from the crack beneath the door to chill her through the thick wool.

When she finally settled and had warmed up somewhat, he spoke. "What do you want to know?"

Did she want to talk to him now? While they were so close? Patrick's earlier revelations meant she had to try to discover more about Amelia and James's mother and why her father may have taken them. "What would you have done in my situation?"

"At what point?" he asked, seemingly unsurprised by her line of questioning.

"I suppose at the beginning."

"When was that? When the men noticed you as a woman and not a girl?"

"I never saw that as a problem."

"You may not have but I would stake my title on the fact that your father did. How long do you think he would have been able to fight the men off? During how many battles did he risk his own life to keep one eye on his enemy and the other on you?"

"I have always held my own in a battle and my father knew that."

"So why did he overlook your skills and see the vulnerable woman rather than the cut-throat pirate?"

A good question. How long had she stubbornly denied what sat right in front of her? But shouldn't the final choice have been hers? Should she not have had more of a say in where she would reside? Her father had a residence: she could have stayed at home and looked after the men who lived there, too old or injured to serve on a ship.

No. She would no more have agreed to that than to London. She snorted and rolled over, forgetting for a moment where she was and how close he was.

"What is it?" James asked, his face only a fraction from hers in the candlelight. *How does he always manage to smell so good all of the time?* she wondered.

"I suppose I wish I was born a boy," she eventually said. "It would have been so much easier."

"But you could have been born a lady. Then you would have had other choices. You certainly wouldn't have known another option lay on the seas."

"I have witnessed the lives of ladies and I would have rather been born a fish."

He laughed then, the sound echoing in the small room. "You have power, Daniella, you just don't know how to use it or where to direct it."

"I know how to use a sword, how to disarm my opponent and kill a man. I can swim, run, ride. Power is in strength."

"Not always. Power can also be in deception; it can be in charm or wiles. My sister can stop an entire ballroom of dancers with the right amount of hysteria."

"I will not use my sex as a weapon and neither should she. It misrepresents women and is probably why the men of London think they can own their wives."

"Ah, a radical at heart then?"

"Not at all, I merely believe women should not be used as property or pawns, or be powerless to change their futures, their lives, the lives of their daughters."

"You are wrong, Daniella. The women of London learn from an early age to manipulate their husbands. Tears, for example, can be most useful under the right circumstance and used sparingly. It is not an admission of weakness but a strong tool and as old as time itself."

Daniella huffed. "I do not cry."

"Ever?" He sounded incredulous.

"No. Well, perhaps if I am physically hurt."

"Not even when you were so ceremoniously dumped on your brother?"

"Not even then. Tears do not alter anything or take back one's actions or change courses."

"You are wrong there also. It works for Amelia every time."

"She manipulates you with salty water and you let her?" She almost laughed thinking of the Butcher cowering before his sobbing sister.

"I let her think she does, yes. I love her enough that if she can make herself cry to change my mind, then it is important enough to maybe change my mind over."

"Perhaps it is genuine despair at her circumstances, rather than counterfeit."

He shrugged. "Whichever. It is effective."

There was no point arguing further so she changed the subject. "And you said she was traveling the continent with your mother?"

"I believe they are somewhere near Italy as we speak. Probably spending all of my money and laughing about it over copious amounts of warm chocolate."

"Tell me about her." She had known he would lie, expected him to, but for some reason it still smarted.

"Amelia?"

"I want to hear more about your family."

"Why?"

"Why not? I feel as though I know nothing about you."

"You don't need to. You only need to know that you can trust me to do the right thing when this is over."

"Can I?" She didn't miss the "when this is over" part. She would no more trust him than she would try to swim with a shark. Now that she knew exactly what he stood to lose in all of this, his agenda, she had to come up with her own backup plan. He would trade her for his mother and sister, if her father did indeed have them, or try to. Nothing was going to change that. It's what happened to her after that that would ultimately decide her fate.

"I think you would like Amelia," he said, a tone of wistfulness in his voice.

"What makes you say that? It sounds as though we are total opposites."

"You have some similarities. You are both stubborn as old mules."

"I'm not sure that was a compliment."

"It was not."

He was smiling. Daniella heard it.

"You are both very determined young ladies. It is a rare trait to have amongst women who were raised to follow their husband's every word and whim."

"But I wasn't raised that way," she pointed out.

"How were you raised? Did your father ever talk of the future with you on those long ocean voyages?"

An answer hovered on the edge of her tongue but she shook her head and rolled back to face the wall again. "We didn't talk about the future at all. My father likes to laugh with his crew, but in private he is prone more to contemplation than small talk."

"Did he tell you stories about his pirating ways before you were born? Where he was born, whether he has family?"

"More leverage against him?"

"Not at all. You keep trying to convince me he is a good man at heart. I merely wanted to understand what drives him."

He made a good point. "He is a good man at heart but I won't try to convince you. When you have your belongings back safe and sound, you will see he has morals and knows what is right."

"And robbing ships and killing men is right?"

"It depends what end of poverty and desperation you come from, my lord. What you would do if everything you held dear was at peril."

As soon as she'd said the words, she longed to take them back. She didn't want to know what lengths he would go to to have his mother and sister back. She didn't want him to think too much on it either.

CHAPTER SEVENTEEN

WHEN JAMES HEARD a strange sound during the night, he opened his eyes, his senses on full alert in the darkness. A sliver of light fell across his boots from the end of the bed but didn't provide enough illumination to see what or who made the sound. In the back of his mind he knew something wasn't right.

In the distance a loud pop was followed by a whistling sound and then a bang that shook the walls around him. He was on his feet and at the window in less than a heartbeat. The acrid stench of smoke filled the air as yet another booming explosion shook the floor. James ducked, thinking the next cannon ball would be aimed at his head.

He tried to peer out of the window but the smoke was too thick, the night too dark. At his back, a muffled thump was followed by a curse and he couldn't believe his stupidity. He had let his defences down and someone had found them.

His hand went to where his dagger was always strapped against his leg but he found only the fabric of his trousers.

"Who's there?" he called.

"Did you think we would never find you, Monsieur Boucher?"

The woman's Parisian lilt sounded at once both familiar yet not. "Who are you?"

"You do not remember killing me, monsieur?"

His eyes stung and his mind reeled. Was this his day of reckoning? "I won't apologize, milady, we were at war."

"Does that give you the excuse to kill women and children?"

Memory once again stirred as she stepped into the puddle of moonlight. Long dark hair billowed down her back and around her face. "Marie?"

"Ah, so La Boucher does remember one of his victims? What about the others? Do you remember all of their names?"

"I did not know all of their names." His chest hurt and his throat filled with lead at that admission. A single tear rolled down his cheek when he closed his eyes. He blamed the smoke. It was thicker now.

Marie withdrew her hand from behind her back to reveal a long sword, its sharp-edged blade glinting as she advanced.

He did not retreat. Not this time. "You are a ghost: you cannot hurt me."

She laughed, the sound still in the air as her form disappeared before his eyes as though it came from the very smoke around him. When next he heard her voice, it was from the direction of the bed. "It isn't you I was thinking of hurting tonight."

He followed her. "You must stay out of my dreams, Marie."

"You wanted me in your bed, James. Do you no longer

want me?"

He squeezed his eyes shut and when he opened them, Marie lay there on the covers, nude but for the blood covering her chest up to her neck, the gash deep, wide, fatal.

"Get out of my head!"

"Do you recall the night you took my life, James?"

"I remember the night you tried to kill me, yes."

She pulled the blanket up to her chin and stared at him, her big brown eyes now wide and scared. Exactly how she had looked minus the shock as he'd driven his blade deep into her chest.

"Do you remember Henri?" Her face changed to that of a small child's. "Or Jean?" The face changed again and again. It was an accounting of his victims. One he'd dreamed too many times before.

"What about the Englishmen who died, Marie? Do you know the names of the boys killed in Bonaparte's name?"

"We are not talking about the casualties of war, *mon cher*. You were an assassin, not a soldier."

When he just about couldn't stand it anymore, he closed his eyes tight again.

"Is that how you survived, James? Did you close your eyes as you murdered them in their beds? Did you turn your back as their houses turned to ash? Did you tell yourself it was all right to kill me because I was your enemy? I think you felt nothing as my life drained away."

"You made yourself my enemy when you tried to kill me. A French woman in the middle of an Egyptian war zone cannot be trusted. I was a fool."

Marie shook her head. "I truly underestimated you, didn't I? I didn't think you had it in you to murder a woman."

"Self-defence is not murder. You were a spy. You were sent to discover my secrets and then kill me. Did you see yourself as a whore for sleeping with me for my intelligence? Did you think I didn't know you were more than you seemed?"

She shook her head again, her face coming back into focus, her dark hair spread across the pillow, her nudity and blood now covered in the virginal white of a cotton nightgown. "I wanted to sleep with you, James. You were the notorious Boucher and I wanted your head on a pike in the town square. I wanted to tell the men of the army that a woman had bested the best."

"But I didn't fall for anything and you were killed. What did the men of your army think about you then?"

This time it was her eyes that squeezed shut against the truth but when she opened them, it wasn't Marie who lay in the bed, it was another woman. Another woman with a lithe and supple body, her flame-red hair almost alive, her wide green eyes betraying a malicious tint. Another woman set on discovering his secrets and then turning them against him.

"What about me, James?" she purred. "Will you kill me if the time comes and then call it self-defence?"

"Leave Daniella out of it."

She smiled then. The blanket dropped as she sat up, revealing the ripped and ruined gown from earlier, her full breasts on display, the dusky nipples peaked and begging. "I want you, James."

He stepped towards her to pull the blanket up but she reached out and pulled him down into a kiss, the honeyed warmth of her mouth like heaven after the acrid stench of smoke.

When she groaned and tightened her grip in his hair to an almost painful pull, he rolled onto his back and pushed her away.

The laugh that followed was not Daniella's. Another change in the shifting moonlight and Marie was back. "You do not like the redhead? You prefer your victims brunette?"

"Daniella would never stab me in the back the way you tried to." His voice was stark in the empty room, his breath harsh between the forced words.

His lie troubled him. Would Daniella stab him in the back? Could she?

The only certainty was that this dream would end the way the dream always did. With Marie lying lifeless alongside him in the bed they had shared for three weeks, blood bubbling from the edge of her red lips and pumping from the hole in her chest.

"How do you know the pirate speaks the truth and isn't using you? How do you know she isn't proving herself to her father by delivering the man who crippled him?"

"You don't know what you're talking about, Marie. Daniella isn't like that."

"Isn't like what?"

He turned on the bed and faced Daniella once again. Marie could not keep doing this to him. It had gone on for far too long. "You have to leave now, Marie."

"Oh?" The taunting laugh came again. "What if I don't want to leave?"

The sharpened tip of a dagger pressed to his Adam's apple and he swallowed despite knowing the movement would nick his skin. "You should have killed me back then, Marie."

"Yes, I should have."

He gripped her wrist hard enough to bruise.

She cried out and dropped the dagger but then came at him again, this time with a sword.

James knew the sword couldn't hurt him in the confined space with no force behind it…and wielded by a ghost. He threw his body on hers, straddled her perfect hips, heard her cries of denial, of love, that he was mad. He'd heard it before. He'd believed it before. He'd nearly died for it once.

"You need to leave me alone, Marie," he shouted, his hands around her neck, her face turning red against the crisp white pillow as she struggled to breathe. Her face changed again then, from Henri, to the unnamed soldiers and civilians, then back to Daniella. He shook her, and her nails raked his arms, his cheeks, his hands where they squeezed.

"You're dead, you need to stay dead!" he roared.

And then she did something she had never done in the dream. She clasped her hands together above her head and brought them down hard to connect with his nose.

Blinding pain, threatening blackness and the sudden buck of her hips saw him on the floor beside the bed. As he lay there on the hard timbers and looked up at Marie wearing Daniella's face, in her hand the small dagger, he wondered if this dream would end differently. He wondered if the woman he had killed had finally found a way to take his life in return.

"WHAT THE HELL?" Daniella didn't know whether to slice him to ribbons with the dagger or hit him again. Her hands throbbed and she rubbed them against her thighs.

When James had begun to talk in his sleep, she'd listened. He argued with someone called Marie. It hadn't taken long for him to start thrashing in the bed so she had got out of it and stood staring at him. When finally he calmed, she hopped back beneath the blankets to try to get some sleep. Then he'd rolled over on top of her and tried to strangle her.

Had he still been sleeping when he attempted to wring the life from her? She rather doubted he just woke up and decided he didn't need her after all. She rubbed the front of her neck, her throat feeling as though she had swallowed rusted steel.

"I'll kill you for that, Marie." He held two fingers to the bridge of his nose as blood dripped over his lips and onto his shirt.

Daniella's grip around the handle of the dagger tightened. She inched backwards to the door but he came at her again.

"James, it's me, Daniella. Wake up!"

One hand slammed into the timber next to her ear, the other wrapped around her throat again. "That's what you want me to believe, but you're a vindictive bitch, Marie. You need to move on."

Daniella shoved with all the force she could muster but he was immovable. If she had been slightly worried when he'd had her in his arms earlier, intent on seduction, she was terrified now. His eyes were glazed and he seemed to look right through her.

She hated to do it but had no other choice. She threw her balance to one side and brought her knee up high and hard and fast.

With a cry of pain, James let go of her and fell to the floor. Daniella jumped over him and crouched beneath the window ledge. If he came at her again, she would push him through it. If it came down to her life or his, she chose hers.

He moaned and writhed but didn't get up again. He was firmly wedged in front of the door and unless she wanted to scale the night-dampened wall in her nightgown then she was trapped in the room with him.

As she looked around for something heavy enough to knock him out with if she had to, he groaned again and rolled to face her, his cheek against the flooring timbers, his hands on the part of him she had hurt the most. Not his nose.

"What the devil did you do to me?"

Her mouth dropped open. "What did I do? I was defending myself against you!"

"What happened?"

She shook her head in disbelief. He really had been sleeping? She'd heard of men who had committed violence while asleep but had never really believed the tales.

"First you called me Marie and then you tried to kill me!" Her throat and neck hurt so much it was a wonder she could breathe at all.

"Daniella...I... God, I'm sorry. Are you hurt?"

"Of course I'm hurt, you ass! You almost strangled me in my bloody sleep."

He rose gingerly, unable to take more than a step before bending and swearing softly. As he approached her again, she held the dagger at the ready. If she shoved it in the side of his neck, he would die. She'd done it before and it required more aim than strength or finesse.

"I'm not going to harm you, Daniella."

"Excuse me if I don't believe you," she retorted, lifting the dagger higher and acquiring a better grip on the weapon.

He changed direction and went to sit on the end of the bed, his head in his hands as he stared at the floor. She relaxed, but only slightly.

"This has happened to me before."

She had to really listen hard to hear what he said—and swallow her horror when she understood.

"The first time was when I was recovering from a bullet wound in my leg. I met your father not long after that."

"What happened?" she asked, not sure whether to believe she was out of danger or not.

"I was in a tent with the other sick and wounded and the doctor gave me laudanum to dull the pain after they dug the ball out. I told them I didn't need the drug but apparently a man doesn't get a choice when faced with an English surgeon bent on saving his life."

He sighed. "I remember sleeping so heavily, I knew I had to be dreaming when Marie showed up that first time to haunt me. She was dead. I saw her die. But when I came to, I found I was strapped to the cot. All around me was carnage. They told me I had risen from my bed and started to chase an imagined foe around the tent. They told me I had stabbed one man and injured five more. I was called home before the army could figure out just what to do with me, their broken assassin."

"Why weren't you imprisoned?"

"It was confirmed by the doctor that having sufficient laudanum in my body to keep three men down was reason enough not to completely hold me accountable for my actions. I did spend my last two weeks as a military man in a prison cell."

"You said that was the first time?"

He nodded.

"How many times have you done it since?"

When he met her eyes, Daniella recognized desolation in them. "A few. I sleep with the door barricaded from the outside some nights, and others I simply don't sleep at all."

"But you have slept these past two nights just fine. Is there something that triggers it?"

He shrugged. "I didn't sleep. I haven't slept in nearly a week. Sometimes it happens when I am under a great deal of pressure or am anxious. I did come up with a handy trick to ensure I do not fall too deeply asleep and that is what I have used these nights past."

"What is it?"

"Usually I sleep on rocks."

"Rocks? I don't understand."

"My bedroll has little sharp rocks sewn into special pockets so that I never get a good night's sleep."

She digested that. "This worked for you in the war?"

He shook his head. "I was still in the prison cell awaiting a decision when the letters came to bring me home. I don't think they would have let me go back into the field as the Butcher after that. Also, I had attacked my fellow soldiers for no reason at all. Most men were scared of me; others wanted to lock me up forever. Hobson was the only loyal man who vowed to fight on with me. My career was over no matter what happened after that day."

"And you were called home before any court-martial?"

"Yes. There was a letter. I'm sure my elevation helped my superiors put my crimes out of their minds." She could almost taste his sarcasm. "*Dear Major James Frank Trelissick,*" he continued as though he read straight from the missive. "*You are being recalled to your family under the most desperate of circumstance. It is with great sadness that I inform you of your brother's and your father's deaths.*"

The anguish he must have felt. All at once his military career over and his family half gone, the title in his hands but smattered with blood.

"Don't feel sorry for me, Daniella." There he went deciphering her thoughts again.

"How could I not?"

He chuckled then but it lacked any trace of humour. "Now you admire me? After I try to take your life?"

"You said it yourself. You had no idea what you were doing."

"I never do. That's the damnedest thing about it all."

She did know how difficult it was to lose control over a situation. "Who is Marie?"

He sighed. "Marie was my lover and a spy and a traitor. I killed her."

CHAPTER EIGHTEEN

ADMITTING IT ALOUD didn't help the way he thought it would have. He'd hoped to hear a whisper as Marie's haunting ghost slipped away for good. Sadly, there was only that same cloying numbness shrouding him as always.

But when he stared into Daniella's large green eyes, he felt the familiar weight of guilt—and a surge of anger at himself. He felt like a dog. Her smooth skin bruised already in the perfect shape of his fingers and thumbs, any other marks hidden beneath that innocent nightgown.

"Please let me check your injuries?"

"I should be checking yours," she muttered but came closer.

He lifted a brow and remembered the exact moment he'd woken from his nightmare. The throbbing pain between his thighs was a sure reminder that things had got very much out of hand tonight.

"I meant your nose," she clarified with a brow lift of her own. "Can I put the dagger down or should I keep it close?"

"You can put it down," he assured her. Nothing could make him hurt her while he was in charge of all of his faculties. He'd told his mother not to worry about his nightmares. Told her they sounded worse than they were but what if he hurt her? Hurt Amelia? At least at home his bedroom door had a sound lock.

Daniella threw the dagger on the bed and he watched closely for any signs of fright or shock on her face, but then she came to kneel before him in a move so submissive he wondered what type of emotion he'd instilled in her with his confessions. "And still you feel no fear?"

"No fear? I thought you were actually going to strangle the life from me. I was terrified and ready to cut your throat."

"I should count myself fortunate that you are a pirate and not a genteel flower."

She threw her head back and laughed. "Never in a thousand years did I imagine you would make such an admission."

God, she was amazing. He wanted to tell her how strong he thought her for fighting him off, for not screaming for help or killing him after she'd disabled him. Never had he thought he would ever meet someone like her.

He should never have fallen asleep. He'd only meant to lie next to her until she'd dozed off herself.

"You'd better cast off your hopes of finding a biddable wife," Daniella told him.

His pulse jumped. "What do you mean?"

"What are you going to do when you marry and still have dreams such as these?"

Hobson had asked him much the same when he brought up the notion of finding a wife. And then once more when they moved into Daniella's brother's stable and passed themselves off as servants. Each night when he found the courage to not sleep on a bed of rocks he asked himself whether he was doing the right thing by his family to even reside in the same house as them.

Now he would give anything and everything he had to be in the same house as Amelia and his mother again.

He had to change the direction of their conversation lest he become even more morose. "I will not sleep in the same room as my wife."

She stopped moving, stopped laughing; he almost believed for a moment that she stopped breathing. "You need to make an heir, do you not?"

Despite the only light in the room being the full moon's glow, and despite their earlier intimacy, the blush was visible on Daniella's cheeks.

"This isn't an appropriate conversation."

"What is the appropriate conversation after midnight with the man who just tried to kill you?"

He'd never known anyone like her. He had to stop his mind from imagining her his equal. He'd already warned himself not to do that.

"A man does not share a room with his wife."

"Ever?"

He shook his head. "Perhaps in a love match but no, a man generally visits his wife in her rooms and then returns to his own."

"You English are a bizarre lot. How does a wife stand it?"

"She is raised to know it as the way things happen."

"What if your wife does ask you to stay with her all night? What if she falls deeply and madly in love with you? Will you tell her about your dreams then?"

"No."

"Why not?"

"Because it is *my* weakness. It is *my* demon to battle and no one else's." Henri's cherubic face flashed before his eyes and he had to close them, had to find a way to bring back the numbness and drive away the despair.

Daniella huffed. "Why do men choose to bury their heads in the sand rather than admit what they did was wrong and move on from it?"

"You don't move on from the lives I took, Daniella. It changes you. Forever."

"Only if you let it. Did you ever kill for the sake of killing? Did you ever stab someone in the heart or run them through with your sword for the joy of it? You aren't the monster you seem to believe you are."

"Not a monster. Not quite. But I followed my orders and not all of those people were dangers to the crown or the war effort."

"How do you know?"

Little Henri had been an innocent victim of the war. James had just finished killing his parents. The Sheppartons had sold British secrets to the French for a paltry house and vineyard on the outskirts of Calais. Hundreds had died because of them. They had thought they'd got away with it too. Until James had been sent back from the front in Egypt to find them.

Their deaths were quick. Clean. Uncomplicated. Until he'd heard the sobbing of little Henri. He'd already lit the fire that would see the house burn to the ground when he'd turned to find the sobbing four-year-old.

It was one of the rare moments when James had felt more than the Butcher's chilled numbness. He'd stared at the child, flames reflected in the midnight depths of his eyes. He'd wanted to say something, anything, to the child. But then he'd fled down the hall, his little legs pumping up and down.

James tried to look for him, tried to find him and get him out of the burning house. He was doubling back in case the boy had too when he'd heard the pop and felt a burn in his thigh. At first he'd thought debris from the growing fire had exploded and hit him, but almost before the truth registered he was falling with the collapsing staircase and had to drag himself from the house.

Henri never emerged. The boy had avenged his parents by putting a ball in James's leg and James had killed him as surely as he'd slit the throats of his family. That was to be his last mission for king and country.

For days he'd sat in that damp, depressing makeshift hospital bed and endured the image of the little boy every time he closed his eyes. Marie's taunting face was nothing compared to a four-year-old fair-haired child's. Years in Egypt and half the continent fighting Bonaparte and it was a small French child who brought the Butcher to his knees.

Coming back to the present, James locked eyes with Daniella again. "Do you see the faces of the men you've killed?" he asked her.

"I don't. When I close my eyes, it's my father's face and the look on it when he—well, when he found me in a...compromising situation that I see. I don't regret the lives I've taken."

When he raised his brows, she held up a hand to stop him. "When it's kill or be killed, I would always save myself and so would you. I believe it is a benefit of piracy—I have very little in the way of a conscience."

When she grinned, James couldn't help but grin back. The minx flat-out lied to make him feel better about himself and he liked her all the more for it. Damn.

"Now please let me check your nose to make sure I didn't break it."

"My nose is fine," he told her, more worried about her neck. He hoped they weren't going to spend the whole trip checking one another's hurts.

Daniella put her hands on her hips and shot him a glare. "It is still bleeding so it's not fine."

He swiped a hand under his nostrils, which brought a fresh sting to his eyes and moisture to betray his words. "It's not broken, just...sore."

She didn't believe him but didn't press the issue any further.

James placed a finger beneath her chin and tipped her head back to inspect her throat. She flinched.

"Oh my God, look what I did," he breathed, running the tips of his fingers over her angry skin. "I am so sorry."

"I've had worse than this and am still alive to tell the

tale."

"Worse? You should see yourself in a mirror. I don't know how we're going to explain this."

"I could wear a scarf?"

James couldn't believe she was still trying to lighten the moment. How was he supposed to look at her for the next few days?

"Besides, we are going to have more than that to explain. You look as though you fell down a flight of stairs. I'm afraid both of your eyes are going to blacken if we don't get something cold onto them. You'd better lie down."

She got to her bare feet and padded across the room to the pitcher of water. Wetting a strip of linen, she returned and glared at him until he did her bidding. Then she set the cool towel over his eyes and told him he had to stay like that for a little while.

"Is this the part where you kick me again for being such a cad?" he asked, a smile on his lips.

"I was serious before, James. This is not your fault."

"If I'd not been in your room, none of it would have happened."

"You would make the lousiest pirate."

He chuckled and then groaned when it hurt the bridge of his nose. He wanted to ask why she doubted his pillaging and plundering skills but was slightly afraid of the answer.

CHAPTER NINETEEN

THE VERY NEXT day once again dawned.
Odd that.

James found himself waking up to wonder why he hadn't been struck down by God Himself during the night. He kept closing and then reopening his eyes expecting the captain to materialize and run him through with his wooden leg.

It would have been a fitting end to a night where the past had had a damned good go at flogging him senseless.

Every muscle in his body hurt. His face felt tight and his eyes would not open all the way no matter how hard he tried. Daniella was right. He was going to have a lot to explain. He rolled towards her on the bed, to see how bad her injuries were in the light of day. Only she wasn't there.

James sat up so quickly his head spun and his stomach revolted. He mentally pushed it all down while he searched for his boots, having taken them off during the night to get more comfortable. He never dreamed the same twice in one night so he assumed they were both safe to sleep after that. She must have waited until he'd nodded off and then fled.

A prickling of dread spread from his nape down his spine. How long had she been gone? Why hadn't he heard her? Which direction would she take and could they catch her up?

The door swung wide while he laced his boots. The relief he felt when Daniella tiptoed her way in was beyond anything. He wanted to kiss her and throttle her.

Was he happy to see her for his mother's and sister's sakes or his own?

"Oh good, you're awake." She stopped midsentence and midstep, her mouth open. "Oh dear God."

"Good morning to you too." He inclined his head and then wished he hadn't. He'd woken like this before, after consuming copious amounts of whiskey and port, tasting as if a dog had squirted in his mouth while he'd slept. But never after a fight. He wondered if she'd half brained him at one stage.

"Your face looks just awful. You should have kept the cold press on it."

He rose and approached her slowly, her eyes never leaving his face as she studied him with pain in her gaze. He didn't have to tip her head back to inspect her neck. He could well enough see the bruises and swelling from there. "You should have put the compress on your skin."

"I told you, I will be fine. You on the other hand need to get cleaned up. Hobson tells me a ship has been sighted off the bay. We need to investigate."

He said the first thing that sprang to mind, his brain trying to catch up and push away other niggling revelations. "The innkeeper said a ship could not get close. The waves are too high and the beach too rocky."

She threw him a look he was beginning to know well. The one that asked how he was still alive and if he was a complete idiot. "I suspect he lied. It sounds exactly what a smuggler might say to keep a nosy lord away from his less-than-legal activities."

James bristled. What in God's name had she done to him? His instincts were one of his best assets and she was ruining them with her distracting presence.

"Where were you just now?"

"We needed clothes."

"So you went out into the inn dressed like that?" He could just about see through the cotton and her ankles were on full display.

"I went out into the hall, yes. I found Hobson loitering there and asked him to find me something to wear." She dropped one arm's bundle on the bed and held the other closely to her chest.

He deliberately ignored the matching bruises on her wrist and arm in favour of an argument. "He wasn't loitering: he was ensuring you didn't escape. He was watching out for trouble."

"Fine, loitering was an exaggeration. He was sleeping in a chair. I could have easily got past him and been on my way. You two really are very bad at this. He didn't even wake while we were beating each other senseless."

James swore under his breath.

Daniella smiled as she slipped behind the dressing screen, unable to resist another jibe. "You are lucky to have retired from the army before someone succeeded in killing you both. Do you think it is age that slows you down?"

"How long does Hobson think we have?" James asked, ignoring her. He made a mental note to remind Hobson what was at stake and on which side his bread was buttered.

"He is having the innkeeper's daughter make a basket of food and Patrick is readying the carriage and horses as we speak. No time at all."

James rubbed a hand over his jaw, grimacing at the stubble covering his cheeks and chin. He no longer appeared the gentleman in any capacity.

Her voice broke into his thoughts once again. "Let me know when you are decent. Unless I can convince you to return to your own room to dress?"

He rifled through the clothing on the bed. There was a clean shirt, fresh breeches and hose, and a coat. "I have everything I need right here."

"Suit yourself."

He wondered what Hobson had found for her to wear as he stared at his face in the looking glass. Dark growth covered much of his cheeks, chin and neck but he left it there. Better to be unnoticeable than clean-shaven and looking every inch a gentleman who had been robbed of everything including his dignity.

Beaten by a woman.

Hobson was going to laugh until he rolled on the floor.

"Did you tell Hobson what had happened to your neck?" he asked as he used the strip of linen to wash the caked blood from his face and the top of his chest. He searched for the nick to his neck from the dagger, wondering if it was part of the dream or if she had actually meant to stab him in the throat. He breathed easier when he found no evidence.

Daniella had said he looked awful and he did. It wasn't even the worst it was going to get. That would come later in the day and into the night. He hoped his eyes weren't going to swell shut. That was all he needed.

Movement in the looking glass had him swivelling, the dagger in his hand before he'd even thought the thought. She made no sound as she moved; there was no rustle of skirts or petticoats to warn him she was there.

"You…" he sputtered, swallowed, inhaled. "You are not wearing that. Who gave you those clothes?" The reason he hadn't heard a rustle of skirts was because she wasn't wearing any. Damn her. Damn Hobson!

"There is nothing else. And anyway, I prefer breeches."

"And I prefer to not draw attention!" When had she worn breeches before? On the ship? With the shape of her calves on display? He damned her father while he was consigning all others to the deepest pits of hell.

"I do believe you are going to have an apoplexy, my lord." Her smile was too knowing in the dawn light.

He lifted his gaze from her tightly encased legs. Could he actually see each individual muscle making up her thigh? "You did this on purpose?"

"I did not. You were the one teaching me a lesson when you cut through my dress. I would have been happy to wear it again today. Well, not unhappy at any rate."

"So find Hobson again and tell him to buy or steal you another dress. The innkeeper's daughter or wife will have clothing they will part with."

"No."

His fists clenched and he took a step towards her. "No?"

"I am comfortable like this. I can run and ride and fight better."

"We are not fighting today or any other day. You cannot leave the room wearing that!"

"I won't be leaving the room. Danny the boy will be." She flourished a cap and then edged him out of the way so she could look into the glass. When she began pinning her flame-bright hair, he still stood, shaking his head and wondering what deity had it in for him so badly that Daniella had been sent into his orbit.

"Hobson also gave me a scarf and there is an oversize coat in the carriage. I'll be your squire. Or footman? I could even ride on top of the carriage again."

The excitement in her voice fuelled the anger in his veins. "You cannot do this, Daniella. You'll fool no one." His eyes travelled along the curve of her spine, the not-quite-white shirt almost hugging the contours of her arse where it wasn't long enough to completely cover it. She wore a waistcoat but her breasts were mountainous beneath the coarse brown fibre. His eyes kept drifting down towards those tight thighs encased in black, and those shaped, toned calves.

He groaned.

"Granted I'll be the prettiest boy you've ever travelled with. A little dirt on my face and the coat over my body—from a distance, I'll pass."

Not bloody likely. "And up close?"

"No one will be getting that close."

James wanted to. He remembered how smooth and supple the skin of her hip was. Would her ankles cross if she were to wrap her legs around him without petticoats to hamper her? Would he feel every inch of her through the suede of the breeches?

"James?" She stared at him in the reflection. "Stop looking at me like that."

"Like what?" He licked his lips but couldn't drag his gaze from her backside.

She turned from the mirror and slapped a palm against his cheek. It wasn't hard enough to hurt but it drew him back to the present. "Pretend I am a boy."

"I'm afraid that is never going to happen." He willed his voice back to its usual cadence but the huskiness had overtaken. What would she do if he kissed her right then? Reasonable thought fled.

He cleared his throat and was about to forbid her to leave the room, perhaps make another suggestion as to how they might pass the morning, when Hobson exploded into the small space like cannon fire. "Pirates, Major. Making for the beach."

Daniella stepped forwards, the cap on her now tightly bound hair. "My father?" she asked hopefully.

Hobson shook his head, his eyes wide when they glimpsed James's battered face. He wisely did not ask questions. "These are real pirates, lass. Not your da."

"How can you be sure?"

"I've seen your da's lot and this ain't them. We have to go now."

"Wait, you can't be sure. We have to find out."

James looked to Hobson, who shook his head so minutely anyone else might have missed the gesture. James turned the dagger in his hand and sheathed it in his boot. "We are leaving right now."

He towed her from the room, all thoughts about her breeches and bare skin forgotten. "Do you have boots for her?" he asked Hobson.

"In the carriage. They'll be a mite big but they'll do."

"We can't leave like this until we are absolutely sure," Daniella pleaded as they fled down the stair. "What about your bags and your clothes? And if it is my father and he wants to trade, we have to meet him halfway."

"Where the rest of his crew can slay me? We meet on my terms, not his. We meet, as you said from the start, in his refuge, which he will protect from violence, including his own. If it is your father, and Hobson seems quite certain it is not, he can give chase. He will have to keep most of his men on the ship or the beach to protect it, yes?"

"Yes," she said. "But—"

"No, Daniella. No buts. We need to leave. I will not have it end like this."

She tugged against his hand, dragging him to a stop. He glared. She glared back.

"I won't go. We have to be sure."

James didn't hesitate. He tugged her hand again until she was off-balance and then bent forwards, scooped her over his shoulder and kept going. She shrieked and lashed out but he didn't pause. They'd stayed too long. He was lucky they hadn't been murdered in their beds. Damn that innkeeper for his lies about treacherous shoals and hidden rocks.

They had to get as far away as they could. As fast as they could. He would not think on why her perfectly sane reasoning suddenly made no sense at all. He absolutely refused to wonder why the thought of trading her back to her father made his gut clench and his chest ache.

Bloody pirates!

CHAPTER TWENTY

RIDING ATOP A man's shoulder had to just about be the most undignified way to travel. Her stomach jarred painfully on James's bones with each of his leaps. He wasn't walking anymore but neither could he run with her. She was heavier than she looked. She smiled and went lax. Like the last time he'd kidnapped her, she had to appear biddable until she could attempt an escape. If it was her father—and really, what other likeliness was there that another pirate followed? It wasn't as though there were an abundance of them floating about, despite what the gossip papers reported—if it was her father, she would go to him and beg him to release Amelia and James's mother. God, she didn't even know the woman's name. Her father would listen to her in this. He would. The blood thrummed in her veins with both excitement and trepidation.

"Hobson, you and Patrick ride behind but tell him to stay close. Give him one of the muskets if he doesn't have his own. We only need to know how many there are and if they appear capable. You are both to shoot anyone who looks or acts or smells like a pirate if they come too near."

Daniella gasped. "You can't shoot at them, they'll kill

you."

"Not while I have you," he pointed out, his voice filled with smug superiority.

"And if it *isn't* my father? Do you think another pirate is going to care if I live or die?" She hated the way her breath huffed in and out as she tried to reason with him.

"We'll all be dead by that stage. It won't matter what anyone thinks."

She could imagine that particular headline. They would all go down in one giant blaze of scandal. The wild and hoydenish sister of a man knighted by the king found dead in her breeches alongside a marquess with two black eyes, also in breeches, also dead.

"Put me down—I'll walk. We can move faster that way."

"Don't need to." James grunted as he set her on her feet. He didn't give her the chance to lash out as he pushed her into the carriage and onto the floor. He climbed in after her and shouted the order to go, to go and not stop for anything or anyone.

"Dammit, let me up," she cried. Every time she tried to sit up, James pushed her back down. She slid on the floor and her head smashed into the unforgiving hardness of timber when they took a corner too fast. A hard lump, most likely to be a boot, dug into the back of her shoulder.

"Stay down and hold on. You are safer on the floor."

"I would be safer if I had killed you when I last had the chance."

He smiled grimly. "You keep saying that, yet here I sit."

Another corner and they both had to hold on, James to

the strap above his head and Daniella bracing outwards with her hands and feet. When James lifted his legs to jam them against the opposite bench right above her body, Daniella took her opportunity. She reached out and with an almighty tug ripped the dagger from his boot.

James roared and reached for the dagger but another corner saw him topple off the seat and land atop her with an *oomph*.

She couldn't breathe. Her lungs were on fire, her ribs hurt: he was crushing her. "Get off," she wheezed as swirling black spots played havoc with her vision. Her fingertips tingled and still she couldn't draw a proper breath.

Her fingers were already lax when James pulled the dagger from her hand. She didn't care. She had to draw breath before she passed out. Once he was up, kneeling with one knee between hers, his breath as harsh and short as hers, he sent her another fierce glare. "Do not try that again."

It took only minutes, though it felt like an hour, for her to regain her lungs' previous composure, such as it had been. Her throat burned and she worried he'd broken something in her chest. She still braced with her bare feet and tingling arms as they barrelled around corner after corner at breakneck speed. Her muscles screamed at her but fury numbed the pain to a persistent ache. At one stage she felt two wheels lift from the ground only to slam back down and still they went on.

There were no words for the way she felt about James Trelissick in those minutes. After the night they'd shared, how could he treat her this way? He spoke of trust yet wasn't it supposed to work both ways? Trying to take his dagger probably hadn't helped her there but he was acting a fool. All of it could have been over and done with had she been able to see the ship. She would have known right away if it was her father. They could have brokered their hostage deal and even now be on their separate ways.

How could Hobson tell the difference between one ship and another? He'd seen *The Aurora* only once in the midst of a battle.

She ground her teeth in frustration.

"I know what you're thinking," he said to her, his voice low but without menace this time.

"I rather doubt that," she bit out.

"You know this was the right move."

"I know you are an idiot. This is your family we're—" She slapped a hand over her mouth but then had to reach out as the carriage barrelled around yet another endless corner.

His eyes went hard. "Who told you?" he asked through teeth clenched so tight his jaw ticked beneath the stubble. "Did you know about them before I took you?"

"No! I did not! But it doesn't matter who told me. You should have. I could have helped you."

He barked with forced laughter. "Now you are saying you would have helped me? That tells me you haven't known for very long. Was it Hobson or Willie? No one else knows."

Not that you are aware of. She would not reveal Patrick's part in it all. She would let James think it was one of his loyal men who'd revealed the truth. "We could have told my brother about your mother and sister and he could have thought of something. He might even have reached out to my father without any of this nonsense."

By his reaction, she could tell he'd thought about it. "Why didn't you ask him for help?" she asked when he didn't answer.

"Your brother and I aren't well acquainted and as far as I understand he is completely in the dark about it all. I paid someone to dig around in his house and put an ear to the ground but it turned up nothing. He is completely oblivious. At least he was."

"What do you mean, you paid someone?"

"Half your brother's household are capable of being bought for the right price and the other half hate him so much they give away their information for free. Germaine could not be trusted to broker any sort of deal. Amelia's reputation would have been in tatters for a certainty."

"What about her life? What if my father doesn't have her? You have wasted precious time."

His jaw tightened again. "This is where the trail led me. There was nowhere else to look."

"So you took me in retaliation, an eye for eye. If something has befallen them, will you kill me in return?"

"I don't have to take your life to ruin it, Daniella. I only have to tell your father that I have bedded you and within you grows my seed. Do you think it wouldn't break his heart to see his unmarried daughter pregnant to his enemy?"

She knew how her father would react to that and it wasn't the type of noose that hangs a man until dead in which James would find himself. He was right about breaking his heart though. She didn't want her father to think her a whore, or worse. What's more, she would not be forced to marry James at the end. She needed to be back on her ship with her men, with her friends, her accepting family.

"DID YOU BUMP your head or did I break your brain when I hit you?" she asked, her green eyes narrowed. "Was it all an act then, last night? The dream? The violence?"

It was no act on his part. But what of hers? Even in his anguish, she hadn't admitted to knowing the truth about his possessions, about his mother and sister, missing on the high seas, taken by pirates. The way she felt about a woman being a man's pawn, she would have revealed earlier her knowledge of her father's hostages.

In fact he wouldn't have spoken to Daniella the way he had if he wasn't in complete agony. Sweat beads formed on his brow and ran in rivulets down his back to dampen his shirt. Inside his boot the stickiness of his own blood was warm and uncomfortable. Not a fatal amount but enough. When she'd ripped the dagger from his boot, the sharpened blade had sliced right through his hose and into his skin.

He'd begun to think of her as a partner in this predicament rather than the means to the end. He hated himself for that. He could not and would not risk the only family he had left for Daniella. A pirate. A wild immature girl with a conniving woman's body.

The space between his eyes throbbed mercilessly and his

head ached along with the rhythm set by his erratic heart-beat.

"I have neither the time nor the patience to keep fighting with you, Daniella. I'll have your word now, as a pirate, as a woman, as a Germaine, that you will not do anything stupid while we make this last dash for the border. Do you understand? Can I have your word?"

"Who gets to decide what is stupid?" A hint of a smile ghosted over her lips but didn't quite reach her eyes.

"Just ask yourself if I would find it stupid and go with that. Actually, I'll have your word that not only will you not try to escape or run, you will tell me every move before you make it."

"That is unreasonable. I will not consent to it. I can give you my word I won't run or escape but that is all."

"It's not enough."

"What do you want from me, James? I will not submit to you. I will not bow at your feet and call you my master." Her eyes grew wide. "That is what this is about, isn't it? It kills you that you can't control me, that you can't control the situation like you did your men in the war. You couldn't control your sister or your mother or your brother and it eats away at you inside."

She knew everything about his brother as well? *Damn.* "I cannot control anything in this cat-and-mouse chase, Daniella. I just want to know your antics won't leave me dead in a ditch somewhere."

"I look after myself." She lifted her chin back so he could once again see the mess that was her neck, the bruises

217

purpling until her throat was almost dark blue. "And if you find yourself in a ditch, it will indeed be because I put you there."

"You were lucky I was…not myself last night. Even you cannot take on a man in charge of his faculties. You cannot take on a group of ruffians without your father or your crew at your back."

"I killed a man two days ago, did I not? I also disarmed you. Twice."

"You did but we were there also that first time. Had you been alone, those men would have taken their turn raping you. They then would have taken you back to their place of hiding and raped you again. The first time you fought back, you would have been tied up or killed. Either way, you would have been raped again and again and again, dead or alive. You had one ball in one pistol and a tiny knife. That is one dead man, perhaps. Much harder to shoot a target that moves than one at your back."

Her eyes turned glassy and flat. "I am not useless."

"I never said you were. Without you, there would have been one more man for Hobson or myself to dispatch. Without you, I have no leverage against your father to get my mother and my sister back."

She did not like that honesty. By the look on her face, she hoped James would say something else. What that something was, he didn't know.

She needed the truth.

It didn't mean she had to like it.

CHAPTER TWENTY-ONE

T HEY DIDN'T GET more than a mile down the road before a bullet hit the back of the carriage, splintering the wood with a deafening crack that made them both duck for cover. When they began to slow, James knew without a doubt they were done for. Nowhere to run and hardly anywhere to hide. It was stand and fight to the death or be captured. Either way they wound up exactly the same. Dead.

He stared down at the finally silent Daniella and wondered how things could have possibly catapulted so far from his plan. "For what it's worth," he started and then paused, unsure of how to continue. "I was trying to do the right thing. For you and for my sister."

"I know you were." The admission hurt her: he recognized that frown now.

"I can try to hold them off if you want to make a run for the tree line?"

She shook her head. "I won't make it very far and we both know it."

The jingle of the harness and the shuffle of the horses' hooves signalled they could go no farther. The carriage creaked as Willie fought to control the beasts; fear was all around them now. James didn't even bother reaching for a pistol. The sound of hooves bearing down and the shouts of men meant they were outnumbered. Perhaps he could bargain for Daniella's life? She wouldn't make it home unscathed but she would make it home. She was resourceful and resilient. Two things he reluctantly admired most about her.

A booming voice drifted along the road. "Come on out of the carriage and show yourselves. You're outnumbered and outplayed."

Outplayed? Odd.

Daniella caught the inference as well and sat up from her position on the floor.

James raised his brow but she only shook her head.

He lifted the glass pane in the door and called back, "I'll first be needing your word I'll get a chance to speak to your leader before you put a ball in me."

Murmurs followed and then, "You aren't really in a bargaining place right now, in case you hadn't noticed."

James would have chuckled had the circumstances been different. "I'll kill the lady myself before I let you get your grubby hands on her."

"No need for that, Lasterton. We need the girl in one piece."

They knew who he was? Bloody pirates. "Will you be taking her back to her father then?" he asked.

"Eventually."

That answer was not good enough. "Do you recognize the voice, Daniella?"

She was thinking about it. Hard. "I'm not sure. I think I do but it's been an age since I last saw him. I thought he was dead. I say we get out."

"No."

She breathed deep and looked him squarely in the eye. "I know you think you have the upper hand but do you not think when it comes to pirates I might know more than you? Please, James, this is not your battlefield and these men do not fight with honour or with pride. You don't speak their language and will probably get us all killed."

As if the men outside had heard her whispered words the one doing the talking called again: "Your men aren't comfortable at the point of my swords, Lasterton, and I can't guarantee there won't be blood spilled if we don't hurry this along. The tide is going out and so should we be."

Dammit. Of course they had Hobson and Patrick as well. Unlatching the door, James stepped slowly from the carriage to stand on the side of the muddy road. There had to be at least two dozen tan-skinned, toothless, filthy ruffians surrounding a paler man atop a fine—probably stolen—horse. He wore dark leather breeches and boots and the brightest crimson silk waistcoat James had ever seen. No shirt, no necktie or cravat.

Despite their shaggy appearances, the pirates were well armed and looked ready to spring into action at the say-so of the paler one.

"I don't believe we've met," James said as he stepped clear of the carriage, arms and hands out to show he was unarmed.

"Darius? *Darius*, is that you?"

"Hello, Little Lamb."

James opened his mouth to ask whether this man was friend or foe when pain exploded in the back of his skull and his world slowly sank into darkness. Daniella's screams were the last sounds in his ears as consciousness melted away into a bottomless abyss of nothing.

"UNHAND ME AT once," Daniella demanded, feeling only slightly ridiculous in her boy's clothes, minus the boots she'd never got around to putting on.

"You are in no position to be making demands, Little One."

"I am not your little one anymore, Darius. What do you think you're doing carrying me off like this?" Lying bent over the pommel of a man's horse was only slightly more degrading than riding on his shoulder, and no more comfortable.

"I'm rescuing you from your kidnapper."

"You're kidnapping me from my kidnapper."

"Every man has to make a living, Little One."

"Would you cease with all the *little one* talk, please? It's humiliating."

"More humiliating than being purchased by a nobleman? Or less?"

"How did you hear about that?"

"I hear everything, Daniella, and the stories worried even me."

"Did my father send you to collect me?" she asked hopefully, trying hard to stretch her body around to see his face. Perhaps they'd made amends and then gone separate ways to get her back?

"Your father doesn't know I have you. Not yet. I did have an interesting visit with your brother, though."

"Does Anthony know where I am? Is that how you found me?"

"My crew intercepted an intriguing letter of ransom but when I presented it to your brother, he didn't seem particularly surprised or worried, more...disappointed."

"You're making a mistake getting involved in this, Darius."

"I can't see how. I'm going to sell a rich man back to his family along with his servants. Sounds like a financially rewarding situation to me."

"He'll kill you for this."

"Who? Your brother? Your father? Or perhaps your titled man?"

"He is not *my* man. He kidnapped me and held me hostage and then dragged me halfway across the country. I was terrified for my life." Embellishing the truth certainly couldn't hurt her cause.

"You didn't appear terrified when my men knocked him out."

"I was shocked is all."

"Being an English lady has softened you, has it?"

Daniella snorted. She was never at risk of turning into an English lady nor was there any danger of her softening. Darius's men had caught James off guard when they'd knocked him unconscious. She didn't like seeing him injured. By her hand or anyone else's. As much as she shouldn't have a real care to his well-being, he was inching his way beneath her devil-may-care act.

"Tell me about the nabob."

Darius was not a trustworthy man. Six years earlier he'd led a mutiny on the decks of *The Aurora*, splitting the crew and their loyalties in half. She herself had disarmed him and sent him overboard with the other dogs. She'd heard talk of his adventures since then, mostly mischief with the occasional ransom run or looting of a navy vessel, but she'd also heard of his death at the hands of the navy.

The years had been kind to him; indeed if anyone had softened, it was Darius. No longer did his sharp cheekbones and aristocratic features appear so harsh and angular. No longer did he resemble the son of the manor house. Fresh air and years in the sun lent him the means to look like a very healthy, very successful pirate. Hopefully the man she had once called big brother was still inside him somewhere.

"My father has something that belongs to him. He got it into his head that he could swap me for his stolen items."

"And those items are?"

"How should I know? Do you think he would trust me with that kind of information? He thinks I am lower than pond scum. He thinks all pirates are the same."

"He said that to you?"

"He didn't have to. It was there in his eyes."

"Should we just kill him now and be done with it? I don't need the ransom that badly."

He was fishing. He goaded her to try to get a more direct reaction like when she'd screamed James's name as he'd fallen. She shrugged as though James's life meant absolutely nothing to her.

The action hurt.

"Did he give you those bruises around your throat as well?"

"We fought."

"He must be some adversary if he is still standing."

"Last time I saw him, he wasn't standing."

"Yes, well, an unconscious man is easier to transport than one able to fight back."

"What stake do you have in this? Do you mean to taunt my father? Kill me? I don't understand your involvement."

"If I wanted you dead, Lamb, you would be. I was bored, no ships to annoy, no treasure to steal, only one kidnapped daughter to save."

"So you're an angel now? Is that it?"

Darius laughed so loudly his horse shied to the left, the reins pulling tight over her back while he got the beast under control. "I would never go that far. I always have my reasons."

Daniella humphed and relaxed as much as she could with her feet and hands tied. She would get no more answers from him and she wouldn't push. Not yet. Not until she figured out what his part was.

When the inn came into view, Daniella thought about screaming for help from the occupants, but discarded the idea. The sea was the quickest way back to her father's hamlet.

The riders fanned out and dismounted one by one, and finally she saw James's prone form over the saddle of a horse being led by another pirate. Hobson and Patrick were trussed up so they couldn't move an inch. Each had murder in his eyes.

Daniella knew how they felt.

CHAPTER TWENTY-TWO

WHEN JAMES FINALLY came to, all was silent but for the creaking of the ship and the sloshing of the waves against the hull. Even though his mind was sluggish and slow to catch up he knew they'd been taken aboard the very ship they had fought to outrun.

It was all over. Amelia and his mother would be at the mercy of a vengeful pirate until the end of their days. He didn't bother opening his eyes, but went over and over in his mind where he'd stepped wrong. What had been his biggest undoing? Was it Daniella? Was it his military pride misleading him into thinking he was in control? She was the single biggest distraction he'd ever encountered—had he simply not seen that she was utter destruction barrelling his way?

The second question trying to bombard his consciousness was had she planned it? At the back his mind from the very beginning had niggled the notion that this was all one bigger trap to land him in front of Captain Germaine and answer for his actions. Daniella had said her father wasn't a vengeful man, but then why had he taken Amelia and his mother in the first place? And perhaps she was vengeful on his behalf, or trying to earn a place back at his side.

He guessed he would soon find out. It couldn't be a co-incidence that this other pirate had turned up that morning. Either Daniella had set him up or he was working for Captain Germaine. Either way, James knew if he didn't do something, anything, he was a dead man.

Opening his eyes as far as he could to the predawn glow, he took in his surroundings. Thank God the swelling to his face wasn't as bad as he'd thought it would get. Expecting to be cooling his heels in a rat-infested hull with the bilge, he was surprised to find himself in a clean, fresh stateroom, furnished with bunks, a desk and two chairs.

His head snapped up and he tried to rise but then the room began to spin and with a groan he was forced to lie back.

Turning his head and willing his limited vision to clear, he saw her. Curled up in the chair, her bare toes hanging from the edge and her hands cradling her cheek, Daniella slept. She looked so innocent, so young and trusting. But looks were deceiving and only a willing pawn slept this deeply once captured. "Daniella?" he whispered, wanting to be careful not to alert a guard if there was one outside the door. Not yet.

No answer. Now that his vertigo had levelled out, he checked the other corners of the room to make sure they weren't being watched.

Satisfied they were alone, he called a little louder, "Daniella?"

This time she stirred, wiped her cheek with the back of her hand and mumbled something in her sleep, but didn't wake.

James swung his legs over the edge of the cot, biting down on his tongue when the room began to spin again. He closed his eyes and waited for it to level out. When he tried to rake his hands through his hair and rub the sleep from his face, he discovered one wrist was manacled to a length of thick chain looped through the post of the bunk: he could only move a short distance in any direction.

He decided to forget subtlety. Forget the element of surprise. Forget truces and partnerships. She'd betrayed him. He had the heavy manacle to prove it and she slept like an untroubled angel.

Slowly and quietly, without taking his eyes from her slumbering form, James slipped one of his boots off, repositioned it in his hand and then threw it at her. Hard.

Within a heartbeat Daniella was on her backside on the floor; she gave one breathless shriek before regaining her wits.

"Good morning," James drawled, his elbows on his knees as he took her in. "Sleep well?"

Storm clouds gathered in her eyes. "I always sleep well until someone tries to kill me!"

"I hardly think one little boot has the ability to take your life, Daniella. You're rather dramatic this morning."

"You could have done the gentlemanly thing and taken the chair."

He raised a brow. "Forgive me. I didn't know I had a choice, considering the fact I was not conscious."

She grimaced again and a look that truly resembled sadness—not guilt—swept across her gaze. But then it was gone. "That was not my fault."

"No?"

"I had no idea Darius would knock you out."

"Next you'll tell me you had no clue he was coming after us?"

"I didn't." She got up from the floor, dusted her breeches off and turned back to face him, hands on her hips. "I'm as much a captive as you."

James lifted his arm. "And yet I am the one in manacles?"

Finally real emotion showed and the sides of her mouth dropped slightly. "That wasn't Darius. That was me. I am unarmed this time."

"I see." He was outwardly contemplative for a moment as shame burned him from the inside. She thought he would hurt her again? "What will you do with me?"

"Darius plans to sell you back to your family in London."

"Did you tell him my family isn't in London?"

"I told him nothing about Amelia or your mother."

James laughed. He couldn't help himself. "What are you doing, Daniella? Turning up your acting skills so I'll believe you're on my side?"

"Your side? Please tell me you don't think I organized all of this?"

"I don't think you did. I know you did. Coincidences of this magnitude are not very likely."

She sputtered but she didn't deny it.

"Answer me this, Daniella. With the exception of last night—" he indicated her throat where the bruises sat "—what makes you think you are safer with Darius than with me? At least you knew my agenda was quite transparent. What about his? Is he a friend? A lover?"

"I have been with you for days. Not once have I been out of your sight. How would I have got a message through?"

"Perhaps at the dressmaker's? Perhaps..." He trailed off. Surely not! "Patrick?"

"What about Patrick?"

"The way he turned up that night and joined our traveling party? Two nights past when the two of you met by the beach? He was sending the signal, wasn't he?" How could he have been so blind? So stupid? How could he have let this corrupted girl ruin everything? "I bet right now he is swinging in a hammock, free as a bird."

"You're talking nonsense now. Patrick isn't one of my father's men. He isn't involved in any of this between you and me. He and Hobson are being held deeper in the ship but I have been assured they will come to no harm."

"Excuse me if I don't believe you or him."

"I am a hostage here as well, damn it."

"Where do you know him from?"

"Darius? Or Patrick?"

"Darius." He was beginning to lose his tightly held temper. Through clenched teeth he asked again, enunciating each word, "How. Do. You. Know. Darius?"

"He used to a part of *The Aurora*'s crew. I have not seen him in six years. Not since he staged a mutiny and lost. I should have killed him then."

"We all have those moments of regret," James said with a healthy amount of sarcasm. If he'd driven that knife into Germaine's chest instead of his leg, things would be so different. "I would have the truth from you, Daniella. Did you know Patrick before we set off on the road?"

"Of course not. He really did find me out walking that night."

"Did you or Patrick signal Darius so he could come to get you?"

"I didn't! You are insufferable. I wasn't even gone long enough!"

"I have underestimated you a couple of times now, Daniella; I won't do it again." Each time she wrested the upper hand from him, or he gave her an inch, he wound up with the injuries of a fool.

"And nor should you but none of this was my doing. I was happy for you to take me to my father and then leave. Your plan was good enough and would have more than likely worked."

"And now our lives are in the hands of Darius the pirate."

"Your life is not in any danger. Neither is mine."

"Do you trust Darius?"

She thought about it for a moment, her bottom lip squeezed between her teeth until she let it go with a sigh, her gaze dropping to the floor. "I trust him about as much as I trust you."

James chuckled but there was no humour in it. They

were in real trouble.

DANIELLA DID NOT want to look at those of her actions that had led them there. Perhaps she should have put her head down in London and accepted her lot. Though of course even if she had, James might well still have taken her as a hostage, so they—Oh, never mind. She needed to keep him calm.

"I promise you will make it home in one piece. Your purse will be a hell of a lot lighter but you will make it home."

"Ladies do not curse, Daniella."

Ah, there was the James she had been getting used to. Mr Proper. Another one of his many personas. As he shifted in the growing light, Daniella looked down and said, "James, you're bleeding."

"You ought to know. You sliced me when you attempted to stage your own mutiny."

"Why didn't you say anything? I could have tended this."

"Should I have told you when we were shouting at each other or when we were being taken captive? Perhaps when I was unconscious I might have found a way to communicate my discomfort? You could have removed my boots before attaching your chains."

"You are very surly this morning."

He sighed but didn't smile as she'd hoped. She went to kneel in front of him and inspected the damage to his shin. It wasn't deep but it needed cleaning. "We do seem to always hurt one another, don't we?"

"In all my years in the army I don't think I shed this much blood."

"You are lying but thank you for trying to make me feel worse about it. I appreciate that."

"You're welcome. Now, can you release me from these manacles or do I present a danger to you?"

"I was protecting myself last night. I know now about your night-time violence but I wasn't sure what would happen while you were so deeply unconscious. They wouldn't let me ask Hobson."

"You didn't tell Darius about it, did you?"

"Of course not. I told him we injured one another when I tried to escape. I told him we fought." She didn't tell him she'd had to talk her old friend out of killing James for putting his hands on her. The purpling around her throat was so vivid now that no one was going to miss it and everyone was going to assume the worst. She couldn't even swallow without pain reminding her of all her follies.

He hadn't fared any better. Around James's eyes the skin was swollen and bruised and his nose looked a fright. Any other injuries sustained were hidden beneath the dark growth of a thickening beard. Long gone was the handsome, clean aristocrat. In his place sat the Butcher, or perhaps a professional pugilist. She only hoped her father asked some questions before he jumped to conclusions when the time came.

Two days.

In two days she would face her father and possibly his

wrath. That's why she hadn't told Darius the truth about her kidnapping. That she'd basically gone willingly with a man she didn't know and continued in his company when her chaperone fell ill. She'd actually not hated the journey. There were times when she'd almost enjoyed herself. Not that she'd tell James, Darius or her father that.

The slice to James's leg wasn't as bad as it looked and had already stopped bleeding, but his hose were beyond ruined so she gently peeled the frail fabric back and off.

"I can do that myself," he muttered, making no move to take over.

"I know," Daniella said. "But it will give me something to do."

She got back to her feet and banged on the door a few times. She ignored James's raised brows and merely arched her own in reply. The door was barred from the outside but, if she knew Darius, a man would be standing by.

Within a tap of her foot against floor, the heavy timbers flew open and a sailor peered in. "What?"

"We need warm water and linens to bind a wound and food and drink for two."

"You what?" Shock met her request but she ignored that too.

"Water, linens, food and something to drink. Hostages are allowed to be reasonably comfortable are they not?"

"I s'pose so," the man finally, reluctantly, agreed. But then he shut the door and locked it again without a yes or no.

"Not a clever lot, those ones," she murmured more to

herself than to James.

"Daniella, can you please untie me now?"

"I don't have the key."

A smooth, unmarred spot by James's temple began to tick and she watched his face grow red. Before he could explode, she explained, "Darius took the key. I couldn't very well ask him not to."

"For the love of God, woman, you make the worst captive ever! You don't fight at all for the things you should and go meekly at the times you could be fighting. If I'm chained to this bed, then I can't protect you. I can't even protect myself."

"Do you want Darius to think there is something more between us than what I have told him? I for one do not need the complication." Though she made the statement, the words rang false and her cheeks heated.

James's quiet voice reached her through her musings. "I'm sorry I lost my temper."

Daniella turned her back on him to look out of the small cabin window. "You're right though. This is not where I planned to be, not what I planned to be doing."

"I think we are both excellent examples of lives not unfolding as wished."

"If you could choose to be anything or anyone, who or what would you be?" Daniella asked him, turning back so she could search his expression for truth or lies. She already knew her own answer to the question but she wondered if he'd thought about it for himself.

"I don't get to choose. Right now I have to be a marquess. I have to care for my lands and my tenants and my family."

"There must have been a time in your life, before your family came into the title, when you thought about the future."

He shook his head. "I was eight, and a naive eight at that. What kind of adventures were you dreaming about at eight?"

Daniella laughed quietly as she leaned against the wall at her back. "I was living my dreams. I spent my days on a pirate ship with the only family I'd ever known. There was nothing else I wanted or needed."

"I dreamed of far-off places," James confided. "I read tales of lands where people ate each other for dinner, where gold glitters in the ground for anyone to dig up and where there are no lords or ladies, only men and women. But those dreams were few and far between even when I was eight. Mostly I dreamed of more. More food. More friends. More for my mother and my father and my brother. We were all happy when word reached us that my father was to inherit. Then I dreamed of having everything money could buy and more. But money does not ensure happiness or safety."

He raked a hand through his already mussed hair. "Amelia has never known how it feels to pull food from the land or slaughter her own dinner. She's never known coarse fabric against her skin or had to do anything for herself. I bet this grand adventure isn't nearly as grand as she thought when they left."

"Why did they leave?" She had to ask.

But James shook his head, lost for words for a moment. "I don't know. One day they were there when I left for my club and when I returned the next morning they were gone. I tracked them to a ship and discovered their route, and then their capture by your father. The ship didn't make it more than a few days out."

"Which seems so odd in itself," she remarked aloud. "My father is retired. *The Aurora* would only sail now for cargo or pleasure but not for pillage. It would be suicidal for all involved."

"Perhaps he ran out of gold? I'd imagine it's costly to live on the wrong side of the law."

Daniella knew that wasn't the case. "You said it yourself, gold isn't everything. No. I can't see that as any kind of motivator." Not since he lost his leg and a portion of his freedom. He'd lost a good measure of his confidence that day also.

Perhaps her father had been coming to get her and something had gone wrong, forcing him in another direction? But that couldn't be it either. Otherwise he would have returned Amelia and his mother and picked her up.

"Tell me," he started, then seemed to rethink his question before finally resuming. "Is this one of those times when I should fight for my life? Or should I go along with it and trust that you actually do know what you're doing?"

CHAPTER TWENTY-THREE

FROM THE FRIGHTENED expression she wasn't adept enough at hiding, James had his answer. She was as much in the dark now as he was. His only hope was the inept navy coming along but then they would probably all get blown up in a ridiculous quirk of fate.

"Never mind," James said, letting her out of answering. For one split second he'd considered handing her the control she kept fighting him for.

The door opened and rather than the guard from before, Darius himself carried in a tray and placed it on the table. "Good morning," he said cheerfully.

Neither Daniella nor James answered. He was glad to see Daniella glare at their captor.

"Come now, Lamb, surely we can put our past behind us and share a meal, can we not?"

"You could leave the tray and be on your way, could you not?" she told him with a scorn that could probably burn had it a spark.

"It's not often I get visitors on my ship. I would enjoy the company."

"You should stay," James said, knowing it was a chance

for them to get more information.

"Thank you. I don't believe we've been formally introduced?" Darius held out his hand but James ignored it.

"You already know who I am, Darius. Do you have a family name?"

"I long ago got over the need for the name of my family and go only by Darius."

He was lying. James let him. "Do you have the key for these manacles?"

Darius looked to Daniella first before answering. She shook her head and then shot James a small look of triumph. Petty little thing.

"Perhaps just for the meal and when I leave I can chain him back up? After all, I am here and I have a guard outside the door. Are you going to hurt her, Lasterton?"

James hated being called Lasterton. It was the part of the title he truly loathed. The name had never been meant for him, reserved as it was for the eldest male child. He enjoyed the responsibilities of the estates and her people but every success in his life had been as a Trelissick. It's who he was through and through. Lasterton came to him only with scandal and grief and madness attached.

He let it go this once. "As long as the lady behaves herself, I believe I can be civil."

Darius let out a bark of laughter and James realized they weren't making a good act of captive and captor. Quite the opposite probably. He wondered if Daniella was aware of the fact that she had moved towards him when Darius entered the room, almost seeking his shelter and safety, even though he was chained and unarmed. He would certainly point it out to her later just to see her squirm.

"Let me clean his wound first," Daniella said, not waiting for an answer before she once again kneeled before him, a bowl of water in one hand, clean-enough strips of fabric in the other.

"What happened there?" Darius asked, gesturing to his injury.

Daniella's lips tightened into a straight, rather pale line as she bent her head to her work.

"The minx thought she could escape me while we were attempting to outrun you." It was the only answer he could give as Daniella tentatively touched him. She ran her fingers lightly down the hair on his leg before wetting a linen strip to wash his skin.

Darius laughed again. Something about their situation was…amusing him? From the lines around his eyes, James guessed he laughed a lot. From the calluses on his hands, he looked to work hard as well. He had hoped for a dandy unable to wield a sword.

"She sounds quite the handful," Darius remarked.

"Indeed," James replied, his brain not functioning as it should. He should concentrate on escape. He should have been forming a plan just in case the opportunity arose. But he couldn't think. Not when the heat from her hand on his calf sent fire shooting all the way to his groin. He leaned forwards on the bunk slightly.

"Tell me more about this virgin auction," Darius said, sitting down and pouring what appeared to be wine into three delicately engraved pewter goblets.

"I'd rather not," Daniella said with a sniff, finally moving her hand from his calf, only to grip his ankle. God, her fingers were slim.

"But it did happen? I'd thought perhaps the tales were exaggerated?"

James cleared his throat and switched his attention back to Darius. "Who did you hear it from?" It had only been a matter of days and if a pirate on the high seas had heard of Daniella's disgrace, then most assuredly all of London had too.

"I have my spies," Darius said, tapping the side of his nose with a wink.

"What are they saying?" Daniella asked, her touch on his leg halting, her grip slackening.

"One story I heard is that you stripped your clothes off right there in a warehouse and offered yourself to Leicester-shire. Another said it was a coachman who bought you. And the third, and this is the story your brother received, said that you must have finally cracked. Apparently you purchased filthy virgins for a sacrifice and hoped to appeal to Poseidon and Neptune to bring your father's ship back on a tidal wave right to London's docks. That's my favourite of the bunch."

James met Daniella's gaze and instead of shame, there was victory. "You should not look so happy about this," he told her. "You are well and truly ruined now."

"Excellent."

James grabbed her by the shoulders and gave her a little shake. The wet rag fell from her grasp. "What are you going to do when the world is at peace, Daniella, and there are no ships to annoy? What will you do when you are forced back to London for some reason or another? News of this calibre will spread across the continent and it will never be forgotten."

Wrenching herself from his bruising grip, she sat back on the timbers and laughed in his face. "I don't care what people say about me—I've been telling you that all along. I am going to be a privateer again, trade in legal cargo. Don't you think rumours and disgrace will follow me forever in any case?"

"That's different. The world is going to think you a whore now."

She shook her head, her bright curls bouncing with her vehemence. "You just don't see it for some reason and I'm not sure if it's because you are a man or because you have everything your heart desires all locked up in your manor house. Not one single gentleman was going to offer for me before all of this started. They were whispering behind my back and cutting me on the street and at balls from the moment I arrived in London. No one was ever going to forgive my upbringing and make a decent offer and I didn't want one anyway."

"My *brother*—" she spat the word "—would have sold me off to one of his cronies, a mere mister either already embroiled in scandal himself or a gentleman old enough not to care so long as he bedded a debutante. What kind of life would that have been for me, James?"

Darius rose and helped Daniella from the floor but James

just sat and stared, feeling the heat of her words. Finally fully understanding the truth of her statements.

"Had either of you listened to anything I'd been saying, you would have heard me try to tell you it would never work. You said it not three days ago. Your wife, God pity her, will have the bluest of blood and be immaculate in every way; there will be not a stain upon her name or her person. If *you* think that way, not even born to your title, imagine what the other men of the ton think."

Darius looked down over Daniella's shoulder at him and asked, "You don't think that way do you, Lasterton? Surely a man of your impeccable character can see a woman as more than a breeding machine and a ball hostess?"

Another change she had wrought in him. He shook his head. He was beginning to see a hell of a lot more than he wished to.

Daniella lifted her hands to her hips. "What about Amelia? Will you make her marry politically or will you let her marry the man she chooses? Or, God forbid, remain single? A bluestocking on the shelf if she wants."

"My sister is none of your business," James told her, finally coming to his feet and straightening up as far as his manacled wrist allowed.

"No, but I'm interested to know how you would feel if she fell in love with a stable boy."

"Amelia would not fall for a stable boy." Of that he was sure. She knew only a gentleman could afford her fine things and servants and luxury.

"I'm asking what you would do if she did."

"I would let her go. As long as she was happy and loved and well cared for, I would let her go."

Daniella laughed. "You, sir, are a big fat liar."

James ground his teeth to stop the reply lingering in his mouth. A stable boy might be all Amelia was good for once word got around that she'd been held by pirates for months on end. James would have to employ a physician to perform the humiliating tests needed to determine if Amelia retained her innocence but regardless the mud would have well and truly stuck and would not be shaken free. What was he going to do? He hadn't thought as far as the finer details. Only that he needed to get them back no matter what and never let them go.

Darius interrupted his thoughts. "Enough with the doom and gloom. Let us sit and eat: you two must be famished."

James nodded though he wasn't hungry at all. Daniella turned back to the window again.

Taking a key from his pocket, Darius approached him, a question in his blue eyes. "If I unlock you for the meal, do you promise not to throttle her?"

"I'll do my best," James offered.

Darius chuckled. "Good enough for me. She does need a good whipping, that one."

He pressed his lips together at the thought of the pirate doing any such thing to Daniella. Flexing his fingers into fists he resisted the urge to knock the man on his arse. He really wanted to hit something. Or someone.

The next hour passed in a blur of small talk, mundane questions and clipped answers, with the ever-rocking ship creaking beneath their chairs. But James couldn't absorb a single word of the conversation. He couldn't get his mind off Daniella's angry words.

She was well and truly tarnished. Not just by her antics in London, he now saw, but by the life she had been born into; it wasn't fair.

Of course she would be free to take a lover if she captained her own ship, but would her deckhands let her? Would they all want a turn? His grip tightened on the goblet, red liquid sloshing over the side and onto the table. She had no sense. She knew nothing of men's minds when they were faced with a beautiful woman. And there weren't many more beautiful than her. Her red hair shone in the morning light, the loose curls draped over her shoulders and breasts. When she laughed, she did so freely. Darius was making a concerted effort to raise her humour. James wished he could make her laugh like that. She was mischief and light all rolled up in one pretty little scandalous package.

He recalled those moments at the inn, right before Hobson had crashed into the room. He'd wanted nothing more than to kiss her.

He gulped and drained his cup in one long swallow and held it out for Darius to refill.

Now he felt like getting drunk. He had nothing else to do and if he could get drunk enough, maybe he could forget about Daniella being whipped by pirates and Amelia being tumbled in haylofts by stable boys.

CHAPTER TWENTY-FOUR

Daniella didn't precisely know why she was so irritable. Forcing so much laughter at Darius's ridiculous jokes had proved to annoy James but had only served to hurt her stomach and heighten her discontent. She continued to use her woman's prerogative to behave irrationally and held on to it tightly throughout the day. After supplying the two with copious amounts of wine (probably hoping to loosen lips) Darius led them up onto the foredeck for fresh air and sunshine. They were far enough out in the icy sea that escape would only be through death in the cold waters.

Hobson and Patrick had been above and passed them in the hall, looking hale and hearty, if a little green around the edges. Obviously neither man was used to the ocean and they weren't handling the transition well.

So now she sat and brooded and cursed beneath her breath. When James took an unlikely interest in the way the ship was maneuvered and the tasks of the individual men, Daniella scowled. Why couldn't he also be seasick and stay in the cabin? When he removed his shirt to climb into the rigging, she looked away. For a moment. But her gaze kept drifting back to him again and again. The look of unadorned pleasure on his swollen face as he lifted his head to the sea breeze was unexpected.

The day her father had come across the returning servicemen's ship, James had been seated on the deck with the other wounded soldiers, pale and listless. By the time Captain Germaine realized his mistake in this quarry, they had already engaged and it was too late to change course. The James of today was not so pale and certainly not listless. The scars on his arms and torso glistened in the sun as the muscles beneath the skin flexed and moved the higher he climbed. She was forced to shield the sun from her eyes as she tracked his ascent, holding her breath when he lost his footing for a moment.

"He's taken to it as though he was born aboard a ship," Darius remarked. He reclined next to her, uninvited and unsolicited. He draped his body over the bench with an elbow next to her shoulder and his legs crossed at the ankles.

"The man seems to suffer from a tad too much arrogance," Daniella stated with a nod for emphasis. She wanted to look back to ensure he'd found his footing but that action would betray her.

"And you do not?" he chuckled.

"You don't know me, Darius. Not anymore. Perhaps not ever."

"I know your kind. You always desire what you cannot acquire."

"Poetry? Philosophy? Come to change my mind and alter my heading?"

"The only person who can change your mind, Daniella,

is you. You talk to him about choices yet you know as well as I do there are always decisions we can make."

"Sometimes those decisions are just plain wrong though, are they not?"

"Ah, now you want to discuss the mutiny?" She speared him with a glare. "I don't need to hear you attempt to justify what you did. You put all of our lives in danger when you betrayed my father and me."

"I wanted more," he admitted with a nonchalant shrug. "I saw what your father had and I was sick and tired of taking orders. But after that day I was taught the error of my ways through sound beatings and torture. It was about then, when a man faces certain death, that the wisdom he once needed seems to dawn on him."

The part about the beatings and torture caught her attention. "What happened to you?"

"After you drove me over the edge of the ship, I floated there in the ocean, surrounded by the dead and dying, clinging to a barrel one of the men threw overboard when you weren't looking, and I wondered the same thing. I was so sure I was going to win I hadn't even considered the consequences did I lose. On the third day clinging to that bloody barrel, about to give up on life, a ship came upon me and the only other man to survive and rescued us. But then we owed a debt so were forced to work it off for a man so evil and cunning just to have him look upon you gave you a chill."

Daniella laughed: he was making it all up to teach her a lesson. "You lie, Darius. If he was so evil, why did he not leave you there in the ocean? Why are you standing here today?"

He met her eyes then, and the solemnity and weight not quite hidden in the depths of his caused her breath to catch. The smile fell from her lips.

"I speak the truth, Lamb: why would I lie to you now? I'm trying to impress on you the consequences for rash behaviour. You never think about what will happen after the fact. Something I never did either, until I was forced to it."

"So this is the revenge you will exact upon me?" she asked, hardly able to hope that would be the extent of it. "Chilling me with your tale and making me think about my actions? James has been doing just that for days without success."

"*James*—" he drew out the name "—has too much invested in you and this situation to see what he did is also wrong. At some time his honour is going to demand he do the right thing."

"You're wrong. I am a means to an end for him therefore his honour doesn't apply."

"That's where you are blinded, Little One. He is a gentleman despite his war wounds and military training. Though he wasn't born to it, every man has it and he has had an abundance of time to have the notion drilled into him. Why do you think he took you to start with? He could have left you on that virgin block and turned his cheek to your fate."

"He kidnapped me to swap me for items my father took. I already told you that."

Darius nodded just once. "Yes, certainly. But you need a man to take you in hand. Perhaps if your passion for the ocean and for your ship could be turned in another direction, you might see the world for what it really is."

"And what is that?"

He shrugged. "For every man it is different. The world showed me your father gave orders and worked sailors hard to keep his daughter safe and his ship on top of the water and not below it. Would I have asked for this responsibility?" He gestured to the men working the deck. "Had I known the cost involved when one loses a man, a friend? The sleepless nights, the endless running and worrying? I'm not so sure."

"I accept that responsibility quite freely. I want it with every fibre of my being and I won't stop until I have it."

"That's what scares me about you, Daniella. You think it's what you want but you have no idea what you ask for. This is not a woman's world."

She stood. She'd had just about enough. "I wish you would all stop treating me like a child, as if a female cannot possibly have a mind or know what she wants."

"But you are a female, not that you ever truly accepted it. As a female, you need someone to protect you and make the decisions the irrational part of your brain ignores."

Ugh. She had to go along with the nonsense Darius dribbled. She might need him after all of it was done. "Would you have me, Darius? If my father truly doesn't want me, would you have me on your ship? Would you let me work alongside your men?"

He nodded, but an instantaneous, dangerous spark lit his

gaze. "I would have you on my ship but I would also have you in my bed. It would be the only way I could protect you from the men. You would be mine and mine only." He stood and leaned towards her, took a tendril of her hair between his fingers and rolled it between his thumb and forefinger. "You have a passion that is very rare in a London lady. It might be fun to explore it."

She slapped his hand away and distanced herself a few steps. "I would as soon bed you as I would kiss a rat."

"I thought you would say that." He laughed but he didn't look as though he had tossed the notion from his mind.

Just then a thump on the deck to her left signalled James had had enough climbing. "Daniella, are you all right?"

Daniella stood at James's back, glaring at Darius but needing a barrier between them so she didn't strike out. There was an irony there, that she felt protected by James and his presence. Even so, she was on *Darius's* ship surrounded by *Darius's* men. She would not be the victor in that fight. "Everything is quite fine."

Darius was still laughing, his guffaws subsiding to chuckles, that mischievous glint in his eye. He was up to something more nefarious than ransom. "Daniella and I were discussing the pros and cons of having a man in her life. Someone to calm her hoydenish ways. I made her an offer should she wish to stay here with me."

"And you had to touch her to do that? I hope she declined your offer?" James asked.

"That is between her and me. Daniella and I are old

friends. I'm sure she told you?"

James nodded and crossed his arms over his bare chest. "She did. But now she is your hostage."

Daniella watched with fascination the play of muscles over James's back. She couldn't look away from a twitching spot right beneath his left shoulder blade.

"When she was your hostage you seemed to be friendly: why can I not also further our acquaintance?"

"Because the lady doesn't wish it."

Daniella lifted her gaze in time to see Darius's mouth split into a grin. "The lady will do as I say while she is aboard my ship."

James's hands dropped to his sides and his fists clenched. "And while I am here, I will do everything in my power to protect her."

"But you are a hostage as well, or did you forget that while enjoying a taste of freedom?"

"Taste of freedom?" James laughed. "I am as much a prisoner on the deck and in the rigging as I am in the cabin. Your cage is large but it is still a cage."

Darius sidestepped and held his arm out. "You are welcome to leave anytime you want. No one is holding you back. No one has chained you to the mast or made you do anything you didn't want to do."

It was time she spoke up. "Will you say that when we are closer to land? When we dock? Do you or do you not plan to ransom us to our families?"

The humour died from Darius's eyes and he breathed deep before he answered. "Him I will ransom. You are a different story. You owe me for sending me over the side of that ship. You owe me for the trouble I had to endure after as well."

"You asked for it when you tried to kill the honest half of my crew."

Darius shook his head but stood his ground. "Once it was clear you were winning, you could have locked us in the hull and delivered us to the next town but you did not."

"I was angry! You tried to cut my throat! I have a scar on my arm where your sword went wide." She began to roll her sleeve up to show him the ugly corded white line there. "You meant business when you turned your weapons on your family."

Darius marched over and squeezed her elbow so she couldn't bare her upper arm. So she couldn't show him the damage he'd done that day.

She was thoroughly tired of being manhandled. "Let go of me," she demanded.

"I would never have thrown you overboard and you know it. Perhaps now I will? Perhaps any ransom your father would pay would not equal the satisfaction I would have by seeing you into the sea."

This was no gentleman teaching her a lesson. Fear took hold, starting in her chest and trickling outwards. "You wouldn't."

His lips split into a predatory smile, one with no warmth or humour, only intent. "I would." He pushed until she was forced to take a step backwards, and then another, and then another.

"Stop," James warned.

Darius didn't listen.

"You're scaring her," James called, starting after them.

"Darius, you're mad—the water is freezing. I'll be dead before the hour is out."

"As I could have been. I wished I *had* died for months after I was found floating. The things he did to his crew would curdle your stomach to hear."

"All right, I'm sorry. Is that what you want to hear?" She began to push back, to try to slow him down but he kept pushing and pushing. Her panic rose. When she let James believe she wasn't scared of anything, she lied. Of course she lied. No one wanted to die. Especially not like this. Not now.

"I don't think there are any words to make up for this."

Her legs hit the side of the rail and she shrieked. "Darius, you've made your point. What good am I to you dead?"

"It would make me feel better." The predatory smile was back as he leaned in close. "Any final words, Little Lamb?"

"Don't do this." Blood rushed in her ears and her mouth dried. She thought her knees might give out. She'd come too far for it to end this way.

"I'm doing it."

Daniella kicked out with all her might, wrenched her arm from his grip and tried to get around him but he threw his arms around her in a hug so tight, she couldn't draw a breath.

"James?" She tried to scream but her words emerged only a half whisper. "Help me."

At first glance it seemed a sick and twisted joke, a man seeking a small amount of vengeance for a slight from the past. It's why he hadn't intervened straight away. But when Darius started pushing Daniella towards the rail, his heart stopped beating altogether.

"Stop," he called out but Darius ignored him. His crew simply stood by and watched, wary but still.

Daniella murmured something he couldn't hear, her eyes wide with fright, freckles stark against pale cheeks, and then she turned wild. He'd not seen her like that, so scared, so vulnerable. She had been so sure they were safe. Had Darius lulled them into thinking they were? Yet again the enigma that was Daniella blinded him to everything else.

Charging forwards James started to punch Darius in the area of his kidneys. He didn't care that his opponent had his back turned. If anyone was going to throw Daniella overboard, it would be James in a fit of rage, not Darius, and not for revenge.

Darius roared and turned to face him, giving Daniella time to scramble away from the edge. James didn't stop. He drove his fist into the other man's jaw and then followed with another punch to his stomach. He just kept hitting him. Darius barely had time to cover his face let alone fight back but James was angry now. He'd wanted to see Daniella fight for her life but when he did, and saw she was losing, he'd seen right through every lie he told himself.

"Enough," Darius said, his hands in fists in front of his face.

"I think I'm going to kill you," James said between heavy breaths, trying to land a punch that would see Darius out cold. "And I think I'll enjoy it."

Vice-like arms gripped him from behind and it was impossible to break away, to make good on his words and rid the world of one more pirate.

Darius tested his jaw, mouth open wide while he considered James. "Take them both below and lock the door. I will decide their fate on the morrow."

CHAPTER TWENTY-FIVE

"**Y**OU SAID YOU would ransom James back to his family! My father will kill you for this!" Daniella screeched as she was hauled unceremoniously down the dark corridor.

"You shouldn't believe a word I say, Little Lamb. I made my living out of lying and I never said anything about a cost on your head, only his."

"Bastard," she yelled, trying her hardest to be free of the grips the sailors had on her arms. "When I'm free, I'm going to come back and kill you as I should have done all those years ago. What were you trying to accomplish with all of that?" Daniella asked and she and James were pushed into the cabin, so far beyond furious she saw only red and nothing else.

"You certainly were frightened."

"You're a madman. What happened to you?"

"Life happened to me. When it is kill or be killed, I will be the one left standing."

A familiar motto to them all. "Don't be so sure about that," she spat. "Now get out. I tire of your games."

He shrugged again and she took hold of the edge of the door and tried to slam it in his smug face. His laughter echoed as he walked away and the door was latched once again from the outside.

Leaning her head against the timbers, she prayed for strength, for peace, for quiet. She didn't pray for freedom. She was doomed.

Because they were headed in the direction of Scotland, she'd been so sure he was returning her to her father as he'd said, but now she wondered. The maniacal gleam in his eyes as he'd held her against the rail was like nothing she'd ever seen in the man she'd known. The years may have treated his appearance well enough but they'd also cracked his sanity.

A curse from behind her reminded her James had just fought to indeed protect her. He was looking through the foggy glass of the window. He rolled his head on his neck and moved from foot to foot.

"Thank you," she said, her hand on his shoulder in the hopes she could show him that she was indeed grateful. Who knew if Darius had actually planned to toss her into the ocean or not?

"What? No 'I can look after myself'?"

She stood beside him and lost herself in the whitecaps. "I wasn't prepared."

When he moved to stand at her back, his warmth permeating every inch of her chilled body, she leaned into him with a sigh.

"I won't let him hurt you, Daniella. Not while there is breath left in my body."

"I know that and I appreciate it. But you also have to think about Amelia and your mother. If we both die here, you'll never get to be the hero and save them."

"This was never about being a hero," he said, his low tone rumbling through her. "I just want them back. I have been so distracted with your presence and so single-minded in my intent, it has made me ignorant to other aspects. It made me blind to the flaws in the plan."

"How so?" she asked, turning to face him, her back against the cool glass.

"When I began to watch you as your coachman, I saw only a spoiled girl crying out for attention."

She swallowed. The gravity of his words, the conviction there, along with the meaning in his expression, all gave her goose bumps. "What do you see now?"

He put his hand against her jaw, his little finger caressing the skin below her ear. "I see *you*. All of you. The pirate, the privateer, the woman. You aren't as strong as you want the world to believe you are."

"Yes I am," she whispered, the fluttering in her stomach like the wings of a hundred gulls.

"Let me protect you, Daniella. Let me show you, you don't have to always be so strong." He raised his other hand to her cheek, the heat and kindness almost searing.

"You won't be my weakness," she said.

"Yet you are already mine."

Her eyes opened wide at his murmured admission but then he touched his lips to hers. Secretly she'd been hoping to kiss him again, to feel his body pressed to hers, to lose herself to him. To escape reality, if only for a little while.

His mouth was gentle to begin with as he traced the

seam of her lips until she was forced to open to him.

She had to remember to breathe when he deepened the kiss, his lips moving, his tongue roaming. He held her head still between his hands as he plundered and explored. Too soon he came up for air, his chest rising and falling with the exertion, the veins standing out on his arms as his muscles tensed from his wrists to shoulders. She ran her hands up and down those arms, feeling the springy hair beneath the pads of her fingers, revelling in the marble beneath the skin.

"Don't stop," she begged, uncaring of how it made her look.

"I can't do this to you, Daniella. I'm a mess."

"I don't care about that."

If he was serious about saying no to her, then he would have moved away; he wouldn't still stand with only a hairsbreadth between their bodies. From that now-familiar ticking in his jaw, she would say he only just retained control.

He placed his hands on her hips but to draw her near or push her away? "I won't be what slides you into ruin."

Taking a deep breath, she said, "I already told you my innocence is long gone. And London society assumes that because I spent my life with men, I spent my nights with them as well. Your piety doesn't belong here, James."

"One of us has to keep a level head." His grip on her hips tightened. She stepped a little closer. Or did he pull her?

"Why? We might both die tomorrow."

"You don't know what you're asking of me."

"I'm asking you to forget everything and everyone and

make love to me."

His breath hitched but still he fought. "You aren't just some woman to be tumbled, Daniella."

Finally she leaned right into him, her soft belly against his hard hips, her heavy, aching breasts against his wide, strong chest. "I want this." She snaked her arms around his neck, her fingers in his hair, and tugged gently until his shallow breath puffed hard against her lips. "Let us have this one night before we face tomorrow."

His control weakened and when she nipped his lower lip he ceased to move altogether. She pressed her lips to his but he didn't return the kiss.

"If we do this…" He pulled back but didn't put space between their bodies. "If we do this and we live beyond tomorrow, I want you to promise me something."

"Anything," she said, pressing her lips to his again.

His fingers drifted from her hips to her backside and before she could even moan with the intense pleasure such a touch evoked, he lifted her against him, his erection cradled between her thighs. He walked her back until her shoulders were flush to the wall and then ground his hardness into her. Sweat beads formed on his forehead as he placed it against hers. "I'll give you this." He finally kissed her, hard, fast, frenzied. "If you agree to become my wife."

Through the haze of passion, of anticipation and longing, Daniella heard the words but didn't believe them. "What?"

"If we are still alive tomorrow at nightfall, you will marry me."

"You can't trick me into saying I do—"

He cut her off with his mouth and kissed her again and a pulsing started deep within her body.

"No tricks," he said, placing soft, feathery kisses down her jaw, his whiskers scraping so erotically she thought she might combust on the spot. "You'll take my name and my protection and everyone will know you are mine."

Which way was up? He didn't stop kissing her, his hands kneading, his hips rolling. He worked her up and up and she craved release. She wanted him inside of her and be damned the consequences. Everything be damned.

"Yes," she groaned as he hitched her up higher and closed his mouth over her nipple through her shirt. Through two fine layers of lawn and cotton, his wet heat played havoc with her senses.

"Your word," he said, his voice muffled.

"You have—" She gasped when he used his teeth as well as his tongue. "You have my word. Tomorrow, if we still live…"

"We will get through this, Daniella." He slid her body back down the wall, gentleness and calm restoring the frenzy. "I'll make sure of it."

HIS SENSE OF honour howled to the wind but his conscience pricked. He smothered the edges of its knifepoint and kissed her again. His hands were everywhere all at once but he wanted her naked. There were too many barriers. He wanted to rip them all down one by one until it was just the two of them, skin to skin, vulnerable and open and raw. He would have her no other way.

He started with the ties of her shirt and loosened the strings.

"Wait," she said, her fingers squeezing until he had to stop.

"It's too late, Daniella."

She rolled her hips against his. "I have one condition."

Picking her up in his arms, he carried her to the bed and placed her on it, following her down until he hovered above her. "No conditions." He placed his lips to hers, kissed her, drank of her. "No more talking." Slowly, gently, without taking his eyes from hers, he slid his hand under the hem of her shirt, up her ribs, to cup her breast, his thumb firmly flicking her nipple until her back arched off the bed. "No more excuses."

Lowering himself down her body, he lifted her shirt and her chemise to her armpits and then over her head, baring her chest to his hungry gaze. He licked his lips. Then he licked her. First one side, and then the other, cupping her weight and kneading, learning the feel of her so if they did die he would go to hell with this memory seared into his very being. When he closed his mouth over a dusky peak, she threaded her hands into his hair and pulled him back up to her face, taking his mouth in a kiss so fierce it was a wonder he didn't explode right then and there.

Reaching down, he felt for the hem of her gown…but was frustrated by her tight breeches. "This is why ladies wear skirts," he said with a curse.

She laughed. "I didn't know that."

Rolling off her, he opened the fastening at her waist in hurried motions, his fingers tangling in the laces, trying not to once again rip the only clothing she had.

She tried to help, taking the laces and undoing them, but he was impatient now. He slid a hand beneath the fabric, his fingers finding soft hair and slick heat. She cried out when he found the nub between her wet folds. "Take your pants off, Daniella."

"I'm trying. You're distracting me."

He withdrew a fraction and stilled, half rolling onto his back. "I can stop?"

She clawed the breeches off, using her feet when the fabric caught on her ankles. He would have laughed but at the sight of her, all woman, all wanton, he bit his tongue and held back. His erection strained and his blood sang.

"As you were," she said, taking his hand and leading it back to her mound.

This time a chuckle escaped and he rolled back towards her as if pulled by an invisible string. "Perhaps I should be grateful you aren't an innocent."

"I hope I get the chance to say the same thing," she said, her own hand trailing down to the opening of his trousers.

In no time he was just as naked as she, the urgency building until there could be only one outcome. He didn't want to hurt her. When he slid one finger into her, she was so tight, so hot, so welcoming, but he was afraid the last thread of his control would snap the glorious second he entered her.

"Slow it down," he whispered as he slid his finger slowly

in and out, in and out, still learning, still memorizing and being mesmerized.

She panted and dragged him into a hard kiss, full of urgency and carnal desire. He ignored the pain in his nose and his face and thought of nothing but pleasure.

"Faster, James, I can't bear it for much longer."

He smiled against her lips. "It's going to hurt, my sweet. You're not ready yet."

Pushing with the heel of her hands hard against his chest, she rolled him to his back and straddled his hips. He grew harder in an instant. He hadn't known it was possible.

"Just how many times did you…ah…lose your innocence?" he asked with a laugh.

The feline grin she gave him made him laugh again but he stopped when she took his member in her hand and directed him towards her entrance. "There was one boy; his name was Jimmy," she breathed, her eyelids drifting closed as she slid down his length, her body greeting his as though they had done this many times before. When she was seated to the hilt she opened her eyes again. "He showed me a few things." She tilted her hips and clenched her inner muscles.

James held on tight to the control he thought he still had.

She bent to trail kisses down his neck, her hair heavy against his chest, her scent everywhere, like cherries and spices. She lifted a fraction at a time and then slid down again, the torturous friction agonizingly unhurried after the urgency of moments before. After about the fourth time, right after she nipped the flat plane of his nipple and ran her smooth hand over the other, that control snapped complete- ly and he flipped her onto her back. "I happen to also know a few tricks." His voice was coarse, husky, unrefined.

"Show me," she implored, her hands relaxing above her head.

He pulled her legs up so her knees were raised, her ankles at his sides, then covered her hands with just one of his own. Gripping her buttock to hold her still, he pushed inside her folds again, knowing now he couldn't hurt her. She was wet and ready and wanted it more than he did, if that was even possible.

As he withdrew, her eyes would open wide but when he slammed back into her with all the force of his desire, she closed them again, her head thrashing against the rough cotton sheet, sweet little noises of pleasure filling his ears. A wholly male satisfaction the likes he hadn't known in an age rocketed in his blood.

Her muscles tightened, her nails dug into his skin but still he held back. He wanted to watch her face as she fell into her pleasure. He wanted to hear her cry out before he lost himself in this moment.

Just when he thought her body couldn't handle any more, just when he thought she'd reached the highest peak she could find, he took her mouth in a kiss not meant to be punishing but harsh in their combined needs, forcing the breath from both of their bodies. He was relentless then, stoking her desires, pushing and pushing until her nails scored his skin, pushing even after he'd swallowed her ragged cries and her legs lost their tension. When he reached heights he'd never before experienced and thought he'd die from the lack of oxygen and rationale, he let go and buried his face in her hair as he emptied his seed deep in her womb.

"Extraordinary," he whispered, running his palms lightly down her ribs, his thumbs brushing the edges of her breasts and then lower still to her hips. He kissed her cheek, her jaw, her neck, her chin. He raised himself up on his elbows just in time to catch the look of intense satisfaction on her face, the silly grin on her lips.

It was the single most perfect moment of his life to date and if he did die tomorrow, he would meet his maker a very contented man.

CHAPTER TWENTY-SIX

D ARKNESS HAD FALLEN in the time they'd spent in each other's arms. Daniella couldn't string a coherent sentence together to save her life and that gave James a thrill he'd never before had.

All the time he'd spent with Marie during the campaign, never had he been this spent. Sure, he was younger and stupider then, full of fire for the battle and a naive desire to serve his country. But this was different. Daniella was different. He had more to lose now than he ever had before but he wouldn't have done anything differently. Well, perhaps he would have bedded the chit before now. They'd had so many opportunities and he had squandered them all in the guise of propriety and honour.

Moonlight reflected from the ocean created trembling shadows and darkened corners for past wrongs to hide away. Tonight wasn't a good time for ghosts and nightmares. James rolled from the bed and lit the lantern, dressing swiftly.

"What are you doing?" Daniella asked with a wide yawn.

"We have to get dressed. As much as I like you like this—" all smooth contours and erotic dips "—Darius will be back soon and he can't be aware of what went on here." Although it would further James's cause. Beneath that wily madman lay a gentleman. He recognized that and wondered what the pirate's story was.

"When did Darius come to your crew?"

Daniella shrugged, the sheet slipping from her body as she rose in search of her shirt. "I was about twelve when we took a ship coming from London. All the lords and ladies were ransomed but Darius wasn't one of them. Neither was his crew. I remember he was wearing servant's clothing: there was an insignia but I couldn't tell you now what it was. He didn't have family to be sold back to and once we sunk the ship, there wasn't a place for him to hide either. At first we assumed he was with a lord on the ship but he confessed he'd stowed away in search of a different life."

"That would account for his speech to an extent."

"What do you mean?" she asked, squatting down and looking under the table and then under the chair.

James swallowed and willed his libido to calm though he didn't stop watching her. "He speaks very well for a servant or even a pirate."

Daniella laughed and turned to him, gloriously naked and unashamed. James held the shirt out to her on two fingers. When she got close, she ignored it and put her arms around his neck, breasts pressed to his chest, squeezing until his head dipped towards hers. "Not all pirates are uncouth or uneducated." She nipped his bottom lip and then snatched the shirt from his grip with more laughter. "My father teaches everyone to read who desires the benefit. Having them learn numbers is an advantage also."

She teased him. He let her. She mocked him to show she had the upper hand even in conversation and he let her. He liked the banter. No London lady would ever tease him so. "Still you don't actually know where he came from at all, do you?"

As she slipped her arms into the sleeves, her movements graceful and sure, James couldn't take his gaze from her. He wanted to kiss her again and again but the soft skin around her mouth was already grazed from the roughness of his facial hair and would only get worse if he were to keep nuzzling her. He almost missed her reply so fascinated was he.

"They all had lives before they came on board. We don't ask questions."

"How do you know which of them you can trust?"

She sat on the edge of the rumpled bed and pulled her breeches over her toes and up her legs. "It's evident soon enough who *wants* to be there, who *needs* to be there and who *shouldn't* be there. My father has a gift for judging a man's character."

"Does he often get it wrong?"

Daniella stopped midway through lacing her breeches and shot him an accusing glare. "No, not very often, but like any man, he isn't perfect." It looked as if there was more she would say on the subject but then she closed her mouth and resumed dressing.

The more he talked to Daniella about her father and the ship and her crew, the more intrigued he became. He'd belonged to an extended family when he was in the army. The sense of camaraderie and brotherhood was most of the reason he'd stayed in for as long as he had. If his brother hadn't cracked and killed himself and their father, he would have stayed. He probably would have died out there in the mud somewhere but he would have died doing something he loved and thought a worthy cause. Who the hell did Bonaparte think he was anyway? As bad as bloody pirates in his book.

But maybe Captain Germaine wasn't as bad as James had believed. He had to hope the man had more than a shred of common human decency for Amelia's sake. If they lived through to the end of all of this, he was going to teach her to defend herself against a man. He might call upon Daniella to do the teaching. Since they were going to be married.

When the time came, she was going to try to weasel out of it. He knew what she thought of marriage and men and belonging to either the institution of matrimony or the flesh and blood aspect of it. Why had she agreed at all? In the heat of the moment? Perhaps she'd finally come to accept that her father was unlikely to let her back aboard *The Aurora*, reputation or no. He didn't mind being her second choice. Not if it meant having her in his arms for the rest of their lives, making love to her wherever and whenever he desired.

There was only one thing he knew for certain. Come hell or high water he would marry her and save her once and for all from herself, from her father, from Darius. She was his partner in every way. If he didn't hold on to her, the rest of his life would be miserable indeed.

Damn, he grew morose when he was tired, and tired he was now. The injury to the back of his head still throbbed, and his muscles stretched with strain from climbing the rigging and then the effort not to hurt Daniella. Seems he needn't worry at all on that score. His smile grew into a grin and when she caught it directed at her, she blushed and turned away, her head down.

"You can't look at me like that," she said, doing her best to smooth her wild curls over her shoulders.

"Like what?" His feigned innocence was tragic. He would have never made a good actor. She started when he draped his coat over her shoulders. He leaned in close. "You better cover it all up just in case I've a mind to take everything off you again."

His spirits were somewhat dampened when the door opened a while later to reveal Darius with another tray of food. He whistled a tune but didn't call a greeting. At least he wasn't neglecting them. But James didn't want him there.

He stepped forwards to take the tray from the blackguard's hands before he came too far into the room. He gave him a little nudge back in the direction of the corridor. "I think we can manage from here."

Darius looked at them a little too shrewdly and smiled, oddly very civil. "I do believe you can," he said, and with a little salute, he backed out and left, still whistling that God-awful tune.

As they sat down to eat, Daniella still smiling and James itching to take her back to bed, he damned plots and scheming to hell and wished for the day when they could leave it all behind them.

MORNING ARRIVED FAR too soon and Daniella found her nerves stretched tighter than the dark sails leading them to their destiny. She fretted over what her father would say. She worried about James and his family and how being married to him would change her life. She hadn't said yes under false pretences but she would not give up the sea. If he wanted her for his bride, there were negotiations to be had.

For months she'd thought of nothing else other than what it would be like to be forced into a union with a tyrant of a man such as any one of Anthony's "friends." Lately she had begun to wonder what it would be like to be joined instead to a man who wouldn't demand complete control over her every whim and fancy. Yes, James infuriated her, sometimes she even wanted to kill him, but at the heart of everything he did was his instinct to protect those he loved. Of course James didn't speak out of love or any such similar nonsense. She was just another female to protect—though the previous night had also made it clear he desired her. She was glad of that.

Yawning in the cold light of day, she hugged herself and stared at the ocean—and land, beginning to come into view through the lifting fog. It would be a cold day, not that it mattered whatever the weather. Nothing would change their course now.

Darius had already announced they were to dock and then take a carriage the rest of the way. He was taking them to Kirkcudbright. Her father should have received word about the debacle and be waiting for them. Now all they could do was follow.

James came to stand behind her and draped his coat over her back and arms; the heat from his body enveloped her and calmed her somewhat.

"Do you think it worth attempting escape once we are on land?" he asked. They—she, Hobson, Patrick and James—had been talking over their options since the other two men were brought to their cabin in the early morning.

Daniella and James were dressed in their days-old cloth-ing, waiting, the atmosphere sombre, moods ranging from fury to resignation. They'd made love all through the night, neither wanting much sleep if they were soon to be killed anyway. She knew his touch, his taste, and his desires. She'd behaved shamelessly, even begging for his mouth and hands on her body and then returning the favour with a willingness that stunned him. Long gone was the time for hiding or acting coy. She was free with James to be the woman she wanted to be. He didn't make her feel shame in the darkness. He worshipped her body again and again and again. Never had she felt this kind of power.

It was intoxicating.

And temporary.

Anything could happen yet. A stray bullet in a fight. The navy appearing out of nowhere and blowing them all to smithereens. This was a part of the planning no one could predict.

"I don't think we should try to escape," she sighed and

leaned back into him, uncaring that Hobson and Patrick saw. What did it matter anymore?

"Why not, lass?" Hobson demanded with a thump of his hand on the table. "Have you both gone soft? Or has being cooped up addled yer brains?"

James surprised them all with a chuckle. "Never had I thought you would ever accuse me of going soft, Lieutenant."

Hobson spluttered for a moment and then sat back in his chair. "So you do have a plan then?"

Daniella shook her head. "The only plan is to let Darius take us to the meeting point. Once we are in the township, he won't be able to kill any of us without causing trouble for himself."

This time it was Patrick who revolted. "I don't think he's going to kill us but to just go meekly to whatever fate does await?"

"Patrick, you didn't see Darius almost throw me overboard yesterday. We don't know what he's capable of. Hopefully I will be sold back to my father and you will all be sold back to James's family. I will make sure his mother and sister are returned to him if they are still aboard *The Aurora*. Then you five will be free to do as you please. We do not want to goad him into further action."

"You are forgetting one pertinent little fact, my dear," James reminded her.

"I haven't forgotten," she replied, a small smile curving her lips.

"Hmm," he murmured his discontent, the rumble vibrating through her body.

"Well, I fer one don't like it," Hobson stated loudly. "Why should we give up now and hand over the control? We should try to escape and negotiate the hostage swap the same as we were going to originally."

"No," James told him. "It's too risky. Just like that day on the boat, when we should have let ourselves be ransomed. Instead we fought and men lost their lives. And their legs," he added. "I'll not take any further risk for the sake of control."

Daniella muffled a giggle with a cough.

"What?" James asked, his arms tightening as he leaned over to intimately place his chin in the curve where her neck met her body. A curve he now knew well.

"If you'd have asked me at the beginning of this week if the Butcher could willingly hand over control, I would have laughed and said not a chance. Look at you now, all grown up into a man."

"Minx. At the beginning of the week I thought I knew what the stakes were, what we were all playing for, but circumstances have altered. Adapting to a changing battle is a required skill for a good major in His Majesty's Army. I should take offence that you'll go with the plans of a pirate but fought so hard against mine from the beginning."

Patrick cleared his throat. "I don't know how you can all be so calm. Who will pay my ransom? My clan know nothing about any of this."

James let go of her, the cold and distance instantaneous, and went to sit at the table with the men. "I'll take care of the ransom. If we survive it all, you'll be free to return to your family with no debt."

He scoffed. "No debt? I'm not a man accepting of the charity of others. I'll pay you back the money somehow. I'll not owe the Butcher."

"Enough of this Butcher nonsense," he said to them all. "I've never cared for the moniker and find I would like to be rid of it once and for all."

She wanted to tell him it made him who he was. He was a warrior and a fighter and any man who met him knew that. It was a time in his life he would never forget or forgive. It was something in him that she loved.

She pulled up short on that single, ridiculous thought. No. She admired him but there was no love there. Nothing worth abandoning her plans for, certainly. There could be no marriage. It was lust. Pure and simple. And lust was no foundation for a life together—especially when that life would undoubtedly trap her in London, inland, under grey skies, away from the sea.

"Patrick." She turned from the window and addressed him, pushing away all traitorous thoughts. "There will be time enough to sort through it all later. First, we have to get free of Darius and find my father. It's the only way we can put all this business to rest."

"I agree," James said, inclining his head. "We need to take this day one small step at a time. I want Darius to believe we have accepted his plans."

"We bloody well have." Hobson was not at all happy but she doubted he would gainsay James. He hadn't yet.

"We are unarmed and outnumbered. If we fight, we die." When James looked to her, a thrill shot through her body, leaving wild energy in its wake. Definitely lust. But his next words warmed her in a way she hadn't thought possible and had nothing to do with wanting to see him naked again. "I for one have something to live for beyond this day and if it only costs me my pride, then so be it." *No.* She pushed the warmth away, but smiled as naturally as she could.

"Ugh," Hobson groaned and put his head on the table. "You are addled."

James and Daniella laughed and when Darius finally entered the room, he wore a look of complete confusion. "You're all in unusually high spirits."

Daniella didn't miss a beat. "I'm hoping my father takes to you with his walking stick before the day is through."

Darius frowned. Daniella laughed harder.

Behind him, one of his minions held in his arms what looked like heavy gowns under his triumphant grin and thick neck. Daniella swallowed and James stepped in front of her.

"Don't fret," Darius said, waving him to stand down. "I merely thought Daniella might like to make herself a bit more presentable when meeting her father after so long estranged."

Daniella snorted. "My father has seen me in breeches before."

"Yes, he has, but the good people of Kirkcudbright have not. I don't think it the best idea to attract more attention, do you?"

She could see his logic but she didn't have to agree with

him. "Very well. You may put them on the chair."

Darius stepped back and let his man dump the dresses. He then executed a bow worthy of a courtier at the feet of his queen. "You have ten minutes."

She didn't want to fall in with Darius's plans but even here, in the sun-warmed cabin, a chill permeated. She would be better served in warmer clothing and she couldn't very well wear James's coat all day.

"Turn around," James told Patrick and Hobson. "If either of you so much as peek, you'll have me to answer to."

Neither man put up an argument as Daniella chose a gown of the darkest blue, which she guessed might fit her. There were no undergarments though she did find a matching pelisse. "You can turn around too," she told James.

"With only minutes to get this done, you are going to need help." He raised a brow, challenging her to contradict him, but any words were futile. As she huffed and shrugged out of his coat and handed it back to him, she poked out her tongue as a protest.

He didn't laugh. His gaze darkened and dropped to her mouth and then lower still as she began to loosen the shirt's laces. As nimbly as she was able, she shed the wrecked and stained shirt and slipped the gown over her head, the weight of the velvet sending the fabric cascading over her body to her toes. If she'd only been able to wash in more than a shallow basin she might be quite comfortable.

James came behind her and began doing up the little buttons, quickly, deftly, smugly. When he was finished, he came so close his breath fanned her ear, sending desire shooting to all the places he'd touched and then some. "Remember what I said about skirts and how you would have no chance had you been wearing one?"

Her heart skipped at least three beats. She nodded.

"Leave your breeches on."

When she turned in the enclosed space, he wore an expression of both raw desire and tension. She wanted to defy him and would have if it had been just the two of them in the cabin for the rest of the week.

When she would have answered, his attention was ensnared by the cut of the décolletage. "Scandalous," he breathed, his hands coming to rest on her ribs, his thumbs tantalizingly close to rising over her breasts.

"It seems to have taken place over my middle name." She laughed, knowing the action of breathing deep would push her further to spilling out. She ran one finger over the edge of the dress's neckline. "Should I find another?" He might never be her husband but by God she was happy he was her lover, however briefly.

He shook his head, his Adam's apple bobbing hard beneath his beard. He closed his eyes for a moment and then, when he opened them, he reached for the pelisse and helped her put it on, buttoning it all the way to her neck. "Much better."

At the bottom of the pile of clothes were a pair of slippers suited only for a ballroom but she put them on anyway. Better than having bare feet.

Within moments, Darius was back. "Come," he said, gesturing towards the door. "I want you all where I can see you while we dock."

"Not worried I'll learn where you put in and come back for you?" Daniella taunted quietly.

"Not at all," he returned in the same sure tone, taking in her attire and smiling.

Arrogant son of a bitch. She hoped justice caught up with Darius and humiliated him—and that she'd be there to see it. The man had far too much self-worth.

"Before we leave the ship, I have a request." James approached her, taking her hands in his.

"What is it?" she asked, her heart in her throat. She'd not seen that look in his eyes before.

He kissed first one knuckle and then the other. "I want you to marry me now, here, on the ship."

No! "But… What about… We haven't properly discussed any of this. Where will we live? How many months of the year and how many sons? We haven't discussed any of it."

"Daniella, I won't die an honourless man. If your father or Darius here ends my life, you'll be wealthy enough to damn everyone to hell, buy your own ship and sail it wherever you please. What does it matter the details or a few hours? You promised me and I'm worried you will find a way to back out when the smoke clears. I need to do this."

Staring into the fathomless depths of his eyes amidst the bruising, seeing the sincerity there, how could she possibly deny him? But. "If this is indeed about honour, I already know you have it. We all know you have it otherwise we wouldn't be standing here right now. I don't want you to do this because you have to."

"I don't have to. I want to. I want you to be my wife, Daniella. I need to make sure you will be all right and not sent back to England to be married to one of your brother's cronies if it all goes wrong."

"I don't need you to take care of me." It was easy for him to relinquish control of one situation but he was asking her to do it for a lifetime.

Darius hit the door with his fist, gaining her attention. "Dammit, woman, marry the man. You might be the only barrier between your father's sword and your lover's heart."

Even though she had nothing to be embarrassed about, her cheeks still warmed at the crude assessment of their relationship. Then the thought came to her. What was marriage anyway? They were in Scottish waters and could be married by a child but at the end of the day it was words spoken. They weren't in a church. They didn't stand before their friends and family and God. Their marriage could be whatever they made it without the church dictating the definition of wife. "All right."

James sucked in a breath. "All right?" he asked, scepticism all over his face.

"I'll marry you and take your money if you die."

He regarded her for a few moments and then his lips lifted and he drew her into his embrace, kissing her hard and fast. When he was done putting on his show, he pulled back. "That doesn't mean you can be the one to kill me."

Daniella laughed. She hadn't even thought of it. This time. "I give you my word."

Darius stepped up and put his hand over theirs. "I proclaim you man and wife before witnesses and God."

James looked up. "That's it?"

Darius nodded. "You don't even need that much ceremony but I wanted to be the one to make it official." He looked to Daniella. "Make sure, when your father asks who was fool enough to join the two of you in marriage, to tell him it was me."

He was getting some kind of sick satisfaction out of it. God only knew why. There was no time to ponder the question further as they were taken above deck and told to sit. They were then bound together with one length of rope so if any one man thought to jump overboard, they would all go. Then they would all drown.

That would be a great start to married life. *Married.* She was someone's wife. She was James's wife. A giddy lightness dissolved the stone in her stomach and she smiled.

CHAPTER TWENTY-SEVEN

IT WAS A three-hour carriage ride from where Darius docked his boat but James had no chance in that time to speak to Daniella at all. No one talked. It was as though they all held their breaths, waiting for the next step in the dance to reveal itself. He wished it would damn well hurry up. He'd told Patrick and Hobson he was happy to hand over control, and he was, but he didn't have to like the waiting. Or the silence.

"So, Darius, have you made contact with Germaine?" James asked, finally having had enough.

The other man nodded. "I have, though not on this run."

"How did he seem to you?" Daniella interjected.

"Old, even then," Darius admitted in a wistful tone. "And I think the good captain has taken a few knocks more recently."

"What do you mean?" she asked, leaning forwards on her seat a little, concern darkening her eyes and her gaze.

"Heard tell that a few months back a great storm swept through this region and wiped out most everything in its path. The captain's home onshore was destroyed, and *The*

Aurora herself so badly damaged he could only limp back here to Kirkcudbright. My spies tell me he met a lady and plans to marry."

Daniella gaped at him. So many changes. Would she even recognize her father?

Darius shrugged. "I only hear the stories. I do not get to judge the validity or accuracy of the news."

James's stomach dipped out, leaving him with an empty hollowness. If Germaine had met a lady in Kirkcudbright and lived there now, where were Amelia and his mother? "But you have spoken to him? In person?"

Darius shook his head and grinned. "Not in years."

James had to draw a deep breath and count to five before he asked his next question. "So what will you do with us if he isn't there? I take it you have some sort of plan?"

"I don't need much of a plan. He is there."

"What?" This from Daniella. James squeezed her hand where it lay in his.

"Plan?" He gestured for the pirate to elaborate.

"I deliver Daniella and the man who abducted her and I have repaid a debt."

"I don't understand," Daniella muttered more to herself than to Darius. Her eyes narrowed. "You were of a mind to throw me overboard."

Darius's grin grew wider. "A ploy. A spot of mischief if you will."

"Explain," Daniella demanded, fists clenched in her lap.

"The last time I was with your father in Kirkcudbright, I asked him could I ever restore my honour in his eyes. His simple answer was a yes. Rescuing you—in more than one way, I feel obliged to add—is repayment of my debt for the mutiny."

Daniella cursed beneath her breath.

Before James could scold her on the language, Darius tsked. "Lady Lasterton would not mutter obscenities."

James understood two things in that moment. Darius was no lowly servant pressed to service on a pirate ship. He had been a gentleman once upon a time and knew the only outcome for an unmarried, unchaperoned scandalous hoyden. James should have heard it the first time he spoke. The second was clearer but no more comprehensible than the first. "You forced me to rescue her from you so I would have her gratitude."

"It worked splendidly."

"So this has all been?" He waited for a suitable answer. He waited for an excuse not to plant his fist into Darius's lying face.

"Meddling," he said, still grinning. Darius then addressed Daniella, who was as tight as a cobra about to strike with her own particular brand of poison. "I really did think I was saving you that day on the road. But then it became clear there was another game at play. A game bigger than any of us."

"You consider yourself Cupid?" James asked with disbelief.

"She needed a push in your direction. When she started asking if she could sail on my ship, I knew I had to do something to nudge her on another course. I will not have a woman on my ship indefinitely. My men would eat her alive."

Daniella shrieked and lunged for Darius in the small space. Patrick, who sat next to the gentleman cum pirate, had to duck out of the way.

"You scared the hell out of me!" she yelled as she tried to hurt him.

James pulled her onto his lap, his arms around her so she couldn't move. "What my wife is trying to—"

"You're a bastard, Darius," Daniella said.

James put his hand over her mouth to stop her next attempt at flaying. "I'm not sure your story is entirely credible." Darius's gaze never wavered so James went on. "You expect us to believe you got involved though you had no way to assess the risk? I could have shot you dead on your horse that day."

"At quite a miserable stage of my life, Daniella and her father saved me and I repaid them by trying to take their ship. I owed it to the captain to bring her back safe—with her reputation intact."

A sudden sharp pain on the palm of James's hand made him growl. "Did you really just bite me?" he asked his bride as she struggled against his grip.

"Was any of it true?" she asked. "Did you suffer torture at the hands of an evil man?"

"No." Damn his insufferable smugness. "I was pulled from the water by a merchant ship a few hours later and delivered to the Americas. There I stayed and worked until I fell in with the good graces of a shipbuilder. The ship I sail now is one of his."

"You're nothing but a hopeless romantic," James said incredulously at the same time Hobson muttered, "Addled, the lot of ya."

"I saved both your hides today. Daniella, your father might now hear you out before he cleaves your husband in half. Lasterton, you have the chance to decide if your precious items are as precious as your new wife. I have cleared the muddy waters. You can thank me later."

DANIELLA COULDN'T BREATHE. Her chest grew tight and her stomach threatened to rebel as her heart clamoured in her ears to the tune of her rushing blood. It was one thing to have entered a makeshift marriage to get herself home and assuage James's infernal honour; it was a different matter when none of it needed to have happened at all. "You tricked me."

"You were enamoured of him anyway. I merely expedited proceedings."

"Expedited proceedings?" she repeated, fury giving way to a shocking numbness.

James twisted her on his lap to gain her attention. "Pay him no mind. What's happened has happened and we'll deal with it after we meet with your father."

"This all worked out very well for you, my lord." At the correct salutation, he frowned. She went on. "Now you get to save my reputation and your precious items, forever the hero."

"Daniella." His voice held warning but she ignored it.

"Is this how your grand plan was to have worked out all along?"

"It bloody well is not."

Hobson spoke up then but they weren't words she wanted or needed to hear. "The major wanted nothing to do with forcing you to marriage, lass. Nothing to do with it at all."

James cleared his throat. "That's enough, Lieutenant. You're not helping."

"Now I have nothing." Not her freedom. Not her ship. Not even her independence. Once again the men around her held all the power while she was thrown back in a cage.

"You have me," James told her quietly.

Her answering nod was slow to come but her heart was no longer in it. For months she had dreamed of having her own life and making her own decisions. She had thought this Scottish marriage as easy to walk away from as her London life, but James obviously had very different ideas.

If she couldn't make this right, all she had left was a bottomless crevasse of nothing and a bleak future without choices. Should she have stayed in London, married an old man and waited for him to stick his spoon in the wall so she could sail off with his money? James certainly was not going to turn up his toes anytime soon.

And what of James? How long would it be until he resented her for all of this? He'd told her he needed a wife as pure as snow. If he took her back to London as his bride what would happen to his reputation? And to Amelia's, if it survived her time on *The Aurora*?

Her dark musings took them all the way into town, where Darius's coachman pulled into an inn yard and brought the horses to a stop.

"This is where our time together ends, I'm afraid." Darius still wore that smug look of triumph and, before anyone could stop her, she launched herself at him again, this time connecting her fist with his nose. She might not be very big or as strong as James, but she knew how to hit a man to make it hurt. He yowled with pain and doubled over, blood dripping through his fingers to fall on his boots.

"If you ever come near me or *The Aurora*, I will not ask questions. I will not invite you aboard for a drink or to discuss the weather. I will shoot you where you stand and then dance on your grave under the moonlight, you arrogant ass."

"Well said, my dear," James added and then switched his attention back to Darius. "You're lucky she got you first. I can't hit a man already bleeding but we'd better not see you again in the near future or the ball that finds your chest may not be my wife's."

Darius raised one hand in a gesture of compliance, the other still on his nose, and then opened the carriage door. "Give my regards to the captain."

Daniella curled her fingers back into fists but James was already pushing her out the door ahead of him. "Just go, Daniella. He's not worth any more of your pique."

"Bullshit," she muttered. "I should have kicked him in the—"

"Daniella," he scolded as he fought laughter. "You're a

proper lady now. You can't say things like that."

She stopped in her tracks causing Patrick to linger in the doorway of the carriage. "Don't think because he made us marry that you own me or can give me orders. If I want to say words like bullshit and talk about bodily harm, I will."

His nostrils flared and she felt a spark of the fight ignite back to life inside of her. Damn him, she would fight this. She would fight him.

All traces of humour fled and he took her by the elbow to propel her farther towards the shelter of the inn. "You are my wife now and don't think you can force me to throw you out using lewd behaviour. I'll lock you in a room before I let you shame yourself again."

"You could try it," she said, wrenching her arm from his firm grip. Even now as they argued, his touch ignited more than a fight and heat pooled in her belly. Shame, not over her external reactions but over her unwanted internal reactions, washed through her to burn her cheeks. "I'll do whatever I must to be free."

"I don't doubt that." His reply was heavily laced but was that sadness weighting his tone? "But I will do whatever *I* must to keep you safe." He came closer and cupped her face in his hands so she almost drowned in his nearness.

Under the inn's wide veranda, he kissed her. Long and slow and delicious. Once again thought fled and she responded in a way no decent lady ever would. Until Hobson cleared his throat behind James, who reluctantly broke contact. Or was it her reluctance that was most keenly obvious between them?

"We should probably get inside before we attract too much attention," Hobson suggested, always level-headed.

Daniella licked lips that tasted of him and blinked a few times to clear the haze from her vision. How did he always manage to both take her wits away and make her want to hurl fire all at the same time?

CHAPTER TWENTY-EIGHT

FOR THE FIRST time in more than a decade James felt whole.

He'd have given his life for his country, but as he stared into moss-green eyes swimming with moisture, he was glad he hadn't. When she licked her lips and had to consciously regain her wits, the beast inside him roared. This was purpose. This was a cause worthy of his last breath. And if it came down to it, she could have it. She could have anything she wanted if it would only erase the sadness from her gaze.

For three of the longest hours in his entire life James had been forced to sit next to a very despondent Daniella. He couldn't comfort her or talk to her or tease her out of it in the confined carriage in front of three other men. It had nearly killed him. For a moment he'd even willed back the battlefield numbness. He'd wanted to tell her he hadn't tricked her—that he hadn't taken her freedom. He would repeat it over and over until she believed him.

"I will get us a room and then we must talk. Agreed?" He waited for what felt like eons but then she nodded and turned away. Lead fell to the pit of his stomach and he almost tasted defeat. Almost.

"Hobson, try and follow the carriage and see if Darius makes contact with Germaine. I want to know where he is before he learns of our presence. If you do find him, set up a meeting for tomorrow, one o'clock in a town square or marketplace. Somewhere public."

As he spoke, he watched for any reaction from Daniella but she had already disappeared into the main entrance of the inn. Her spine may have straightened slightly but he couldn't be sure.

Convincing the innkeeper they weren't vagabonds took some effort and in the end James had to hand over his heavy signet ring to secure their lodgings and meals. "I will be coming back for that," James assured him with just the right amount of menace. "If you fence it, you'd better be a crack shot on the fields."

The man swallowed but nodded before setting his wife to the task of taking them upstairs. He and Daniella had a room at the top of the long, steep stair, Patrick and Hobson right next door.

"The lady might like a bath sent up," he said to the mistress of the house.

She shook her head. "Not up those steps, milord. There's a bathing house out back with hot water on the flame all day and night and a tub big enough to swim in if you've a mind to it."

"That will be more than adequate, thank you," Daniella said, before squeezing the lady's hands in hers and thanking her for a fine room.

James had seen much better but at least it was clean and

warm. He eyed the bed and longed to lie down and close his eyes for a few hours. But there were things to do that could not wait. Seeing to Daniella's comfort topped the list.

"Would you like to rest first or bathe?" He wanted to say so much more but he couldn't seem to find the words or the strength. Her despondence should have fired him into action but he found it contagious.

"You needn't mollycoddle me," she said, turning her back to peer through the window. Did she search for her father or a way to be rid of her husband?

"Let me be the gentleman, please. As much as you mightn't wish it, I care for you and for your comfort."

Her head dropped slightly and he thought he heard a betraying sniff but then her back stiffened and she spoke. "Bathe first and then rest. Hopefully Hobson will find my father and we can resolve our situation. I should like to at least be clean before then."

Resolve our situation. Why did she make it sound so final and so impersonal?

He'd found his other half. She would never bore him nor he her. Life would be a constant challenge of wills but he looked forward to it. He looked forward to a lifetime with her.

"What is it?" she asked.

He must have worn his need as a mantle and she'd glimpsed it. He shook his head. No good would come of blackmailing her with his desire. It would be best if she chose him of her own accord. "Nothing. Come, let's get cleaned up. We can talk over supper."

DANIELLA DIDN'T WANT to do anything with James. She wanted to be left alone to wallow in misery. To contemplate her undoing and scheme a way out. She may not have had easy or clear choices in London but she did here. Her father was near and he would protect her. Right after he horse-whipped her for her actions to date.

She groaned.

"Did you say something?" James stopped on the stair. He was a stranger to her. No longer did he place his hand in the small of her back to guide her. He walked ahead. He didn't look at her as though she were his next meal. He barely looked at her at all. She supposed it was better that way. When the time came to say their goodbyes, it would be easier. If she was still there to say a goodbye.

The cleanest way to cut ties would be to simply disappear. James had left plenty of opportunities for escape open but she had needed to stay with him then.

As soon as she learned her father's whereabouts, she would climb out the window and be gone. It was the only way. They could forget being married, she was sure their witnesses weren't about to admit anything anyway, and each go their own ways. She would set Amelia and her mother free and send them back to him before he even knew she was gone. He would get what he wanted and be done with her. Then she would cut the ropes anchoring *The Aurora* and set a course for China, or the Americas. She would find the exact opposite side of the world from England and make it her home. She would exchange her Jolly Roger for a merchant letter and travel distant coastlines plying legitimate cargo.

It was a heady dream but she didn't feel it in her heart or her head. She was exhausted to the point where her head hurt and it was an effort to put one foot in front of the other. Her one constant, unhelpful thought now was that she didn't want to be alone.

She followed James to a sturdy wooden structure behind the inn on the edge of a dense forest. Daniella would have said it looked more like a hunter's cabin but the inside was mostly occupied by an enormous tub. She didn't have the strength to study how it all worked and since it was already full of steaming water, she didn't care much either.

"I'll be fine now," she said to James as he was closing the door and barring it. "You don't have to stay with me."

"I have no other pressing engagements right now." He grinned and she tried to grin back with a matching nonchalance. Hot moisture burned her eyelids but she willed it away. Here was neither the time nor the place to shed tears.

"I won't escape."

"I know. You gave me your word and I trust you."

That caught her attention. "You do?"

"Of course I do. Would I have tied myself to you otherwise?"

"I'm not really sure of anything anymore."

"You're not sure of me?"

When she didn't answer straight away, he gestured for her to turn so he could work on the buttons of her gown.

"We have a connection, you and I." His fingers worked

but he was in no hurry as he lowered his voice and spoke only to her and not at her. "Since the moment I kidnapped you we have been on this path together. It may have felt as though we were at odds but we always wanted the same things. Freedom and family."

"And now we've both lost our freedom."

"I don't see it that way. I'm hurt that you do."

When the gown sagged, she turned back to face him. His eyes were so full of regret she nearly took back her words. "How did you think it was ever going to work?"

"Why did you say the words if you were never fully committed?"

Wrenching her gaze from his, she paced to the tub and lost herself in her reflection on the surface. Her hair was a mess, her face dirty and her appearance more that of a beggar woman than a lady. "I suppose I got carried away. You made it all sound so easy."

"What changed then? Darius? What he said about pushing us together?"

When she didn't reply he came to stand at her back and she longed to melt into him. Just this last time to share something beautiful before he too realized their folly and walked away.

"Nothing has changed for me since this morning, Daniella."

Everything had changed for her. Before this week she'd discarded notions of love in favour of sailing the seas. She'd never considered herself wife material and therefore never considered having a husband. When no offers for her hand reached her brother, she'd steeled her resolve to be independent. To lean on her crew and her family rather than chase fantasies and emotion.

The promise she'd made to be his wife hadn't precisely been forced from her mouth but the proximity of his body and his own promise of pleasure urged her to make concessions. Thinking back, she'd had a condition of her own but when he kissed her all rational thought fled her mind.

Her only truly happy moments from the past days had been in his arms. Nothing else could touch her while he was—not even the prospect of a life on her beloved ship. It was the part she would miss the most when they separated.

She didn't want to think or speak anymore. Sliding the gown down her arms, she stepped from the fabric. Without breaking eye contact, she loosened the ties of her breeches and pushed them all the way down and off her feet.

His intake of breath was his only movement. It was almost as though he dared not move lest the moment slip away.

"Say something," she urged him. His stillness was a worry.

"You're beautiful."

A reluctant smile tilted her lips. "I'm a mess."

"A beautiful mess." He stepped towards her. She didn't stop him.

Their lips met but this time there was no rush, no urgency or frenzied coupling. Daniella pressed her body to his and with a groan he wrapped his arms around her back and held her close.

As she'd desperately hoped it would, the world around her ceased to exist. It was just her and James and the exquisite pull he managed to provoke with a mere kiss. Though this was no mere kiss. Right down to her toes she felt his passion, his promise, his heart and soul. If only they were enough.

When his fingers skated up her hips beneath the chemise, she shivered. That fluttering feeling once again took over her insides and when she breathed deep, she inhaled his masculine scent mingled with the smell of fresh water and cut wood.

"Touch me," she whispered as he feathered kisses over her jaw and down her neck.

"Not yet, love." When he pulled back, he gripped her hem and raised it over her head, leaving her completely naked and thoroughly dishevelled. "You'll catch your death."

"I'm not cold at all."

His gaze dropped to her pebbled nipples and Daniella finally found the strength to smile in earnest. There was that hungry look. He'd admitted once that she was his weakness. Perhaps now was the time to take advantage?

"I'll just check the temperature is right."

He gulped. She smiled again and gave him her back. Bending at the waist, she dipped a hand in the heavenly water, swishing it back and forth. When next she looked over her shoulder, he was almost undressed, only his boots and breeches in his way, his jerky movements frantic.

With a giggle at odds with her earlier melancholy—how did he *do* that?—she climbed into the water and sank back against the tub, the water up to her shoulders. She sank farther, getting her whole bedraggled head under the surface. If there was a heaven waiting for her, this was it. James loomed over the side of the tub and she sat back up to look at him.

"Move forwards, love." He used the endearment now as though he might actually mean it.

She did his bidding and he slid behind her, water sloshing over the edges in every direction.

"You're going to make a mess."

"Do you care?" he asked.

She shook her head and leaned back, guiding his arms around her.

At first his embrace was calming and safe but as he traced lazy circles on the skin over her ribs, closer and closer to her breasts, she felt less calm and a lot more of the pull.

She longed to arch her back so his hands would end up where she needed them the most. She was free to be her wanton self with him. The previous night had shown her he enjoyed it when she took charge, when she told him exactly how she wanted him to touch her, what she loved and what she didn't.

Sliding her palms over the backs of his hands and threading her fingers through his, she pulled one hand up and sent one lower. He caught on quickly, placing open-mouthed, hot kisses against her shoulder while cupping her breast. He flicked her nipple with his thumb and then rolled the nub. This time she did arch and then brought herself completely flush with his abdomen and chest, his hardness nestled against her bottom while his fingers played havoc with her sex and her senses. She gave a wriggle. He cursed. His other hand dropped beneath the water and before she had time to wonder at his next move, he entered her with one long, strong finger. With the others, he found her centre in her folds and rubbed gently up and down. She cried out when he added another finger and sped up the motion. Water sloshed and Daniella stifled her wild sounds with two hands over her mouth.

She needed more. She needed him to fill her until she felt whole, until she couldn't take anymore. She reached for him beneath the water; he chuckled when her hand wrapped around his length.

"Slow down, Daniella. We have all the time in the world."

"I don't want slow. I want you now, inside me."

He lifted her slightly with both hands under her backside. "Turn around. I need to see you."

She was willing to do anything he wanted when they were like this. It scared her.

Daniella maneuvered herself so she was staring into the bottomless depths of his gaze, a lazy smile on his mouth beneath his beard. He lifted his knees and settled her back against them then he leaned forwards and took one nipple into his mouth while he cradled the other, running his fingernail over one peak while grazing with his teeth on its twin.

She rolled her hips and he had to stop what he was doing as he closed his eyes with a long, low moan.

With two hands she pushed back on his chest and repositioned herself over his manhood. This time he didn't stop her, just kept his eyes closed as he filled her.

"You'll be the death of me."

"I'll be needing you for a few minutes yet." She cut off his reply and his surprise at her teasing when she placed her lips against his. His beard rasped, once again heightening her senses. She delved her tongue into his mouth, drank of him as though he was the elixir of life.

When her pace became too slow, he gripped her hips, held her up and plunged into her over and over, the pleasure building until her nails bit into his shoulders. With one final, deeper than expected penetration, her world fractured, exploded, ignited. He caught her screams in his mouth and her body in his hands as the room tilted sideways. Or perhaps that was her?

He didn't usually get the last word in but in this she could find no argument, no reply.

"We were made for each other, you and I."

CHAPTER TWENTY-NINE

"**H**OBSON?" JAMES CLOSED the door of the little dining room and then sat at the low table. He couldn't believe he was about to start this conversation but his thoughts were in turmoil and he needed the advice of his old friend. He and Daniella had soaped and rinsed and made love until they were wrinkly, and now she was upstairs drying her hair by the fire. As soon as they left the bathhouse she had mentally withdrawn from him, leaving him cold and anxious.

"I couldn't find the captain, Major."

"Couldn't find him?"

"Oh, they know where he is but they aren't saying."

"They?" He couldn't keep up.

"Sodding captain just about owns this town. He'll know we're 'ere, I'll eat my hat if he doesn't."

"I do believe I am in over my head."

"Only now, milord?"

He swallowed a sharp retort and instead sighed. "When did it get out of hand do you think?"

"Perhaps it was the day you disguised yourself as Her Highness's servant? Or perhaps it was the day you snatched her from the virgin's auction block? You shouldn't have married her," continued his outspoken servant.

"I know that," he roared, upsetting the silverware in the table when he slammed his fists down on it. "Don't you think I know that? God, what a mess. I should have waited until after this was all over and won her properly."

"She was no innocent, James. You did not have to marry her at all."

"I did have to marry her. My honour…I…" How could he explain that he loved her? How could he tell his friend he couldn't give her away any more than he could cut his own throat?

"She didn't ask to be married. She wants to be back on the open ocean with her father. You've complicated every-thing."

"Would I really make such a terrible husband?" He stood so he could pace.

Hobson shook his head but followed his progression around the room with his eyes. "You would make the right girl a fine husband. But Miss Daniella isn't the one for you and you are not the right man for her. She'll see you as a trap if you take her back to London."

James's stomach sank even lower. Of course Hobson was right. She'd never consent to living in London and he had to be there to take his seat in the House of Lords. There was no way he would let her live year-round in the country while he was in the city, so close yet so far away.

"What do I do now? I can't just hand her back to her father and say goodbye."

"It's what she's wanted all along, James."

"What if she wants something different now?" What if she actually wants me? The nightmares, the scars, the damage, all of it?

"Did you ask her?"

"Not in so many words."

"Seems that should be the place to start."

"And if she rejects me?" He couldn't meet Hobson's gaze.

"Then you go back to London and you find yourself a real wife and you forget all about the Germaines."

"It's all so wrong. So, so wrong." Why couldn't he have her and his family? Why couldn't she be his family? Marrying her was the only part of this entire scheme that felt right. Where was the mistake in that?

"Ask her to write a letter, lie and beg and plead and you'll have your annulment. You both have more than enough scandal around you, even a divorce isn't going to hurt much."

"And if she won't?" he asked, as he picked up a little paring knife and tucked it in his coat pocket. He wasn't lifting the silverware but he felt vulnerable without some kind of weapon.

"Make her. Your life depends on it and so does hers."

"You're right," he agreed half-heartedly.

By why did he have to be so right?

DANIELLA STOOD STILL against the dining room door, two

hands clapped over her mouth.

Annulment.

How could he? She might have been planning to run, but marriage was his idea from the start. She tried to be grateful for her own plan, for being denied only something she hadn't planned to keep, but felt only terribly hurt. How could she fall for his lies? How could she fall for him?

She didn't notice James had opened the door until she looked up and saw him staring at her with the same tortured look she knew must be mirrored in her own eyes.

"How long have you been standing there?" he asked, his hand outstretched, reaching for her.

She swallowed the hurt, defiant to the last, and stepped back. How dare he? "Long enough."

"And?"

How could she respond, torn as she was between her need to break free and her desperate hope that he loved her…maybe even that he wouldn't let her go?

"You have to know this is the only way forwards. I… It's the only way."

"I'll write your letter, my lord. Thank you for freeing me from what was obviously the biggest mistake of your life."

"Don't be that way, Daniella. If you gave up your notion of being on the seas, we could make this work. You could appeal to your father for my mother and sister and we could all go back to London."

"And live happily ever after? For how long?"

"What do you mean?"

"I told you from the start, I'll not live there indefinitely."

"What of the heirs I need? What of my life? You won't yield anything yet you expect me to?" He gripped her shoulders and forced her to meet his gaze.

"Why should it be you getting this marriage *and* the life you'd already planned? Why must I give up everything and you nothing?"

"I won't have an absent wife. I won't sit at home like a milksop and pine for you. Never knowing whether you live or if some cold-hearted bastard has driven a sword through your chest. I want all of you or none of you, no in between, no shades of grey."

"You can't have all of me. I belong to my ship, to my crew. I belong to the sea the same as you belong to your title. We were foolish to think we had a choice in this."

James let her go and raked both hands through his hair until the strands pulled and the pain he felt magnified tenfold. "You do have a choice and you're making the wrong one. You could be happy with me, Daniella. Really, truly happy with me. I would treat you like a queen but you won't even give us a chance."

"It's all about what you want and how you're going to get it. How do you know you can't be happy with me? On *The Aurora*? We wouldn't have to pillage or steal. We could deck her out a merchant and trade. We could be happy that way too."

"I have responsibilities in London. I have a title and a family and, damn it, I'll not throw that all away. You speak of your crew as lives in your hands but what about my tenants? What about the men, women and children who need me? Would you leave them with that uncertainty? Because I'll not do it."

"Let someone else do it," she cried. "Just as your father stepped up, surely there is someone else for your stupid title?"

"It doesn't work like that. I'd have to be dead for that to happen. This is my chance to show England that I'm not the Butcher, that I'm as good as my word. I can make a difference in the House of Lords and for my people. I can campaign behind the scenes so the next Bonaparte doesn't take the lives of another generation of boys."

Her expression softened, defeat in her eyes. "A noble thought, but England doesn't care about you, James. That is a one-sided love. How did she repay you for your years of service? With nothing more than nightmares. What does she promise you in return for your obedience and fealty? She won't keep you warm at night as I would have. She won't hold you in the night as I would have. She sure as hell won't give you obedience or fealty in return. The moment you falter, they'll eat you alive. You, your sister, your mother, your name."

"You're wrong. You play the game and you are rewarded. What will happen to Amelia if I stay here with you? Would you climb out of your cage only to put us in it?"

Daniella shook her head. He was right: it was hopeless. "I need to think on it."

She'd been featherbrained enough to spend an hour imagining her father returning James's family, not angry with her for her childish stunts because she was a happily married lady. He would give her the ship and her husband would sail alongside her. Now she had to finally admit that for the foolishness it was. She wiped angry tears from her eyes and cheeks and set her feet, one after another, down the carpeted stair to the hall below. She'd blatantly ignored any other outcomes because it was too painful to think of her father pushing her away again, after everything she'd done to get back here.

"Daniella!"

She ignored the shouts from behind her and kept going. She had to be alone with her thoughts and her devastation. She threw all of her weight behind the inn door and blinked against the sunshine but still she didn't stop. Bleak despair resettled like a boulder in the pit of her stomach.

"Daniella, stop!"

"Why? So you can lock me back up until my father comes for me? Or so I can write your damned letter and absolve you of everything?"

"Please, we need to talk about this."

She whirled around so suddenly in the middle of the road that James had to skid to a stop to avoid smashing into her. "What do you want from me? I can't do it your way and you won't bend at all."

James considered her before saying, "Can't? Or won't?"

She was silent for a time as she thought of her answer. Won't. If she had to choose one, it was won't. That life wasn't for her. *But how do you know?* Whispered on the wind. "Please, you have to know this won't work."

"Give it twelve months, Daniella. Let me show you the

possibilities."

She was about to give in, about to tell him she would try because now that she'd spent time with him, she wasn't sure she wanted to spend time without him. His gaze lifted over her shoulder and a different kind of tension stiffened his spine. "I don't believe it."

She spun around. "What are you looking—?" There, on the side of the road with a wide smile on his face was her father, leaning heavily on his cane, arm in arm with a pretty blonde woman on one side and a heavily pregnant girl on the other.

Daniella's heart gave a *thump-thump* and then ceased beating altogether. "Papa?"

She stepped forwards, her hand out, a lump in her throat and tears now falling unheeded down her face. But then an iron-strong arm wrapped around her middle and pulled her back.

"What are you doing? Let me go!"

"I can't do that, Daniella."

"Papa?" she shrieked and kicked out with all the fury she had singing in her veins.

CHAPTER THIRTY

"DANIELLA, CALM DOWN." Was he really seeing what he was seeing? Surely he'd fallen down the stairs and split his skull? He must have died there on the floor and gone to hell.

Hobson exploded from the door of the inn behind them and James passed Daniella to him. He ran across the street, heedless of animals, carriages, people. Without warning, he barrelled into Captain Germaine, knocking him off his feet. Or rather, foot. They went down and as they did James landed a right hook to the older man's jaw. After sliding a few feet, he regained his balance, prepared to attack the man again. "Get up, you filthy dog."

A screeching reached his ears over the blood pounding there. He ignored it all. He would have satisfaction and he would not stop until one of them was dead. "Get up!" he raged. This was all Germaine's fault. As he approached to kick the man, his mother appeared and threw her body over that of the captain's.

"Mother, run! Take Amelia and get to safety."

She met his gaze with worry, with concern, with...shame? "What are you doing here, James? How did you find us?"

"I'm rescuing you. I'll kill him for what he's done to you both." He wasn't ready to look for Amelia in the growing crowd. Once was enough to know someone had taken advantage of his sister. He would kill that son of a bitch as well.

"What he's done? What are you talking about?" Why didn't his mother look scared? Why did she protect her captor?

"Have you lost your mind?" Daniella shouted as she threw herself to her father's other side.

"What did you think would happen, Daniella? That I wouldn't notice my pregnant sister and not demand an accounting?" He addressed Germaine who now sat on the ground but hadn't yet risen to his feet. "After you die, the man who raped my sister is next. Do you understand me, old man? Now get up."

Germaine stared at him in confusion. "Raped your…?" He seemed very dazed as he turned his face to Daniella. "What are you doing here? Who is this boy? What is he talking about? What happened to your neck?"

James wasn't hearing the words he wanted to. "Are you going to deny keeping my mother and Amelia prisoner all these months?"

Amelia stepped forwards then and took their mother by the shoulders and helped her from the ground. "Mama, we knew this might happen, and now we are making a scene. Shall we take this discussion somewhere more private?"

"I say we settle it right here, right now," James suggested

with a growl, his fists raised.

Daniella jumped to her feet and came at him. "You can't kill my father. I won't let you."

"You can't stop this, Daniella. Perhaps if my sister wasn't sullied and increasing, things could have been different. We could have tried to find some middle ground where we both win. But that—" he pointed to Amelia and her distended stomach "—does not lie."

"I'd hear my father's version of events before I let you stab him again." She held her arms out but stood fast.

"Stalling, my dear? I will go through you to get to him, wife or not."

"You'd harm your own wife to get at her father? This isn't England, James. Your title is no protection. Here you would be tried, found guilty and hanged before the day is out." When she stopped, thought a moment, and stepped aside, he gulped. "On second thoughts, go right ahead. Perhaps I will be taking your money by day's end after all."

Didn't she know by now he would never harm her? He'd lost control. Again.

This time it was Germaine who spoke. "I do believe there is quite a bit of explaining to do but not here. I'll see the women back to the ship and then I'll return."

"Over my dead body. The women stay."

"Not here. Not with you. If your mother wants to return with me, she can, but I'll not have Amelia subjected to it."

"Fine. But Daniella stays with me."

"I will not," she interjected, making to join her father.

James took her by the arm before she'd travelled two

steps. "My wife stays with me. I won't have anyone sailing off before this is sorted. If you don't have a damned good explanation, I will call you out and put my ball in your chest."

"Very well," Germaine agreed. He gave Daniella one long hard look before he ushered James's family away. Out of his sight. God, he thought he might actually be sick. He'd spent so long searching for them and they were walking away.

"You have two hours," James called after them. "After that, I cannot be held responsible for what follows."

He waited a few moments until they all piled into a carriage farther down the street and were off before he turned to the woman he held in his hand. Expecting another fight, he was surprised to see fresh tears.

"He hates me," she whispered before crumpling into him, a woman who had nothing left in the world.

THE ONLY THING that hurt more than seeing his sister pregnant and distressed was hearing Daniella's gut-wrenching sobs. He'd tried to hold her, but she'd lashed out at him until he was forced to take her to their room and have Patrick watch over her.

She'd said it was all his fault. He was beginning to think maybe it was. Why did his mother look so healthy and happy? Why did his disgraced sister have colour on her skin and a happy glow about her? Had he been wrong? They looked as far from prisoners as Daniella had earlier that morning.

In his mind he recalled the wording of his mother's letter, the part about not looking for them. He'd thought her forced to write the letter but perhaps she had been merely coached about the wording?

"Another drink, Major?" Hobson held a bottle of scotch in the air but James shook his head. One was enough to revive his senses after the shock he'd had.

"What do you think just happened out there?"

"Unclear," came Hobson's single-word reply.

"But they actually looked happy, did they not? I wasn't imagining it?"

"Perhaps they were just happy for the moment? Maybe a rare visit to town for something? Jumping to conclusions isn't going to help."

"And Amelia? What of her?" He lifted his gaze to his friend's. "Did you see her?"

"Aye. Baby will be along any day by the looks."

But whose baby? He wasn't very good at the arithmetic behind reproduction but it didn't take a scientific man to figure it out. His grip tightened on the empty glass while he raked his other hand through his hair. She must have had her innocence ripped from her within days of being taken from the sinking ship. He would demand blood for this. Nothing less would cease the howling in his veins. Not even Daniella would be able to stop him avenging his sister's honour.

"God, Daniella..." The devastation in her eyes when her father just walked away from her was almost too much to bear on top of everything else.

"No coming back from that," Hobson pointed out before emptying his glass down his throat.

"If this were the battlefield, I would have killed him on the spot. He deserves no less."

"This isn't war, Major. It's people's lives. The Butcher in you was never able to make the distinction. You can't put a ball in someone here and not suffer consequences."

"I suffer consequences every time I close my eyes," James pointed out.

Hobson went on. "As do I. Always when I took a life, I knew it for what it was. Before the boy in the fire, did you ever think about the people behind the faces?"

"They were our enemy, Hobson. It was kill or be killed." She'd said it so many times—Daniella. He'd thought it an excuse to absolve her of her guilt but he'd said the same words. Exercised the same excuses.

"Yes. But you are no Butcher now: you can choose a different path. One that doesn't end with one less body on this planet."

James stared at him. Hobson was right, as he was always right. He was hearing the whisper he'd been listening for all these months: the ghosts were leaving. He took the first real breath he had since Marie came for him in Egypt.

Oblivious, Hobson continued. "Anyway, let's see what the captain has to say for himself first. Then we'll decide on our course. The father of that baby will need his reckoning at the very least. That should help ease that temper of yours."

They were interrupted then, as Germaine and his mother entered the room. No propriety, no knock, just solemn faces and a tension to make them all buckle under the pressure.

James stood as the captain saw his mother into a chair and then he sat and faced her. All he wanted to do was squeeze her tight but he doubted she would welcome his embrace. She held the same expression Daniella's father had. Was it shame? Indifference? He didn't like it no matter what it was. Foreboding settled with the chill in the room.

"Mother, will you tell me what is going on?"

"You should never have come here, James."

Not the words he'd expected and he took each one as if a blow to his chest. "Did you honestly think I would just let you go? You had been *captured* by a *pirate*."

She raised her brow but ignored his words and went on. "Now half this town will think Amelia's baby a bastard."

"Unless she married in the last six months, that baby is a bastard, Mother."

"That's not the story we put around, though." Her fingers twisted in her lap until the skin on her knuckles went white.

"We?" he asked, trying to have a care for her obvious nerves but frustration was tipping him to intense anger.

"'Twas my idea, lad," Germaine told him. "How about we start at the beginning rather than at the end, though, before you get all red in the face and think to knock me down again. Won't happen a second time."

"Richard," his mother warned him in a low tone. "We need him to listen."

"You are the woman he is going to marry. Aren't you?" One of the pieces fell into place. He nearly vomited. Right there on the toes of her shoes. His stomach was a whirling storm and little beads of sweat coated his palms.

His mother nodded. "We have spoken of vows, yes."

"I don't believe this." James stood and resumed his pacing. He only stopped to get Hobson to fill him another glass.

"It isn't what you think, Lasterton. None of it."

"He's right, son. I don't know how it went so far as it did. I thought I would write you a letter and you would forget about us for a time."

He stopped dead in his tracks, incredulous, injured. "Forget you? The only family I have left in this world? What kind of man do you take me for?"

Germaine stood and wobbled on one leg; James's mother reached her hand out to support him. James looked away before he could see if the older man took it.

His mother went on with her story. "Amelia came to me and confessed she was with child—"

He stopped pacing again, fell into his chair. "Before you left?"

"It's the reason we left. Neither one of us could face the scandal. Not after your brother and your father... You'd worked so hard to lift us out and she was too afraid and ashamed to plunge you back in."

"You should have come to me. *She* should have come to me."

"She barely knows you, James. You were gone for so many years and when you came back, you were changed. Even I didn't know you anymore."

But... But... He loved his sister. They had been so close.

She had to know he would do anything for her. Had the Butcher nonsense scared her or had it indeed been his manner, his nightmares, his grumpiness?

"So your option was to run away? Where does *he* come into the story?"

"It seems the ship we paid for passage on was not as she seemed. Only two days out and she began to sink. If Richard hadn't come across us, we would have been lost."

James emptied his glass again. He breathed hard for a few moments as the liquid burned all the way to his soul and then he asked, "So you rescued them? You didn't take them to get at me?"

"Get at you for what, lad? I don't even know you."

James looked into the captain's eyes, saw the confusion there, the blankness. "I was the one who took your leg."

"You were?" they both said at the same time, the rough pirate captain and his genteel mother as one. He cringed.

"It was my men on the ship that day, the one you tried to take in the Channel. We fought, I stabbed you."

"I killed that man," Germaine said with a shake of his head. "My sword cleaved him in two before I pushed him into the water."

"A flesh wound. I figured my odds were better in the water than on the ship."

Germaine sank back into his seat with another shake of his head. "I don't believe it. So you thought I took the women as what? Revenge?"

"To punish me, perhaps, for your lost ransoms. When Daniella told me about your leg—" he winced but went on

"—then yes, it did seem as though you might wish for revenge."

His mother spoke next. "Why do you travel with Daniella? You said she was your wife."

"I'll bet she trapped you in one of those schemes of hers."

"You've heard about them?" James couldn't believe it. Her father had known all along but never put a stop to them?

"Of course I have. I bet you came here to get out of it? To give her back?"

"Would you take her?" It wasn't the best question but after the look the captain had given her earlier, he wanted to know what her fate would be if he did decide to let her go. As if he even had any say in it anymore.

"I'd have to now, I suppose." He sighed. "I wanted better for her. I thought together with my money and Anthony's title, it would be enough to make some forget her past."

"Why not let Daniella live here with you, in retirement? You could have found her a nice husband and seen her happy."

Germaine shook his head. "It was never my plan to live here at all. The men and I were to disappear, to live in isolation and only sail for the pleasure of it. I wanted Daniella to have the glittering balls and the privilege. I wanted her to be safe from further persecution."

"Let me understand," James said, trying as hard as he could to keep his temper in check. "You knew Daniella was ruining her chances at a match, but you did nothing? I don't understand."

"I knew she would rebel, but I thought she would settle. I would have sent word to her but the storm rolled through and the ships were all too damaged to sail. And as Amelia nears her time, I can't leave them. Daniella is a woman in charge of her own life but your sister is a scared girl."

"No one of any worth was going to offer for her," James said in a fury. "No one. Do you know the men your son was considering as suitable matches to be rid of her? Doddering ancients and ambitious commoners."

Germaine frowned. "No. I did not know of them. I can see—I should have—"

"James," his mother said hurriedly. "I want to stay here. We both do, Amelia and I. Not as pirates—Richard gave all of that up. He is…" she looked down, pink staining her décolletage and cheeks "…a good man. I am happy for the first time in—well, a good while. And in any case, Amelia can't possibly return to London with a baby and no husband. Even if the ton believes the stories we could make up, the truth will come out eventually."

"What am I supposed to tell them then, Mother? You've given it all up for a ship's life? Or should I tell everyone you died at sea without an explanation of how you got there?"

"Tell them we died at sea on a voyage to escape the grief and scandal: it's the only way. By next season, a new scandal involving a different family will top the gossip. They will forget about us. We've taken on new names. No one here knows who we were."

James couldn't believe his ears. He wanted to scream and shake her and ask *What about me?* Was he simply to forget them too? All alone in that big house with only the servants to fill the empty rooms? Had she no thought at all to how he might fare if they'd actually died at sea? He willed his voice to calm, to convey the disappointment he could no longer conceal. "I know who you are. I know where you are. Asking me to forget is selfish and beyond anything anyone has ever asked of me."

Germaine thumped his meaty fist on the table again. "Tell me about Daniella. How did she come to embroil you in her mess?"

"Did you not get any of the missives I sent ahead?"

"If I knew the extent of it, would I be taking a leisurely stroll through town, boy? How did you get her here?"

"We came by road some of the way, but actually, a man named Darius delivered us this morning."

"Darius? I don't understand. What was that cur doing anywhere near my daughter?"

Now he cared? "He *did* get my message and thought he was saving her."

"From what?"

"Not what," James explained. "Who. He thought he was saving her from me. I kidnapped her so I could trade mother and Amelia away from you, and Darius thought he was rescuing her."

"Were you already married at that stage or not?"

"Not. That happened this morning as well."

"My head hurts," his mother complained, looking between James and Germaine. "This is all too much for one afternoon."

James had to agree with her completely.

"I would like a moment alone with my daughter," Germaine asked. "Please."

"You can speak to her but I won't let you take her with you. Not yet."

"So you do want me to take her back with me?" he asked, green eyes only a shade lighter than Daniella's flooding with concern.

James had fully expected a bloodthirsty pirate but in his place stood an old man with only his daughter's best interests in mind. Every day must have been a battle for Germaine, to watch her amongst his crew. Eventually something would have gone wrong. If James were in his position, he would have offloaded Daniella after the first mutiny with Darius. A ship was no place for a woman.

And London was no place for her. She'd wither and die a little inside every day there. He could no more watch that happen than he could watch her walk away from him. She kept talking about not having choices and being driven to desperation but now she did. She could leave with her father, forget he'd ever come into her life. Or he could fight for her. Show her he could make her happy. He just needed a grand, crazy gesture to convince her.

"I'm not giving her to you or anyone else. Daniella is mine. I just need to convince her." He just needed to persuade her he was the one man in her life who might be able to give her everything her heart wanted. Now that he'd realized he could.

"Excuse me," he said and rose from the table, from his

mother and her new and very unsuitable beau.

He took the stairs three at a time even though it hurt his entire face with the jolting. He had to talk to Daniella, to find out if the damage he'd done to her, hell the damage they'd all done to her, was irreparable. If he begged for her forgiveness, would she give it to him?

He burst into the room with no finesse at all, his chest full of words he wanted her to hear before she got it into her stubborn head to ignore him, but then he choked, coughed, swore. She was gone. The room was empty.

He was too late.

CHAPTER THIRTY-ONE

F OR A WOMAN who never cried, Daniella had given the practice some decent exercise. The skin of her face was tight and hot, her neck hurt, her eyes were scratchy and her whole body ached. She cursed her father and her brother and life itself for the rough ride given to her.

"Come now, lass, 'tis not the end of the world."

"Piss off," she retaliated. She was done with kindness, with propriety, with men, even if Patrick had helped her escape the inn. They rode the last miles to *The Aurora* even now. She tried not to wonder how her father and her husband were getting along.

"You know I can't do that," he called back over the jingle of their mounts' harnesses.

"Fine. You helped me. What do you want in return?"

"When we get back to your ship, will you give me Amelia?"

"*Give* you Amelia? She's not a toy. James has searched for her for months. Did you see her today?"

He nodded and gulped, steadying his mare over a rough bit of ground. "Aye. I saw her. She needs to be somewhere safe for the birth the child, not a ship surrounded by strange men in a foreign place."

"It's your baby then?" she asked.

Patrick actually blushed and turned his face away. "I didn't believe her when she came to me. I told her to try her tricks on another man and as good as threw her out."

"But you and she obviously…" She trailed off, thinking the actual words unnecessary.

"Aye, just the once. 'Twas silly and brash and exactly the stunt my father said would land me in a pot of boiling water."

"It's landed you in more than that. When James finds out it was you, he'll skin you and leave you for carrion."

"He isn't going to find out. Not yet. Not until I've had the chance to make it right with Amelia."

"Do you love her?" Daniella asked, fresh tears burning her eyes; she shook them clear and focused on her horse's path. Love was a silly notion for fools and debs.

Patrick said, "If she'll have me, I'll make an honest woman of her."

"And if she won't?"

"I'll fight until she does."

It was good enough for Daniella. "I'll speak to Amelia. I won't make her go with you but I can try to make her see what is in store for her and the child aboard a ship."

It had been too much for her mother. One hundred and forty-eight pounds her father had paid her to leave Daniella with him. It was one of her earliest memories. Her mother had had enough of life on the seas, of living with men and the constant rock of the vessel. No parties to attend, no friends, no fine things and sometimes no food or fresh water. She wanted to leave and was going to take Daniella with her. Her father forbade it. Her mother said he would have to kill her then.

The captain had gone to his little chest beneath the bed, unlocked it and poured out its contents. A pearl necklace, an amethyst ring and one hundred and forty-eight pounds. Her mother disappeared at the next port.

Emptiness clung to her very being and she couldn't shake herself free of it. Why did no one want her?

JAMES STOPPED ONLY to ask the direction to *The Aurora* and how long it would take to get there. It was another twenty-five minutes before he got the details from the captain, who was unwilling to cooperate until James vowed not to do Daniella any harm when he found her. He had to swallow what was left of his dignity and explain his nightmares to account for her injuries. Explain that Daniella could look after herself and that it was she who had given him his two blackened eyes. It was no small feat. He still wasn't sure the captain or even his own mother believed him about any of it but they consented and gave him the information he needed.

Another twenty minutes passed while horses were haggled over and saddled.

She already had over an hour's head start. How long did it take to ready a ship for sail, providing the storm damage had been repaired? Surely she would also need time to convince her father's crew to leave without their captain?

Germaine and his mother agreed to stay at the inn and give James the chance to speak with Daniella alone. He'd had to grovel for that, on his knees. Thank God he had little pride left.

Had he not shown her in his actions how much she meant to him? He'd married her damn it and still she ran. Perhaps her ship and her independence really did mean more than anything else in the entire world and it wasn't an act? Why couldn't she just bloody well see what he could offer her?

James swore a blue streak as he mounted, Hobson on a horse behind. When he found her, he was going to tie her to a chair and make her listen. Make her see he would do anything for her if only she would stay at his side. Surely she would listen then…

CHAPTER THIRTY-TWO

TIME SEEMED TO stretch itself out until minutes felt like hours before her beautiful ship came into view. Docked in an inlet big enough for two ships if neither one needed to turn around, in water calm and almost clear.

It wasn't her father's usual place to dock but then Darius had mentioned the ship sustained some damage in the recent storms. She found the humility to be grateful for the pirate's intervention: without it they'd be headed for the wrong port and James have thought her the worst kind of trickster.

She hoped her father had already completed the repairs. Once she was on board, they could weigh anchor and leave this wretched land behind.

Her father would forgive her. He had to. After this, she had no place left to go.

As they neared the ship, Daniella slowed her horse to a walk. Shock took hold and devastation ate her soul in one mighty gulp.

She couldn't believe what she was seeing. A nightmare? Yes. But was it real?

Of the three towering masts, only one stood. There was no evidence the other two had ever been there. Even from a distance she could tell half the railing was missing. No men worked her deck. No shouts or orders reached her ears over the horse's hooves thudding on the earth.

The majestic ship she'd spent her life on was as broken and as silent as a dead man.

"That's what you've been fighting for?" Patrick asked. His tone didn't mock or condemn. She wondered if he was as stunned as she was.

Daniella only nodded. She didn't have the words to explain to him how beautiful *The Aurora* had been. How other captains coveted her and a king had once tried to take her.

Readying herself for more heart-wrenching pain and even more damage, she kicked her heels to the mare's sides and took off towards the wreck. Perhaps it wasn't so bad as it looked? Perhaps the masts had been dismantled to allow for the repairs?

But it was worse. So much worse.

She wasted no time sprinting up the plank but the side she'd seen from a distance was far better than the other. Darius hadn't exaggerated when he'd said the captain had limped her there. She wasn't seaworthy at all. She was barely liveable.

"Is it possible Amelia isn't here?" Patrick asked, completely oblivious to her turmoil.

"It's possible there isn't anyone here," she replied. But her father would never leave the vessel unmanned. Not even in her current state. *The Aurora* meant more than that to him. It was their home. Their way of life.

One step towards the stern and a barely muffled scream

split the silence. It was long and loud and the pain it carried made Daniella wince and duck. Both she and Patrick drew their daggers at the same time. Daniella would have given almost anything to have a sword in her hand instead of the short unfamiliar blade.

"Wait," she told Patrick as he looked for the stairs to go below. "I know this ship better than anybody. I'll go first."

Patrick shook his head and started tiptoeing across the deck. "Not likely, lass," he whispered to her without a backwards glance.

He was going to get himself killed.

Another scream, this time lower in volume but not lacking in intensity. Daniella followed Patrick down the short narrow stairs into a darkened corridor. She waited for him to keep going but he seemed stuck fast.

"What are you waiting for?" she hissed.

"I can't see a goddamned thing," he hissed back, his frustration palpable.

Daniella pushed past him. "Follow me." The pitch black didn't bother her at all. The next scream did.

"Amelia?" Patrick bellowed down the passageway.

"Thank you very much," Daniella said with a shake of her head. They may as well have announced their arrival with a brass band.

As men usually did, Patrick ignored her warning, her words, her, and pushed ahead into the dark.

Daniella went straight for the captain's cabin. If the women were guests aboard the ship, it would make sense for them to share the largest space. Dagger at the ready, she pushed the door open and then sprang back into the shadow. Not a man seemed to notice her presence. Hurt and anger and pride kicked each other trying to get to the surface. Was she now invisible as well?

Finally one sailor turned his head but then turned back. He then seemed to come to his senses. "Dani?" he asked, breaking away from the group hovering about the bed.

"What the hell is going on, Hoste?" Why did seven of her father's men cram their bulks into the small space leaving the decks unmanned? Leaving her ship completely defenceless?

Another scream and Daniella fought her way to the bed as the men stepped back almost as one.

Amelia. The young woman writhed on the bed, her dark honey hair plastered to her forehead with beads of sweat as she forced out one breath after another and then another. Tears slid down her face and onto the pillow as she cried out, her arms around her belly, her knees drawn in protectively.

Amelia's eyes, when she managed to focus them on the newcomers, held shame and hopelessness and a fear so great Daniella also took a step away.

"Help me," Amelia begged on a broken sob. "Make it stop."

As though shot from a cannonball, Patrick exploded into the room, a curse on his tongue and a tension in his stance. When he saw Amelia, nothing else registered.

She shrank away as he approached the bed, the fear turning wild in her eyes as she appealed to the other men in the room for assistance. Shuffling back on the bed as far as she could until her body was flush with the wall, she once again covered her mountainous stomach with her hands. "Get out," she said to him, the father of her child.

"Amelia, you cannot mean that," he protested as he fell to his knees on the timbers. He reached for her; she tried to back away again.

"Get him out of here," she cried as pain once again ripped through her and she doubled over with another scream.

Daniella gazed around at her family, her father's sailors, the men she'd known all her life. Not a one made a move. They all looked to her for orders as though she had never left.

"Hoste, Lion and Woodhead, fetch linens, hot water and brandy. The rest of you get out. You'll not want to see what happens next." She'd watched the delivery of a baby just the once. She'd wanted to look away, to leave the room, but her father wouldn't allow it. He'd wanted to her to assist, to hold the poor girl's hand as she wailed into the night. Daniella had thought he kept her there on purpose, as a warning, such was the torment it had imprinted on her soul. Amelia's screams bought it all back in an instant. They had to do something. The baby was coming whether she wanted to be there or not.

"How long ago did the pains start?" she asked as the room slowly cleared. She needed to know how long the woman had been fighting her body and her babe.

Before Amelia could answer, Farrar, her father's bosun, stopped in the doorway and indicated Patrick. "He staying or going?"

"He's staying," Daniella said forcefully. "He can see where his actions have led."

Jenson, the ship's cook, also stayed. "I've been caring for the girl so far. I can help," he offered, his serious gaze switching back and forth from Daniella to Amelia. "She'll have a rough time of it."

Patrick stood and turned on the spot, his arms out as if to ward them all off. "You'll not touch her, none of you. I'm taking her off this ship right now. It's no place to birth a child."

Jenson leaned back against the wall with all the nonchalance of a man who knew the outcome of the argument already. "I have six more men outside that door who would beg to differ."

Exactly what she did not need in that moment was a pissing contest. "Stand down. Amelia is not going anywhere."

"You told me you would give her to me," Patrick accused.

"I told you I would ask her what *she* wanted. Look at her, Patrick. Do you think you could move her? I'd wager she won't even let you touch her."

"I'll take that wager," Amelia muttered from the bed. When three sets of eyes were on her, her spine straightened and a show of defiance lit her features. "I asked him—" she indicated Patrick with a point of her trembling finger "—for help once and he denied me then."

"I've been trying to make up for it ever since. Why do

you think I'm here?"

Amelia tried to sit up, tried to collect some of her forgotten dignity, but another pain gripped her and she screamed again. Patrick ignored everyone and took her in his arms. She held on to him as though he was the anchor and around them raged a hurricane. Burying her face in his dirty shirt, Amelia sobbed and begged him to take the pain away.

Jenson moved to the foot of the bed and began to lift her skirts.

Patrick pulled his dagger and pushed the man away with one hand while he tried to hold on to Amelia with the other. "What the hell are you doing?"

"We need to know if the baby is coming," Jenson told him, not budging an inch.

Daniella moved forwards then too and placed her hand on Patrick's outstretched arm. "We need to know how long she has laboured. The baby could be in trouble. Amelia is tiring quickly." Any fool could see it.

"They are right," Amelia said with a groan, rolling to her back and letting her knees fall apart. "He is coming. Just get him out, please."

Jenson flicked her skirts up with no more preamble, with no more argument. He removed her drawers and Daniella had to just about hold Patrick back. She wondered if he even knew exactly how babies were brought into the world.

"Be still," she told him as she also bent to look. Already she could see a small amount of white-blond hair atop a barely crowning head.

"He is nearly here," Jenson told them all as he pushed his

sleeves up to his elbows.

Hoste slipped into the room with steaming water and clean linens and then left again. Jenson washed his hands and then bade Daniella to do the same.

Her hands shook. This was not supposed to happen. Where the bloody hell was the brandy?

"I'm so sorry," she told the other woman as she readied the linens. "You should have been at your home dealing with this, with a doctor, with your brother and your mother around you. You should never have ended up here."

Amelia shook her head, her hair splayed around her. She opened her mouth to speak but Patrick cut her off. "If anyone is to take the blame for this mess, 'tis me. I should have listened to you when you came to me. I was a coward and a cad and a dunderhead. I should have married you right then in the church down the road from the club. We would right now be with my mother and my sisters and a midwife. Our child would not be born out of wedlock. He would know he was loved from the first instant."

Amelia's cinnamon eyes, eyes the same as James's in every way, opened wide. She panted, "He has been loved from the first instant. By me."

"He is *our* son, Amelia. I made a mistake, the biggest of my life. I was never worthy of your heart then. I should never have taken advantage of you but I was so taken with your beauty and your kindness and your passion for everything in life. And when you came to me, I was confused and drunk and I made the wrong choice. Not days later I realized and went to find you but you had gone and I thought your brother had found out and done away with you."

"Done away with her?" Daniella asked. "You honestly thought he'd killed her?"

Patrick nodded. "I did at first. The Butcher and all that. It's why I followed him when he took you."

Daniella gasped. "It was you in the garden that night watching the house?"

Amelia spoke up then. "What? What? My brother…would never…harm me."

He turned back to her. "Then why did you disappear so suddenly? Why did you not ask him for help?"

Yet another pain gripped her and this time instead of screaming, her eyes rolled back and a long low moan rent the air. Her back arched off the bed and her fingers curled to fists. "Please make it stop," she begged again when her stiffened body softened slightly. "I'm sorry. I'm sorry. Tell James I'm sorry."

Daniella took Amelia's hand in hers and said, "You can tell him yourself when you introduce him to your baby."

"He'll…never forgive…" she managed.

"Then you don't know him very well. He kidnapped me to have you back."

"You're…his wife…"

"We were married this morning. On board a ship in the middle of the ocean. Now you breathe. Right down as far as you can."

A thought came to her as the girl obeyed. "Amelia, Patrick will marry you right here, aboard this ship. No disgrace. No shame. Only love."

"He doesn't…love me. Or the…baby."

Patrick leaped to his feet and roared, "The hell I don't!"

Amelia jumped, her eyelids snapping open as she stared at him. "Just…honour."

Patrick held her head up so she could see him. "I do love you. I don't go about bedding random virgins, Amelia—I made a mistake. You can spend the rest of our lives taking it out of my hide but please, for the love of God, marry me, be my wife, let our child have my name and my lands and my people for his family. You'll be treasured as a Laird's lady and our son will have a title and a castle and pride."

"You…betrayed me. Can't…forget."

"You don't have to forget, my love, you only have to say you'll be mine."

Another contraction, so much more severe than any of the others Daniella had witnessed, took hold of Amelia then. Patrick held her down while Jenson barked orders. Daniella did everything she was told to and then took Amelia's hand in hers. "Take courage. Give your babe a name. Don't curse him to—to the fringes of life."

She'd never allowed herself to think like that at all. Perhaps that was why she yearned for her shipboard family. None of them belonged anywhere else.

"Please, my love, please say the words before it's too late," Patrick implored Amelia.

The blank look in her light eyes was frightening but then clarity appeared momentarily and she nodded. "I'll be your wife."

"Thank the Lord," Patrick sighed.

"Excellent, man and wife, et cetera, et cetera," Jenson said as he readied linens and took away soiled ones stained with the brightest of blood, then gathered his patient up so she was relatively upright, though her head lolled. "Amelia, sweeting, you're going to have to push as soon as you feel the next big pain. Do you understand? You're going to have to push as hard as you can."

Daniella continued to stare at the blood: there was so much. Surely something was wrong. She shook herself and moved closer to help support the labouring girl.

"I can't do it," Amelia cried, her head thrashing on Jenson's shoulder. "I don't know what to do."

Jenson's voice was soothing. "Just listen to your body. The baby grows impatient and wants to meet you. Just push. Now! Hold your breath and push!"

CHAPTER THIRTY-THREE

J AMES HAD NEVER been so terrified in all his life. The blood-curdling scream from *The Aurora* wasn't anything he hadn't heard before, but now it was coming from someone he loved.

He reined in and slid from the too-small saddle in one unsteady movement. He and Hobson had had to separate just in case they were going in the wrong direction.

So much time had passed. Anything could have happened.

He didn't slow down as he ran on to the ship via the wobbly plank. But then he had to stop. He didn't know his way around this ship. He didn't know where Daniella was or who she was with. He had to pause; he had to think.

"'Ere, 'oo the fuck are you?" a voice rang out from behind him.

James turned and faced a wiry little man. His fingers flexed and curled. "Where is Daniella?"

"She's below."

Spying a door, James pushed the man out of the way and took off at a run just as another scream reached him. He was going to kill the man who dared touch her. He would burn the boat to the waterline, as he'd wanted to do all along.

Before he got too far along the below-decks corridor, he came to a wall of burly sailors. None looked particularly vicious or scary but all were definitely guarding the door at their backs. The room from which the awful sounds were coming.

"Stand aside," he ordered them.

"Who are you?" one asked as he crossed his arms over his chest.

"James Trelissick. Stand aside. I'll not let you hurt her anymore."

"You can't stop it, nabob," another chimed, standing shoulder to shoulder with the first.

This time James's fingers curled into fists and he stepped forwards. "You will not stop me getting to her."

"Are you sure you want to take us all on? One little gentleman against the five of us?"

Stepping from one foot to the other, James rolled his head and cracked his knuckles in front of his stomach. "I'll give it my best shot." He would never go down without a fight. Not when it came to Daniella.

"I'll take him," one offered as another said, "This should be diverting."

He pulled his arm back, ready to let loose, when he was grabbed from behind. At such close quarters, and in the dark, he should have checked his back for more opponents. His arms were held at his sides as one of the sailors, a burly ginger-headed man with a full beard and huge hands, approached.

"Knock his teeth out, Lion!" one of the men yelled.

James thrashed with all his might, tried to kick out, to knock his captors off balance, but it was no use. He was outnumbered and unconscious of his surroundings. He'd charged into battle without any information, none of the facts. The Butcher was well and truly lost.

Just as he squeezed his eyes shut, tensing for the blow that would surely break his nose for good and loosen his teeth, a wail filled the air. This was no blood-stopping scream. It was the sound of a baby crying that reached his ears.

"Amelia?" He'd not stopped to think of his sister. He'd wanted only to find Daniella and tell her he loved her. Convince her the only place for her in the world was at his side.

Another cry from the other side of the door and his heart swelled with emotion.

The two men holding him suddenly let him go and he dropped to the floor with a thud as they surged towards the cries, all thoughts of fighting forgotten.

The door opened and another man filled the space. Questions fired off all at the same time. "What is it?", "How is the lass?", "What of the boy?".

The only reply came with a toothless grin. "It's a girl. A wee little red-faced lass with the palest hair you ever saw."

A collective sigh reached his ears and the tension dissipated in smiles and pats on the back. The toothless stranger looked down at him, his brows raised. "Another one?"

"Too many strangers for my liking," the first spoke

again. "This one claims he's Trelissick."

"You'd better come in then and meet your niece."

Dare he? Would it be easier for Amelia if he went back to London and told everyone she'd passed away? He could mourn her for a year and then start his life fresh.

On his own.

Alone.

With none of the people who made his life worth living. For so long war and the fight both inside him and for his reputation had ruled his every move. Now what did he have? The House of Lords? His clubs?

That was no way to live. He would not treat his sister as the rest of London would. He would tell everyone the child was his baby to a mistress. Amelia could settle in the country with the babe and no one would ever have to know.

He climbed to his feet and slowly approached. It was an effort but the ends of his lips lifted into a forced smile as he stepped over the threshold.

Amelia sat up in the huge bed, small, pale, tired. And Patrick? Patrick sat next to her with the bawling bundle cradled in two hands, staring down at the baby as though she was the greatest miracle he'd ever seen. Confusion set in.

Daniella stood by Patrick and smiled with undisguised happiness, moisture glistening on her eyelashes much like the last time he'd left her. Only this time, she was truly smiling. She was truly happy. Was it the baby or was it the ship?

James cleared his throat and they all looked up at once. They turned possessive, wary and—yes—afraid, respectively. Guilt greater than any before swamped him. Forget the

Butcher's deeds. He'd ruined Amelia's life by being absent and unapproachable and he'd ruined Daniella's by thinking he knew better than her. By thinking he could control everyone and everything. All he'd wanted was his family's happiness.

"You came," Amelia said with astonishment. Not happy astonishment though.

"I'm sorry I didn't get here sooner," he joked, trying his hardest to defuse some of the tension in the room.

"I…" his sister started but then her gaze dropped.

"You don't have to tell me now, Amelia. Explanations can wait. Are you all right?"

"I think so," she said with a nod.

Daniella stepped forwards, her gaze serious, all traces of her previous smile gone. "We should probably discuss some of the turns of events of the day."

"What is Patrick doing here?"

"Patrick is exactly where he should be, with his child," Daniella said.

James was even more confused than he had been before. It made his head ache. Again. "What?"

"That night on the beach, when you caught me sneaking about? Patrick told me why he was really with you. It was the night I discovered what your stolen items really were. Or rather, who."

"*He* told you?" James switched his attention back to Patrick, who had yet to say a word.

He finally spoke. "I did tell her. After I tried to kidnap her away from you."

"I beg your pardon?" Fingers of dread squeezed at his nape.

"Patrick had the same plan as you: roughly the same motivation as well as it turns out."

His pulse raced and the room swayed ever so slightly. He should have known there was more to the Highlander's sketchy story. Why had Daniella so completely blinded him? *How* had she so completely blinded him?

"Perhaps we should start at the beginning?" Amelia offered.

But James suddenly found he just didn't care enough. Not now. Not yet. He wanted to take Daniella away from there and say what he'd come to say. Amelia was safe. Patrick was at her side, where he assumed the young man had been at some other stage in the last nine months. He'd seen his sister as a girl, fragile and innocent, for so many years, but there she was, pale with exertions only a woman could survive. She and Patrick could look after their own. Right now, he needed to concentrate on his wife—make amends for all the ways he'd fucked everything up.

He moved closer to Daniella and whispered in her ear, "Perhaps we should leave these two to their moment?"

"You aren't angry?" she asked.

He was furious. Beyond furious, but it wasn't at the top of his list of current anxieties.

EMERGING ABOVE DECKS into the sunshine, Daniella almost fell under the weight of it all. She was exhausted. Her chest was so tight she could hardly breathe. But she had to make him listen. "I'll sign your papers. I'll absolve you from the marriage and you can go back to London with a clear conscience. You can find a proper wife and start over."

She watched the ocean to avoid his eyes. On a day where her thoughts and emotions were in absolute turmoil, the sea was calm and soothing—just as it had always been. This was why she could never leave the water. It was her home.

James took her by the shoulder and turned her, crowding her against what was left of the railing at the backs of her legs. His eyes were fierce, his grip bruising. "I won't have it. I'll not let you ignore what is between us."

"You were the one who wanted an end to it. You were the one who talked incessantly of pure wives and blue-blooded babies!" The rage she'd thought spent burst back to life. She shoved him in the chest so hard he staggered. "You can't have it every way, James. You can't have everything you want!"

"Yes I can," he objected. "We can make this work, but you are so scared you won't even give it a chance."

"Scared?" she scoffed, crossing her arms over her chest. "I'm not scared of you."

"I don't want you to be scared of me, damn it. I want you to see me. See that I love you and know that I will fight for you. What do I have to do to convince you I can make you happy?"

"You don't love me. You do this out of honour and call it love so you can sleep at night."

The bluster left him then and his shoulders dropped.

"Why are you fighting *me*, Daniella? You already know how I sleep at night. I don't. Yes, I'd pictured for myself a pure wife, but I also pictured one who wouldn't argue when I left her bed to barricade myself in my room. I never imagined meeting a woman who would knock me on my arse over and over."

"I do feel it," she freely admitted. "The connection. But I also know it will not last. It cannot last. If I return to London with you, the ton will crucify you—you know they will."

"My brother killed my father and then himself. My unwed sister just gave birth to an illegitimate child. I am *the Butcher*, for God's sake. We will do what the other scandalous members of the ton do: we'll ignore those who cut us and we'll waltz the night away and kiss on the dance floor as fodder for the gossips. I want you as you are right now, secrets, schemes, exactly as you are, minus the only thing holding you back. Look at what you fight for. Your ship is in pieces. You are wrong to want solitude on the sea. As I was wrong to want society's approbation. I see it now, all of it. All I care about is you. If the only way I can have you is to stay, then I'm staying. We can live on your damned ship."

"For how long?" she asked. Why couldn't he just leave her be? Her heart was splitting in two and every word he shouted at her only made it that much worse. "How long until your responsibilities come to find you? What about your mother and Amelia? Your tenants and your House of Lords?"

"Your idea. I can have someone declare me dead so the

title can pass to yet another distant cousin. It will not be easy but it can be done. Mother is staying with your father if I had to guess. Amelia... Well, I don't know what will happen there."

"Amelia will go with Patrick. Her husband." She waited for his reaction.

"Impossible." Not what she had expected.

"Just now. Before the birth of the child. The same words we spoke to one another. They are married."

"As are we."

"Not for long," she reminded him.

"What a mess," James muttered beneath his breath.

"Indeed."

But then he said the last thing she ever thought he would. "I want you to give me one year."

This was the conversation they had started earlier and she didn't want to revisit it again. "What good will that do?"

He shook his head but then came close, crowded her again, put his hands on her arms again. This time his grip was soft, reassuring. He stood too close and her walls began to crumble. "Give me one year to change your mind. To show you what kind of future I could give you. We'll retire to the country in wedded bliss, gossip be damned, and I can show you a life with me will be just as rewarding as a life on the ocean."

"I can't. You know I can't do that. I won't be bound to the land."

"My estate is on the coast."

"I beg your pardon?"

"I live by the sea, you beautiful fool. A short trot down the cliffs and you are standing in the water."

She stared at him, angry, hopeful. "And you didn't think to share this information with me before now?"

He looked sheepish. "Yes, well, I didn't think it would help, being an estate and not an actual pirate ship. It will be difficult and I'll have to spend some time in the city—and you might even find the place sufficiently pleasant for the occasional visit, being a married woman—but I think we can make it work. If at the end of the twelve months you are still miserable and yearning, I will go with you. We will find a new home—buy an island plantation for ourselves and leave an agent running things here. I'll not leave you now I've found you."

"You're impossible. It's impossible." But once again hope bloomed in her mind and in her chest.

"I want you to be mine, Daniella. Only mine, for the rest of our lives."

The hope deflated. "You can't own me, James. I won't belong to you. I have been fighting my whole life. Fighting to be better, to do better, to be worthy of my place on this ship. What if I don't know how to stop fighting?"

He shook his head but in his eyes his smile radiated his own hope. "You already belong to me in the same way I belong to you, heart to heart, no chains. Tell me you aren't my equal in every way and if we disagree over this or that, we'll fight each other. But then we'll kiss and make up. Tell me you don't want me to kiss you and love you and make you feel whole. That's what you do to me every second of the day, Daniella. You made me *feel* again."

Heat flushed her cheeks and tears burned her eyes. Words lodged in her throat. Was he right?

She was scared. More than that. She was terrified. If she said yes and it was awful, how would she survive? But if she sent him away, regret would take over her life and tarnish everything she did. Of course she loved him. He offered her the world and she hesitated. She was an idiot.

Her lips curved and she closed the distance between their bodies. "I do love you, James. You're everything I'd never thought to wish for. I don't know how you're going to make this work, but I'll give you your twelve months."

He cradled her face in his hands and bent his forehead to hers. "I'll be having more than that, but it's a good place to start, my love."

EPILOGUE

Four very short months later

"I MADE A mistake," Daniella said as James held her hair and she cradled a bucket on her lap.

"Oh?" he said. She hated the way he answered her with those two little letters. He knew he was right and was attempting very poorly to hold back the smugness.

"I think it's time to move back to the house."

"But you love this ship. You swam naked in the moonlight and sold your fictional virginity for a life on the seas."

She'd thought the boat the perfect romantic gesture, docked a short way from the main house, their bedroom for all intents and purposes, James's attempt to keep her happy. Something in which they could escape, every year or two, so she could show him the islands and waters he'd dreamed of as a child; so they could both relish the sun and the wind and the enormous ocean that fed her very soul. But now? "You just want me to say you were right and I was wrong." The wind howled all around them, each gust causing the ship to pitch and the lantern light to tremble. It wasn't the only thing pitching and trembling.

"Indeed I do, Lady Trelissick."

"I won't do it," she said, right before the retching started again. The constant rocking of the little ship set her stomach to heaving. Never in her life had she imagined suffering seasickness.

"The sickness will pass. Amelia said hers lasted for around nine weeks at the beginning of her pregnancy. She also said she fared far better on land."

"She would say that." Her sister-in-law didn't share Daniella's love of the sea. But then she didn't have to now that she spent her days in the Scottish Highlands in a drafty castle, the only water in sight a loch too cold and deep to enjoy.

"Your father also said your mother spent far too much time vomiting when she was on the ship carrying you."

"He exaggerates because he wants me in the house and not out here. He's worried about the gossip."

"There won't be any gossip. My staff don't talk to others about the inner workings of the house."

"What about the girls?" They'd both quite forgotten about the virgins she had purchased while they gadded about the countryside getting kidnapped. Until they'd arrived home. James's butler was still having conniptions over it all.

"They still aren't speaking to anyone but you. Each time I enter a room, they flee."

"You do have an awful reputation," she reminded him with a grin, as she leaned back in his arms and let his warmth flow through her. He rarely dreamed of war anymore. Not when he was in bed with her, anyway.

"I do?" He laughed. "What about your reputation?"

"Apparently the rumours about me are wildly unfounded. Not one person seems to be able to find a single witness to any of my supposed scandals. For some reason I am being celebrated as a rescuer of slaves and a matchmaker above reproach."

"Hmmm," he murmured in agreement as he placed a kiss on her collarbone. "Not sure how they all came to that conclusion."

"I think your riches may have had something to do with it."

"Never," he said into her hair. She heard the grin in his voice and couldn't help but grin in reply. Though she had been as sick as a dog for days, he always managed to lift her spirits. His baby in her belly also made her smile every time she thought about it, sick or not. She would live anywhere, in a cave, in a house, on a boat, in a field in the open, as long as he was there with her. As long as he loved her then, as he did now, she knew they could overcome anything they faced. Together.

THE END

Did you enjoy James and Daniella's story? Support the author and leave a review!

Join Tule Publishing's newsletter for more great reads and weekly deals!

If you enjoyed *The Road to Ruin,*
you'll love the next book in....

THE DAUGHTERS OF DISGRACE SERIES

Book 1: *The Road to Ruin*

Book 2: *The Slide into Ruin*
Coming September 2020!

Available now at your favorite online retailer!

About the Author

Bronwyn Stuart is a multi-published, award-winning author of both contemporary and historical romantic fiction. Her latest Regency series, Daughters of Disgrace, will be released July 2020 by Tule Publishing. She and her shoe collection share a house in the Adelaide Hills with her husband, kids, dogs and cat. She's a sucker for a love story and a bad boy.

You can find out more at www.bronwynstuart.com

Thank you for reading

THE ROAD TO RUIN

If you enjoyed this book, you can find more from all our great authors at TulePublishing.com, or from your favorite online retailer.

TULE
PUBLISHING

Made in United States
Orlando, FL
09 September 2022

22186016R00219